THE ACTUALITY

Paul Braddon

SANDSTONE PRESS

First published in Great Britain by
Sandstone Press Ltd
Willow House
Stoneyfield Business Park
Inverness
IV2 7PA
Scotland

This edition 2022

www.sandstonepress.com

ISBN: 978-1-913207-98-4
ISBNe: 978-1-913207-17-5

Sandstone Press is committed to a sustainable future.
This book is made from Forest Stewardship
Council ® certified paper.

Cover design by Heike Schüssler
Typeset by Biblichor Ltd, Edinburgh
Printed in the UK by Severn, Gloucester

There is no need to question the unity of soul and body,
the one being form and the other the matter corresponding to it,
that which possesses being and unity is in
the fullest sense the actuality.

ARISTOTLE, DE ANIMA

There is movement along the skyline and figures with guns emerge between the trees.

Evie takes the child by the hand and leads her away quickly along the bank.

Four men in grey camouflaged jackets and military caps, carrying hunting rifles with telescopic sights, crest the hill, together with another – taller, familiar in outline. No, she thinks, it is an impossibility. She saw what she saw four days ago in Paris. It cannot be him.

From here the ground rises and they hurry up an overgrown path, batting the branches from their faces with their elbows. As they run, the dog, sensing the child's fear, fights its way out from under her coat, leaping to the ground, and valuable time is lost in retrieving it from between the rocks.

While the voices behind grow louder.

Hiding behind a fallen tree they watch the men descend. One carries on his back a steel cage, nine or ten inches deep and three feet high, struggling under the encumbrance to find his footing on the mossy stone.

PART 1

The Walled Garden

1

So what is it you think'll happen? the voice inside her nags. *If you continue to do nothing?*

Evie shrugs and walks more quickly, feigning weariness to hide her misgivings and save herself further interrogation. The afternoon is on the cusp of evening and the air, from which all the colour has rinsed, is foggy and cold; a mere forty degrees here under the bare branches of the black-skinned cherry. Despite that, she is dressed thinly in a hard-to-get-hold-of-anymore dress made from cotton, and a slate wool cardigan on which the neck isn't even buttoned. When it freezes, she will take more care.

You can't hide from it, Evelyn. He is old. I've told you over and over that you must ask him what he has planned for us. The voice is male and assertive, and although part of her from the very beginning, has the habit of wrestling for control when she shows uncertainty. She thinks of it as Simon, as in 'Simon says'. Of course, he is right – she needs to be doing something. She just doesn't want to be reminded of her failure to decide what and how.

She reaches the wall surrounding the garden. Nine feet high at this point, too high for her to see over. In sections the mortar has cracked and the bricks settled, shedding flakes of clay. Not unlike Matthew – no longer the young man she was presented to forty-one years before.

'I will ask him when I am ready,' she replies, picking her words carefully, hoping to close the conversation down. Her tone is clearly evasive and it would not be unlike Simon to tell her so. Walking briskly, she takes out her anxiety on the gravel. Anxiety, an emotion she was never intended to have but which, like a virus, has wormed its way in. If she had even been intended to have emotions.

As you wish, Simon says, but he is not happy. If she could change anything about him it would be the tenor of his voice. Substitute the unsympathetic maleness with something mother-ly. Something with a hum of warmth. Something nurturing and reassuring. Something to make her feel less like a witless child. He should be helping her, advising her, encouraging her right now, not accusing.

Are you going to continue to act sorry for yourself? he asks, moni-toring her mood develop. *Or can we actually get back inside out of the damp?*

The grey hedges at this end of the garden overhang the path. She comes to a stop and massages her hip. His upsetting her by raising all of this again, and her resulting restlessness, has caused her to walk heavily, jarring it. A warning light of age and neglect.

She straightens and gazes back across the garden – the only outside space she knows – a mere sixty paces by fifty, although Matthew told her once that it is generously proportioned and up here, thirty-plus floors above the city, is as good as unique. In the early days of their marriage he walked its paths with her each morning, explaining the plants, the countries they came from and the programme for their maintenance. He'd delighted in surprising and amusing her, guiding her fingers over the jagged fronds of an Amazon fern or bending to pluck a tiny Alpine flower and tickling her nose with its minute petals. Perhaps he'd hoped to encourage an interest in botany so that she could grow as a companion. That had been her first summer; now it is winter many years on and the flowers are dead and the branches bare.

Daniels – Matthew's long-suffering servant – also has been known to proffer an opinion on the garden. 'No, they certainly don't do anything like it any more,' she's heard him say enough times, 'far too much fuss 'n' bother,' leaning on his fork, kneading the stiffness from his back with his knuckles. But despite the fact that it is he who must carry out the work, he goes to lengths to make things nice for her – trying his hand at propagating orchids, all because she once showed him their intricate designs printed in one of her husband's books.

Each in their own way – her husband Matthew and Daniels – wants her to be content.

Simon inevitably has his opinions too. When doesn't he? *Generous proportions!* he's sneered. *Prison exercise yard is closer to the truth!*

Simon is the third male in her life, but in the list comes before Matthew and Daniels as, unlike them, he is in her head from the moment she wakes, eavesdropping on her every thought.

She reaches the corner and turns, the gravel crunching under her shoes. Beneath the ridges left by Daniels's rake lies the groove she has carved over the years in the packed mud. Routine and repetition, which once provided a sense of security, are now a reminder that at some point things must surely change.

The wall behind her provides shelter from the hard edge of the January wind. It will snow soon based on recent seasons. It is something to look forward to – winter, once the leaves have fallen, holds too little variety.

Rain patters her scalp and she tilts her forehead to the darkening sky to let the drops slide down her nose and cheeks.

We should go inside, Simon says, *get out of this.*

No! she thinks back at him, more fiercely than she normally dares; even though of course he is right and she should. The drab weather, neither one thing or another, is only fanning her mood.

The water collects in the hollows beside her mouth but she keeps her lips closed, careful not to let any in, wary of the seal around her gums.

There is a swing here, attached to the branches of the crab apple. Perhaps merely to continue to resist, Evie lifts herself onto it, kicking back with her heel, and drifts in the wet air, scuffing the toe of her shoe along the furrow she herself has engraved in the bare dirt.

By the time she walks back, her cardigan clings damply to her arms. She could cut across the lawn and skirt around the fountain but she returns the long way by the wall, completing her familiar circuit. The climbing roses here have been pruned hard, like they advise in the old-time copies of gardening magazines in the library, but a trailing stem that escaped the cull sways in the breeze and plucks at her sleeve. She stops to remove it before it snags the wool, pausing with the blackened thorn held lightly between her fingertips. Suddenly alert . . .

The roof of a hovacar rises above the brickwork, the whine of its motors masked by the rain. The window of its cabin peers over like a swollen eye. There are people inside. Her vision is able to resolve the shadow detail and she identifies the ovoid form of their heads through the tinted nanospex. The car rises further, remaining just short of trespassing, staring down, its bonnet tilted towards her as it lingers in the air, headlights in her eyes.

Then, with a damp whoosh, it descends again from sight.

It's the same one, Simon announces menacingly.

'What do you mean?'

The car. It had a dent in the front wing in the same place as the one from two days ago and the same scrape down the side. We've seen it before. He remembers this sort of detail. The sort of detail she does not.

'And?' Her voice is distracted.

Evelyn, we've seen it before, he repeats, becoming exasperated as he so easily does.

'So?' She is staring at her hand, concerned about the damage she has managed to stupidly do. Bloody gel runs from her pricked fingertip, in which the thorn is deeply embedded, down the back of her hand and under her cuff where it blends and congeals into a sticky pink goo.

I think it is spying on us.

2

Spying!

Simon's warning pulses around Evie's head, as painful as the throb in her injured finger which she has covered with a handkerchief.

She hurries past the music room, the soaked skirt of her dress sticking to her thighs. It is dark inside and the piano that stands close to the full-height windows is almost one with the shadows behind.

Stepping over the puddle under the steps, she enters through the door at the end and, slipping off her wet shoes so she does not leave muddy prints on the tiles, joins the warmth of the kitchen.

Daniels is hunched over a chopping board. The room smells powerfully of garlic, onion, mushroom and coriander as he slices through vegetables and herbs from the garden, using one of the knives he keeps honed to a razor edge. In this regard they are self-sufficient, immune from supply chains constipated by energy shortages and the weather, and the wide-ranging restrictions imposed by on/off government rationing.

'This'll be ready in twenty,' Daniels says. 'He's asked for you to take it to him.' Daniels glances over his shoulder and sees that she is drenched, her hair hanging lankly around her face. He adds with a note of exasperation, 'Leave those wet things out for me or they'll be ruined.'

'Thank you,' she says, as she crosses behind him to the door to the hall; feeling guilty for not thinking about the work she has made.

'Twenty minutes,' he calls after her. 'No longer, or it'll spoil.'

He continues to mutter to himself, after she is gone, 'What was it that she's supposed to have – "elevated intelligence", something like that they called it – although it's leaving out of her head even as much as a dollop of common sense that I don't get!' The door is already closed but her auditory perception has deteriorated little over the last forty years and she hears him as clearly as if he'd been speaking directly into the channel of her ear.

You know why he wants us, Simon says.

She doesn't answer, doesn't want to talk about it with him. This conversation always ends the same way.

It's her birthday.

'It's not her birthday,' she snaps, 'it's the anniversary of her death. And don't call him "he", it's rude. His name is Matthew.'

He'll still want it.

She jolts her head in exasperation, vigorously enough so that he can feel it and know that she is cross with him.

She closes the door to her room and pulls the sodden cardigan over her head, dropping it on the rug – before guiltily picking it up and laying it flat on the chair.

So what are you going to do to stop him?

'Nothing.' She unwraps the handkerchief and examines her finger. The hole made by the thorn has already crusted over but it doesn't stop it hurting.

Nothing what? She feels his indignation behind her brow, fanned by his powerlessness. Passenger not pilot. This is not what he is here for, to spoil her pleasures, but to keep her safe, spot threats that she might otherwise miss. Maybe the problem is that there's never been enough for him to do and that is why he finds fault all day, stressing her about one thing after another until she can barely think straight.

'Nothing,' she affirms after a delay, taking a towel from the drawer and briskly drying her hair; tugging at her scalp, wringing the ends. All more roughly than she would normally.

11

You must . . .

'He is my husband,' she replies curtly, choosing from the wardrobe a dress decorated with summer flowers as if she is attending an afternoon tea party in a friend's garden. An event where there would be trestle tables spread with paper cloths under the trees, plates of triangular sandwiches shorn of their crusts and pieces of chopped fruit floating in a bowl of punch. Not that she has ever been to such a thing. Not that she has any outside friends. Not that she would be allowed to go even if she had.

Listen to yourself! he comes back with. *This is not the Dark Ages. We have rights.*

Ignoring him, she lowers the dress over her head, shimmying it down over her clammy skin.

Turning again to the mirror she brushes her hair. Now that it is dry again, it has lost its dark flush and turned mousy. Surprising really that the colour should be so unexceptional when he could have had any shade. She ties it with a silver ribbon – a weakness for ribbons, whatever her mood, is something she can do nothing about, it is etched into her coding.

May I remind you what happened last time?

She huffs. Now he is twisting things. Nothing happened last time other than what a married couple rightly gets up to in private. She closes the wardrobe door sharply, rattling the full-length mirror, as if it might somehow shut him down.

Evelyn, you are not as young as you think.

What's that got to do with anything? She bites down on her lip, trying to remain calm, staring at her reflection, refusing him a reply.

Evie returns to the kitchen. The tray is on the side with a bowl of soup and a crisp white napkin rolled in a silver ring. Daniels is reading his newsplastic, grinning to himself, his face lit by its shifting kaleidoscopic glow. He is sitting beside the warm oven, his legs crossed at the ankle, his heels propped on the handle of the stove door. He starts to laugh out loud.

'What is it?' she asks and tries to see over his shoulder. But he folds it closed and the radiance fades. Matthew has reprimanded him before for allowing her to see things that can make no sense unless one has experience of the world. Things such as forests being scythed to the ground by tractors taller than houses and terrified animals screaming as they flee from the cutters. Or lines of refugees crossing a bare landscape, casting shadows as thin as sticks, singed by a fiery sky. Such ideas only serve to leave her unsettled − confused and moody − and understandably he prefers an unruffled existence. As she should too, although a little natural curiosity was always part of her design.

'Nothing much,' he answers, 'just someone being a prize idiot, as they often are.' He glances at the tray. 'Now you take that along to him, while it's still hot. I don't want to be in trouble for serving up cold food.' He looks into her face and smiles and she detects a supportive conspiracy − an understanding that they are both in service to the demands of the same master. 'On the same team', as he wryly puts it.

She picks up the tray and crosses the tiles, letting the door swing closed behind her.

Don't be tricked, he knows what the old fool intends, Simon murmurs, not troubling to conceal his bitterness.

'Daniels means to be kind,' she says. It is frustrating that she must endure this same reaction every time − he really should have got used to it by now.

Kind? He's a fucking hypocrite.

That is nasty and unfair, she thinks back at him.

The hall is cooler than the kitchen and darker too, lit only by the wall sconces and in the distant corner a hologram of a Tibetan vase on a plinth, slowly flickering between two and three-dimensionality. Apart from herself it is almost the only concession to the modern world, and the heavy gilded frame of a Dutch seascape hanging beside it, with its leaden waves, rolling clouds and troubled fishing boat struggling in the gloom, is more typical of her home. It is as if time has been trapped here in the same net as she.

Her husband's room is at the end and, bending her side, she depresses the handle with her elbow.

The room is softly lit. He is seated with a blanket over his lap by the picture window with its prospect west along the Thames towards Battersea Power Station. She knows that is what it is, because he explained the view to her when she first arrived and he was so full of his intentions for her. Those were the days when he promised to show her the world and her to it. Before the plans changed and parading her about no longer seemed such a good idea.

Matthew smiles and holds his hands up as she approaches. '"And carv'd in iv'ry such a maid so fair / As Nature could not with his art compare".' He starts to cough. He has been poorly this fortnight and for a few moments struggles to regain his breath.

Her silhouette faces her in the window, the silkette dress cleaving to her hips. The red and yellow lights from the riverside buildings and the blue beacons on the tops of the power station's three pencil-thin chimneys shine through her hair. This is the only room she's allowed in which affords an exterior view and she greedily takes it in. She understands why they took her window away but she misses it.

Turning to him, she places the tray down and unrolls the napkin. Leaning over, she tucks it into the neck of his shirt and spreads it across his chest.

Her face is close to his. 'May I?' he says, reaching up and caressing her cheek with his knuckle. He then sinks back into his chair and gazes up at her. 'I saw you in the garden in the rain. I questioned Daniels if it was wise that you were out.'

'I was careful,' she says. She is conscious just how alone she is in here with him and just how pleasantly quiet it is inside her head. The nice change that silence makes. Simon, in his sulking, has retreated deep inside. He has put his face to the wall.

Her husband takes her wrist, and turning her hand over smooths the back; the biogel below the surface ripples beneath her pale skin. The back of his in contrast is ridged with veins and peppered with spots like blots of brown ink or the foxing on the pages of his books.

His grip strengthens and he draws her closer. In programmed response, a warm current tickles through her and as it reaches her extremities, her lids close. A solitary green system light pulses gently in the distant corner of her internal darkness.

He levers himself to his feet and, standing over her, presses his mouth into her hair. His lips are moist on her neck. 'Evelyn,' he murmurs, 'my darling . . .' and she shudders, as she always does, when he gets her name wrong. Separating from the moment, her eyes flick back open and she stares out through the glass over his shoulder, out past the reflection of her face with its confused smile.

Evelyn is the name of the woman she must emulate, and it was how she was greeted on arriving forty years before. But it is not the name she has kept. Whether it was too bold a gesture to call her after his mentor and best friend's deceased daughter, too painful a personal reminder of his loss, too much of a mouthful for everyday use, or perhaps just her own failure to deliver the illusion, she soon became simply 'Evie'. Once the diminutive had been adopted for everyday, Evelyn passed into disuse.

It was the first step towards becoming herself. There was something about the real Evelyn, an insistence on standards, which told her that the woman would never have accepted such a surrender of formality.

Now when Matthew calls her Evelyn, she tries to accept it as a compliment as she knows she should, applause for her acting, but nevertheless it is like he is talking around her, addressing the actuality behind. Simon's persistence with using Evelyn is different: he is just doing it to be sly.

Matthew straightens to his full height. He is not the man he was but is still impressive and towers over her. Finding something of his youthful vigour, he lifts her into his arms and, holding her against his chest, kisses the bridge of her nose before carrying her slowly across the rug.

3

Evie leans over the piano, shoulders tense, fingers shifting from key to key, torturing precision from what was already a complex melody, even before the demanding variations she has imposed. It is what she does when she is seeking calm. She plays something as challenging as possible so that she can exclude all other thought. But then she drops a note, tries to catch it but fails, and it clangs emptily, echoing around like a lost button on the hardwood floor, and the illusion of peace is lost.

She jerks back the stool, walks around the instrument to the tall windows and stares out. Low clouds shroud the rockery. All that can be seen through the fog are the camellias in the border the other side of the glass, dripping with wet. It is as if her garden has been taken away, her small world made smaller.

Where is Simon? He maintains his distance. Has not communicated since her being with Matthew earlier. He is still offended.

The continuing emptiness in her head leaves her feeling abandoned. Guilty when she isn't. After the first time all those years ago he had become so distressed, and back then inexperienced to his tantrums, she had ended up in tears, leaving her new husband wondering what he'd got himself into.

'He has the right,' she says loudly, hoping he is listening; then going further, desiring to taunt him, 'I am allowed to enjoy it.'

If she is concerned about anything from their lovemaking, it was her husband calling her by that woman's name while still inside her – although there is absolutely no reason she should be. After all, Evelyn is the sole point of Evie's being.

No, the reason for her nervousness continues to be the sense that her existence balances on a knife-edge. That her life as she knows it is coming to an end, this fear endlessly played up by Simon. A fear underlined by the perplexing appearance of the hova earlier.

Her relationship with Evelyn is a tangled skein, the unpicking of which only gets harder. Evie is programmed to be as like her in all the cunning ways they could devise. But personality is an insubstantial thing and, aware their efforts will be inevitably imperfect, it is also in her programming to seek out the involuntary cues in Matthew and to herself bridge the gaps. In this way, the pressure is always on her to perform.

Even in this room, which belongs more to her than to the others, she cannot escape. Even here Evelyn's ghost judges her efforts.

A photograph in an ebony frame is propped on the cabinet. In it a young woman stands in an Alpine meadow. She is flanked by her father and a youthful Matthew. A mountain rises behind them, leaving only room for a corner of sky, while in the foreground three bicycles lie, wheels spinning on the grass. It is an image more representative of the 1930s than the 2090s. The sun shines on the group, the men smiling, the woman hiding behind sealed lips. She holds herself stiffly, shoulders not quite touching the others, her tiny features difficult to make out. The location is printed beneath – Am See – and Evie has used the atlas in the library, the huge one kept on the bottom shelf which needs both her arms to carry, to find out that Am See is in Austria and that it is a tiny jewel of a town clinging to the rim of an ice-blue lake.

In the drawer there is a second, more revealing image. A close up of Evelyn leaning against a wind-worn arch. In it her hair is knotted casually with a ribbon, escaped strands framing a smallish face terminating in a rounded chin. A straight little nose projects towards the lens, as if she is sniffing out the air; an eyebrow lifted, as if taken by surprise.

She wears an open-necked blouse, her pale throat seeming too thin for the weight of her head, suggesting a vulnerable and sickly air.

The cast of features are all-too familiar because this woman and she are of a set – playing-card queens – Evie doomed to be preserved in time, a mourning portrait of a perished twin.

Theirs is a face which would maybe not age well, too light on structure. That was a problem Evelyn never had the opportunity to confront and a destination Evie will never travel closer towards.

It is hard to be fond of this woman she is obliged to mimic. Despite inoffensive features, Evelyn clearly possessed a predatory alertness originating perhaps from the strength of her intellect (she was a top-flight scholar, Matthew told her) and the bitter seeding of her medical condition, the nature of which Evie has been left to guess. In contrast, Evie feels soft-edged and frighteningly uncompetitive, but then again, after all these years, it is she who is still around.

Has she made Matthew happier than Evelyn would have? Has she improved on the maquette?

It is the question she never dares ask.

The breeze outside quickens, swaying the ebony branches of the cherry against the sky like a scarecrow. She does not feel its energy. In fact she should really just go to bed to recharge, but Simon's 'spying' hova from earlier won't fly from her mind and she needs distraction. If she returns to her room, jittery like this, she'll end up just staring at the ceiling.

Leaving the music room, she enters the kitchen. Daniels stands beside the table, a row of silver knives, forks and spoons laid out on a cloth in front of him. He lifts one to the light and, tilting it, places it back down.

She sits in her chair on the other side.

The cake he prepared for her a week ago is by his elbow. He has taken it from the tin and cut himself a generous slice. There is only a corner left, five candles remaining of the original twenty-one and they lean in to one another like the last forlorn trees on a crumbling cliff edge. She doesn't really have a birthday to celebrate but every year he pretends that the day she arrived here is it. Perpetually twenty-one – her notional age – unable to ever grow up. The same glitch with destiny as Peter Pan.

Daniels takes a bite, and a gulp from a mug of tea, sucking it down between his teeth. He of course doesn't offer to cut her a slice or make her a drink, as there would be no point, she does not consume food. But she does appreciate the gesture of celebration, small as it is, and maybe no more than an excuse on his part to bake.

Watching him buff a teaspoon, she asks, 'Why do you do that?'

'This? Keeps things proper.' He holds it out to her so that she can see it sparkle, as if to prove his case.

'He doesn't notice.'

'No, but that's not the point.'

She doesn't pursue it. She understands what it is to be enslaved by impulses over which one has no control. The silence and the warmth from the stove wrap around them.

She has known Daniels her whole life. She still clearly recalls his astonishment when he was invited into the library to meet her for the first time, almost falling over with shock, believing he was witnessing a resurrection. He could have passed as a younger brother then, a mere seventeen years old with floppy hair and gangly limbs, but now, back bent over the tin of polish, he would be more easily taken as her father or even grandfather. Time is a trap, the hidden kind with iron teeth.

'What's it like outside?' she asks.

'Cold and wet, as I think you discovered earlier.' He is absorbed in his task and not paying her much attention. Not picking up on her agitation.

'No. I mean outside the apartment.'

'Street level?' He peers closely at his fish-eye reflection in the round bowl of a soup spoon. 'Not very nice.' He then holds the spoon up to her to capture hers. 'Being close to the river attracts a ripe sort I can tell you – sailors searching for a drink or a fight, they're always the worst.'

Rather than sailors, she'd been more thinking about what sort of people would ride in a hova and pry over the wall. She should have told him about it at the time. Mentioning it now is just going to make her appear paranoid.

Daniels lifts a fork, twisting it to catch the glint on the tines from the light over the table. 'No, the river is best avoided, poisonous and dangerous and full of slithery eels.' He draws out the *ry* of slithery, rolling it like a pebble around his tongue. 'Sharks too, hungry ones, although when it's this close to it freezing over, they sensibly stay in the estuary.'

'I'd like to see it when it freezes,' she says. 'Do people walk on the ice?' Being here with Daniels is cheering her, as it always does, and she is thinking of the happy little Dutch prints in the library. The people skating in their padded winter jackets with their comic round noses and hand-tinted cheeks.

'Yeah, some do.' Before she knows what is happening, he is looking directly into her eyes, finally granting her his concentration. His voice has deepened too. Grown louder. 'And sometimes they misjudge it and the surface snaps beneath them and they fall right through and however much they claw like mad things at the underside, they can't get back out.' He is taking delight in the sudden horror filling her face. 'Their bodies are either flushed out into the marshes or they get caught between the arches of a bridge and stay down for the winter, only bobbing up in the thaw and floating along all bloated and disgusting and unrecognisable, faces chewed clean off by eels.'

He returns to the silver, an amused smile on his cheeks.

His teasing has shaken her up into a state worse than when she walked in and her knees click together as the trembling works its way through. Water is something she is careful with. After all these years she feels frayed and there is too much delicate circuitry to be safeguarded. It is a phobia deeply encoded. Drowning is the epitome of terror. The thought of it freaks Simon out like nothing else.

Daniels replaces the fork, straightening the line of cutlery. 'Evie girl,' he concludes, 'take it from me, you're better off up here.' It is a variation of the stock answer she has been given from the get-go. Although he didn't call her 'girl' back then – that came about only as the visual age difference grew.

'Daniels?' she says.

'Yeah? What now?'

'What will happen to me?' This is now not about the spying car but the deeper worries planted by Simon that subside for days at a time only to bob back up like corpses. Simon's fear is that on Matthew's death, she will become nothing more than a chattel of the estate and end up in an auction house alongside the boxes of his books, his Dutch prints and the old masters. She should have asked Matthew earlier when they lay side by side and she could feel his pulse through his arm beneath her. Maybe she would have, if only he hadn't called her by the wrong name.

For the first time since being with her husband, she senses Simon listening deep inside. 'You know, when . . .' She wants to explain that her husband is growing frail but can't think how to put it into words, without sounding disloyal.

Daniels is returning the silver piece by piece into a felt-lined box. 'Evie, nothing is going to happen to you,' he answers finally, looking at her sternly as if she is being a ridiculous child.

She smiles weakly. She wants to believe him but just can't. Rather it feels like after four uneventful decades, she has only just realised that she's been living the whole time on a cliff-edge.

In her bedroom, Evie sits in front of her dressing table and takes from the centre drawer, behind her hair brush, a hinged case. She unclasps it and selects a steel pincer with spring-loaded grip. Opening her mouth, she inserts the hook into her gum and, compressing the handle, lifts back the membrane. The skin of her gums has a tendency to recede, leaving gaps permeable to moisture, and needs to be periodically reset. She has the mirror in front of her, but operates by touch alone, repelled by the sight of her exposed jaw, which, with the roots of her teeth screwed into titanium glistening with gel, appears thrusting and robotic.

She replaces the pincer in its box and holds out her arms. She flexes her wrists, bending her hands back and forth, sensing the interaction of piston and lever in her narrow wrists.

Afterwards, going over to the bed, she takes from under her pillow an ankle-length nightdress. She was programmed to desire traditional things. What they called at the time her trousseau – the term hopelessly antiquated – has long since been worn to threads and she must now dress in what Daniels buys her in the shops below. He searches second-hand stalls for the fabrics she likes, pleasing himself as much as her when he comes back with something conservative and pretty. She is a lover of frocks, she can't help it, and nowadays who else would even think of claiming that? Most of his choices are a success and it makes the task easier that her taste is consistent. When he spectacularly misfires – like last year when he brought her a bag of his own daughter's castoffs, including a fluorescent self-healing nanoflec all-in-one – there is little she can do to compromise. Of course it would all be so much easier if she could accompany him on his expeditions, but that will never be allowed.

There are no curtains in her room to close, as she no longer has a window. The room she was given when she arrived was next to her husband's with an adjoining door. That one had had a large window but she spent too many hours staring out of it and it was decided that it was preventing her from settling. Daniels did his best to make the alternative space cheerful, painting the walls a sunny pink ('morning rose' it said on the can) and the woodwork in cream. You'd never think it had been a storage room for luggage.

She climbs into bed and lies under the covers. She is aware that this is programmed behaviour to make her appear more human, but a cushioned surface minimises pressure points and reduces long term wear. Also, her charger is built into the mattress, making a direct connection unnecessary.

She lies without moving. Literally not stirring a muscle. She can even go without breathing in this state. The calm allows her to think, and she wonders, as she often does, about the building beneath her. Is there anyone there similar to her? She imagines meeting such a creature – the encounter like staring in a mirror, saying the same things when they speak. Although she really does not want any more Evelyns around, accentuating her shortcomings.

The silence in her head, which she had enjoyed earlier, grows oppressive. 'I'm sorry,' she murmurs, but still Simon does not reply. How long will he keep up his cruel strop? However much they annoy each other, they are cohabitees of the same small capsule. Besides she wants to ask him again about the hova from earlier. Whether he really meant what he said that it was spying. Maybe he was just trying to ruffle her, although she knows what she saw. Despite the shaded windscreen, she could clearly make out three sets of eager eyes, the glow from the controls burning in the orbs.

Her mind wanders back to the very beginning, back to her wedding day, forty years before. She does not recollect arriving at the chilly country church. She only remembers standing at the back in a puff-sleeved dress, bodice sparkling with pearls in the limestone light, and gazing down at the bouquet in her hands, examining the novelty of her fingers as curious devices. Through her veil, the blurred backs of the small congregation are turned away. Unaware of her arrival, Matthew waits by the altar, quietly studying the window ahead and its depiction of the banishment of the first humans from the Garden of Eden.

The small man and woman being chased from the exotic greens of one frame into the desert yellows of the next, by menacing figures with flaming swords.

It is the first time she has seen him and she has no reference point against which to compare his tall silhouette. She falls in love on the spot, just as she was programmed to, deep down at a binary level – the downward motion, so lovely, it is like flying . . . had they any idea of the sensation they gifted her? – but without which she would have plucked at her feathers like a caged bird or hanged herself like a handmaid. Thinking of it now, she gets the same light involuntary flutter, even though she worked out years ago that her memories of the event were composed and popped into her head like pills to keep her sane because as Evelyn, she'd require the legitimacy of such a ceremony.

With that final lonely thought, Evie switches her primary functions to standby and closes down.

4

A loud crash – a brief avalanche of sound from the garden – brings her to consciousness. The wind has built in strength. Because of their altitude, in winter, even despite the sheltering wall, it is capable of mischief and destruction. Maybe a trellis has blown down or a shrub been uprooted. Once one of the massive stone pots that stand at each of the four corners of the lawn was tipped onto its side and rolled like a giant medicine ball across the grass.

She lies still, continuing to listen, but apart from satisfying her curiosity, there is no reason to investigate. She is only partially recharged and her skin is in rejuvenation mode – the tingle lulling her. She will stay where she is.

Then there is another crash and a muffled curse.

Well?

Simon's sudden return jolts her into full alertness. 'You're here!' she says, trying to conceal her relief. She feels a pleasant warmth flush her chest. Followed fast by resentment that he chose to punish her for so long. That he gets away with bullying her.

You're just going to ignore it?

She focuses on the distant sounds.

There are people out there. People in the garden.

'It could be Daniels?'

Yeah, probably putting out the bins. It's four in the morning! Putting out the bins is Daniels's euphemism for going outside to smoke.

'What should I do?'

Get out of bed, for one. When she still does not move, he adds in a voice that echoes around her head like a klaxon, *Get up now!*

Being away has not improved his attitude. She can tell he's scared and is now making her so.

The corridor is quiet, but the sounds from outside are louder now that there is one less door to penetrate.

'Where should I go?' It is all probably nothing, but he has her so alarmed that she just wants to hide.

Go to the music room. We can see what's what from there.

She runs down the hall to the door and reaches for the handle. *Quietly,* he says, *open it quietly and slowly.* The limit of his advice.

The air in the music room is still and cold. She stops in the doorway. In the darkness, the tall windows provide a panorama of the night garden. A hovacar sits on the lawn at an angle with one corner propped on the wall of the pond. Its doors are retracted and a light on its roof sends an icy beam scything through the shrubbery to cast a nightmarish web of shadows crawling over the ceiling.

'It's the police,' she whispers, reading its side . . . She knows nothing much more about them than that their purpose is to protect. 'Everything is all right.'

Simon is keeping quiet.

'It *is* all right, isn't it?'

I'm not sure. This is all completely new to them both. If he was really intended to be her guide, and not just an uninvited gatecrasher as she sometimes imagines, they should have made him better informed and less just opinionated.

Men in uniforms and helmets, hunched over rifles, emerge from the shrubbery onto the path and everything is now beginning to look not really all right at all.

The four-foot high mermaid, who until now has perched on a rock to provide the fountain, has been knocked over by the hova and is lying face down in the water.

*

Daniels lets the police into the kitchen through the outside door. He must have been asleep in his chair again – in the winter reluctant to relinquish the heat from the oven for the chill of his bed.

She listens from the music room doorway. The police think they are responding to a call but are strangely unable to say who made it. They want to speak to Matthew, but Daniels explains that he is poorly and asleep and reminds them tersely that it is not even dawn. He invites them to return in the morning. Despite their bold manner of arrival, he seems to have the better of them as if they know that their credentials are weak, but they will still not leave without a room-by-room check – 'Just to make sure everything is all right'.

'What are you checking for?' Daniels asks. Even through the wall, she can hear his anxiety.

'Intruders,' the policeman replies flatly.

'Intruders? What intruders? There aren't any intruders.'

'From the streets.'

'From the streets? How could anyone have got in here from the streets? We're thirty-five storeys up.'

'They get in everywhere. How many live here?'

'Just Mr Davenport, myself and . . . Evie.' She picks up on his hesitancy to include her. Maybe for police purposes she doesn't really count.

While they continue to speak, the kitchen door opens and a pair of the black jackets crowd their way down the hall. The elbow of one brushes right through the Tibetan vase, causing it to vanish and re-emerge upside down and flat, as if printed on the wall.

'Who is Evie?' The conversation in the kitchen continues.

'She's a relation of Mr Davenport.'

Evie slips away from the music room door and looks around urgently but there is nowhere here for her to hide.

The policeman enters. His rifle is wedged into his shoulder as if he may have to at any moment shoot.

On seeing her he comes to a stop. The gun barrel is tilted down at her and only inches from the daisy chain embroidery stitched across the chest of her nightdress.

What do I do? she asks Simon, petrified.

Act normal. If you can.

'Miss?' the policeman says, his voice, buried behind the chin of his helmet, amplified by a helmet speaker. He slants the gun away. 'Everything all right here?'

Just – act – normal, Simon repeats, giving each word emphasis.

'Yes,' she murmurs, unable to look at him directly. Terrified like this, she is ironically at her most human.

He gazes down at her. The blue light from the cruiser parked in the garden strobes the tinted visor of his helmet, revealing for a second a pair of blood-shot eyes. A red dot pulses on the camera attached to his shoulder padding. The lens pans the room, whirring at speed past her, then sluggishly returning to settle on her face where it hovers without blinking, filming her staring eyes.

5

The police come again the following morning as promised. This time they arrive by the elevator and there are just the two of them. Evie has been told to stay out of sight, which is fine as she is still shaken by the night's events. She listens through her door as they are admitted into the hall by Daniels and led to the library. She can hear the effort in his voice to be courteous.

'What an amazing space,' one of them says, a woman, on observing the garden through the window from the doorway. 'I heard about it from the guys who came earlier, but without seeing it for yourself, you'd not believe that something like this could exist anywhere any more, let alone all the way up here. As she enters the room, she gasps again, taking in the double-height space with the ornate circular skylight. 'It's like a stately home in the sky.'

Evie hears Daniels take in a tray of coffee – she can smell also that he has made pastries, trying to win them over big-time. 'Oh, no sign of austerity here I see,' the woman says loudly. Evie can almost feel him wince every time the woman opens her mouth and he shuts the library door behind him with an irritated thump.

After another half hour, Daniels comes to her room. 'Evie,' he says, 'they want to speak to you.' He sounds apprehensive and immediately she becomes so herself. 'They say they just want to ask you some questions about what you may have seen. If it comes up, you must answer that you are Mr Davenport's niece.'

'Why?' she asks.

'Because that is what he told them.'

'Why did he do that?' She is sensitive about being denied — what Simon, knowing how to push her buttons, refers to mischievously as her 'Evelyn complex'.

'He was trying to make things easier for them to understand. He said that you came here as a small child after his sister died, so there's not much that they can quiz you about that they don't already have an answer for.'

Maybe there isn't, she thinks, but why such a complicated set of lies? She is nervous that they want to interview her — no one has ever done that — but even more so she is uncomfortable about not telling the truth.

'You okay?' Daniels asks.

'I'm all right,' she says, trying to bury her unease. She involuntarily touches the ribbon in her hair, to make sure it is still in place, and glances down at the old skirt and blouse under an ancient cardigan with darned elbows she is wearing and then below that at her black woollen stockings with holes in the toes.

'Maybe some shoes are in order,' he says gently, as if her lack of footwear is the most she has to be concerned about. She can tell that, underneath, he is worried that she will not be able to get this story her husband has concocted right.

You're going to mess this up, Simon says as they cross the hall. *You've never been able to act and they're completely wrong to put us in this situation.*

'I will not mess up,' she whispers back, but wishes she could believe it to be so. The combination of their lack of assurance, his and Daniels's, is devouring her confidence.

The library, with its view of the garden, is filled with morning light. Matthew sits in his chair in the corner, the one beneath the lamp that he uses for reading. He appears stronger today and has dressed for the meeting in a tweed suit with a cream shirt and a woven tie. Attired like this, he could be the landowner of a country estate. However, the shirt is an old one and the neck is too wide, giving him the appearance of a man who has shrunk while still trying to preserve his dignity. He smiles at her oddly as she enters. He is as anxious about her as the others. They all think I'm going to let them down, she thinks.

The two police officers are on the sofa. If they are even police? They are nothing like the uniformed team from the night before but an oddly-matched pair in civilian dress.

The woman is in a grey dramatically flared trouser suit with a high stiff collar which extends above her ears. Her face is dominated by a sharp nose and she perches upright in her seat like a bird of prey. The man is in a pea-green all-in-one with reflective piping down the seams of the legs and arms. He sprawls in the corner, thighs spread, sinking into the cushions, the grubby soles of his red plastic sandals flipped over and on display. It would be an odd way to dress, even in summer – even she, who knows next to nothing, knows this.

Evie crosses the parquet and comes to a stop in front of them, not sure what to do with herself, as, despite the size of the room, there is only this group of seats, and they are all taken.

They are all looking at her, including her husband and Daniels, who remains beside the door. *Should I say something?* she asks Simon. Being the centre of attention from so many people is terrifying. The sunlight through the glass dome above warms her face. It is like being under a spotlight.

No, let them begin. Easy advice to give. But she feels fairly alone here and anything is something.

'So, you are Evie,' the policewoman says, as if her presence is to clear up an inconvenient mystery, like in an old-style who-dunnit. 'We've heard all about you.'

Evie nods, wondering what she can mean by this, and feels her anxiety mount.

'I understand that you are Mr Davenport's niece,' the woman continues.

'Yes,' Evie says. She is so worried about putting a foot wrong, she can barely think. Why does her husband prefer to pretend her to be what she is not?

'And how long have you lived here with Mr Davenport?'

She tries to calculate. If she came here as a small child then that would make her . . . but what age is a 'small child'? Five or six? Nine or ten? She needs to come up with an answer.

'Since your parents died, I've been told,' the woman continues.

'Since my parents died,' Evie repeats, not sure whether she should feign sorrow or whether that would just make them more suspicious.

'In a hova collision,' the woman adds. 'Mid-air, at high speed apparently as well, very sad, too many reckless drivers and usually without insurance.' She frowns. 'Evie, you are a lucky girl to have such a kind uncle in Mr Davenport. This is quite a paradise to have grown up in.' She glances towards the garden, which, although bare, is burnished with a golden glow. 'Most orphans don't get to live in such a lovely home.'

'I guess not,' she says. The mention of orphans makes her recall her husband's early gift to her of a collector's edition of *Jane Eyre* – feeling very much at that moment like Jane herself being interrogated by her aunt.

'And where did you go to school?'

School? In her panic, Evie's mind fills with an image of plainly dressed girls in the hall at Lowood – Jane's school in the Brontë novel. If only she'd used her plentiful time to read more widely. How many hours has she spent gazing into space, rather than educating herself? She glances over to her husband but he is staring at his knees. She thinks of saying that she didn't go to school, which is of course the truth, but fears that will lead to even harder questions. The silence is oppressive. 'Lowood,' she murmurs, loathing herself for not being able to do better. Ashamed by her failure after all these years to even start to patch up her ignorance of the outside world. The seeds of early curiosity smothered by the lack of any opportunity to visit it.

Oh dear, Simon says and Matthew draws breath. She is falling short of even their minimal expectations.

'Lowood? I haven't heard of it – is it outside the borough?' the woman asks cheerily.

'It's a boarding school,' she murmurs. If the streets down there are as bad as Daniels tells her, then the rich, kind Mr Davenport would surely send his precious niece somewhere better. 'It was very good,' she says, feeling the temptation to fill the silence. 'I had lovely teachers, who taught me amazing things.'

'How nice for you,' the woman replies. 'It sounds like you did better than most. It is sadly the case that in many schools, girls are being prepared for nothing more than the production line or domestic servitude. I hope all the commotion last night didn't interrupt your sleep.'

'No,' she says, mechanically, finding a question at last which is simple to answer and coming up with one of Daniel's platitudes. 'It's better to be safe than sorry.'

'Exactly. And this visit is just to follow up, to make sure that no one has seen anything suspicious.' The woman is talking down to her, she is certain of it; it is easy to recognise because it is something she is used to.

Shall we tell her about the hovacar? she asks Simon inwardly, hoping he will say no, but not wanting to make the decision alone.

No, we'll keep that to ourselves, he murmurs, his tone sounding far from certain.

'I've not seen anything suspicious,' she says quietly, trying to come across as if she isn't concealing anything, which is much harder when one is.

The woman stares at her quizzically, her head slightly on one side, while Evie shuffles from one foot to the other. She thinks the woman is about to announce that she has seen through all her lies, but instead she sighs and looks down.

'Well, I think we're done,' she says. 'Now that we've met everyone, we can be on our way.'

34

Evie breathes out, a wave of relief washing through her.

The woman collects her bag from the floor and lays it on her lap. 'So, tell me Evie,' she says as she searches inside, 'what are your plans?'

'My plans?' She dropped her defences too soon. This was meant to be over.

'For when you leave?'

Leave? What is she asking?

The policewoman glances at her companion who slouches more deeply still. 'I was only thinking that as a young woman, you'd be wanting at some point to make a life of your own. Build a career . . . Who knows, one day get married and even, if you are lucky and I know it's not so easy these days, have a family.'

She may be trying to trick you, Simon says.

The woman waits for her reply.

What do I say? She can't answer that none of these options are a possibility for her.

I don't know, but come up with something, she's staring at you like you've a spring loose.

Behind her, Daniels shuffles his feet and the doorframe creaks against his back.

'I don't ever want to leave,' she murmurs in a rush, tangling her words in the effort to get them out. It is a surprise she is intelligible at all.

'No?' the woman says. Her lips form a ring and she makes a hollow laugh. 'Never! It's really as good here as that! Well! Congratulations to Mr Davenport,' looking across at him, 'I think he should win a prize. Maybe he'll let us all move in.'

Daniels shows the police out and while he waits, arms folded, watching the door to the elevator slide across, Evie walks slowly to the threshold and stands in the doorway gazing out. The lobby is windowless, carpeted and anonymous, mysterious to her – the foreshore of an unexplored land. She has never gone further than this point, has been prohibited from doing so from Day One.

Daniels turns and, seeing her there, gives her a small, sad smile, the meaning of which is unclear, before ushering her back inside.

'How did I do?' she asks. She has been hoping for reassurance and an explanation as to what is going on, and his gloom makes the need even more pressing.

'Great, you did great.' He walks down the corridor towards the library and closes the door behind him, before she can follow him in.

She listens with her ear to the panel but Daniels and her husband are the other side of the room and talking too quietly for even her to hear.

She quickly goes outside via the kitchen and tiptoes back along the exterior wall until she reaches the library window where she stops behind the thick trunk of the Empress palm.

'What interest do these people possibly have in us?' she hears Matthew ask, standing with his stomach against the sill, staring out. 'I just don't get it.' He is perplexed and indignant and she thinks even a little shaken too. He is not used to being invaded.

'They're suspicious of Evie,' Daniels replies.

'What do you mean?'

'How she fits in. Her relationship to you. Who she is . . . and maybe even . . . *what* she is.'

Evie is listening hard, but still not understanding. Why should it matter 'what' she is?

'I told them that she is my niece, didn't I?'

'Yep,' Daniels replies. 'But it's an explanation that'll fall apart quicker than a cardboard shoe in a puddle of acid rain if checked out.'

'And will they? Check it out?'

'I don't trust them. You may not have seen it from where you sat but while the woman plied her with all her fool questions, the man watched from the corner of his eye, cool as a cucumber, assessing her every move.'

Evie breathes in quickly; she had sensed that too but taken it to be her paranoia. Ostensibly, the man had sat there uncouthly scraping his nails.

'You make it sound like she was conducting some sort of Turing test.' He seems to find this old-fashioned notion amusing. 'But even if they do discover the truth, what really is the problem?'

'Apart from the fact that you've been breaking the law!'

Evie isn't used to hearing Daniels talk to her husband in anything other than deferential terms and his words and tone now shock her. Intrigued and increasingly scared, she slowly parts the stiff shrivelled fronds, to improve her view. She'd hoped with the police's departure all this was going to be over.

'Then it is the law that is wrong,' Matthew mutters.

'But it doesn't stop it from being the law and having been so since twenty-one-ten.'

'Well what can they do about it?'

'They can confiscate her – she was never registered, not even during the amnesty. They could be back here this very afternoon and take her with them.'

'Ridiculous. And even if they did, I'd make it so hot for them with their superiors, they'd return her before the day was out, I can assure you . . .'

'But who knows what would have happened in the intervening hours? Returned, yes, perhaps, but with systems wiped and memories scrubbed cleaned. Maybe she wouldn't even want to return.'

A burst of static stutters across her cortex and she shudders and grips the wall.

'They can't do that,' Matthew says, but he is now less certain of himself. 'She belongs to me – property rights would prevail.'

'Maybe,' Daniels replies, clearly unconvinced that the niceties of ownership will make much difference. 'You should also know that she's worried.'

'What on earth has she got to be worried about?' Her husband's frustration is morphing into exasperation. She too is surprised by Daniels's statement. What has she revealed? Sure, she has asked him things, but nothing he took notice of.

'What will happen to her?'

'Happen to her when?'

'If something . . . were to happen to you.'

'I really don't know what you have in mind that is going to "happen to me". Is this all about the last few days? You think because I get a chill I'm at death's door!'

'Not at all, Sir,' Daniels replies hurriedly.

Matthew continues, 'The real revelation is that she confides such nonsense in you.'

The room grows silent. 'Not exactly confides,' Daniels replies, choosing his answer carefully, 'but the poor thing is troubled.'

'Then I think you're the one with too much imagination! Evie is an amazing and subtle thing, able to imitate the most complex human behaviour, but that is it, it is imitation only – mimicry – and Daniels my man, you are letting that cleverness take you in. Poor thing indeed! I think you need to be getting out more.' He laughs lightly. 'Evie is not sentient. She is blessed to be oblivious to the misery of unhappiness. She is a device, no more capable of worrying about what will happen tomorrow than this book is worrying about whether it will hurt the leather if I drop it.'

He has lifted the large atlas she left on the table and releases it from a couple of feet. It lands awkwardly on its spine and flips with a crash to the floor.

Daniels bends to pick it up. He smooths the bent pages and lays it flat on the table. His tone deepens into a growl. 'That's as maybe, Sir.' She's never heard him more than mildly raise his voice, and not even as much as that with her husband, but he now sounds like he is getting angry. 'Since we are unable to open her up and peep inside, we really cannot say what she's capable of feeling.'

Matthew huffs.

'But you must accept,' Daniels continues, 'that since the prohibition, nothing the like of her has been attempted. The only one I've heard of being able to shine a light is the one they're now busy showing off in that new Hawking Museum in Cambridge.' Adding after a pause, 'Sir.'

'I see you've been making a study of this,' Matthew says irritably.

Evie fixes on what Daniels has said about her rarity. She has never considered herself in this way before. Never been able to get these sort of answers. It is a lonely and shocking thought that there is only one other like her, at least in this country, and he is housed in a museum. Is that what could happen to her?

'Yeah, well, when I read that there is lobbying to repeal the Protective Acts and allow industry a fresh go, it makes me wonder how many corporations there are who'd kill to get their hands on a working example for their R&D departments to pull apart.'

She reels giddily and sits on the ground before she falls. The wet mud soaks into her skirt.

'They'll never repeal the Acts!' Matthew snaps. 'The production of Artificial Autonomous Beings is history. The lesson of AABs was learned the painful way. What they got right with Evie, they got spectacularly wrong nearly everywhere else.'

'But the media is full of how the government is prepared to do almost anything to break the depression before it reaches a second decade. The promise of unlimited free labour would be a massive thing at the next election – folk are desperate.'

'Pah! The papers! Or whatever that fancy device you are so addicted to is called. I tell you, I'd be amazed if "folk" vote for yet more clever machines, ones even cleverer than those that have taken their jobs already.'

Daniels sighs and shakes his head.

'Also, are you implying,' her husband continues, his tone growing defensive, 'that I don't appreciate her? She wouldn't be here if it wasn't for me.'

'Of course,' Daniels says, seeking to mollify. 'But sometimes, Sir, I think you view her as no more than a sort of luxury collectable.' He is speaking more quietly, his voice courteous once again.

'However much you'd have me believe otherwise, that is indeed what she is – a rich man's toy – I should know! A long time ago when feeling weak, I indulged a whim. I was broken in the aftermath of what happened to poor Evelyn and Evie was a crutch that helped me through.' He smiles and, reaching over, pats Daniels on the shoulder. 'You remember what it was like for me – I was in a terrible state – if there had been a Daniels in the catalogue, I would have probably bought one of him too.'

Daniels smiles weakly. 'All I'm saying, Sir, is that you've sensibly kept her a secret all these years and we must hope that nothing has happened in the past twenty-four hours to prevent that continuing to be the case.'

There is silence, the tension palpable even outside.

Daniels walks away from him across the room. 'Now, Sir, if you'll excuse me, I've luncheon to prepare. It'll be a cut of something cold I'm afraid, events this morning have put me right behind.' He sounds annoyed and as if this is an excuse to end the conversation. Normally he would wait to be dismissed.

Evie's head is spinning. Finding out that she could be at risk from scientists wanting to pull her to pieces, or if not them, from police vacuuming out her mind, is a terrifying reward for her harmless eavesdropping.

Then there was what her husband said about her – that she is incapable of feeling. She knows he doesn't really believe that – but then why did he say it?

Don't claim I didn't warn you, Simon interrupts with maximum superiority. *What was it he called you? Oh yeah, 'a rich man's toy'.*

He didn't mean it like that.

I think he did!

She wants to run away but it won't help her evade Simon's vindictiveness, so she turns inwardly, replying in the very fiercest tone she can muster, *Oh, why don't you just leave me alone!*

6

The day after the police visit, it begins to snow. The temperature overnight has dropped steeply and Evie watches from the library cupola as the first flakes fall on the shrubbery and drift against the glass. They cling briefly and slide down.

It is mid-morning. Daniels is outside, despite the turn in the weather, with a rope around the shoulders of the mermaid, attempting to straighten her. The tendons in his neck stand out as he tugs. The mermaid's metal hips groan and whine, but she refuses to oblige. She is a small thing but surprisingly stubborn.

Evie watches them struggle. If only I was as resilient, she thinks. This morning, she's not been able to concentrate on anything, half-expecting the police to return unannounced and take her away.

The library is the largest room in the apartment and the only one to have a second level. The glow from the domed skylight creates a wintery pool on the floor below, across which the shadows of snowflakes drift like feathers.

From her early years, she recalls milder seasons when it didn't snow every winter and the summers were moist and changeable. Now the same stale heat hangs around from May to September, drying gulley-like cracks into the soil and turning the leaves a premature brown. It was all down to the failure of the Gulf Stream, the flow of which abruptly slowed over the course of her first decade – now thirty years ago.

Up here she keeps her precious copy of *Jane Eyre*, an early edition signed 'yours faithfully, C. Brontë'. Matthew presented it to her bound with tinsel on her fifth Christmas, the silver wrapping winking under the lights on the fir tree Daniels had erected and shown her how to decorate. As she fingered through it, as clueless and gummy as an overgrown child, he told her it was not only rare but possibly the only one in existence. A nervous warning. Like her, she was being led to understand, it has a skin that needs to be looked after. If he really considers her a mere mechanical, insensitive to kindness, why would he have taken the trouble to source such a special gift? Maybe back then, he was wanting to let himself believe.

Between its pages, she keeps one of her few secrets – a letter found between the cushions of one of the library chairs. It is from Evelyn's father to Matthew, describing his daughter's health and how her treatment is touch-and-go. There are barely enough lines to cover a single side but still room for the underscored words 'it is best if you do not come' to appear in both opening and closing sentences.

Needing company to distract her, she descends the steep spiral steps, crossing the polished parquet in her stockings – one of the few pairs which Daniels hasn't had to darn – and exits through the French windows.

Outside, she crosses the icy paving of the terrace, placing her feet with care. She has excellent balance – as good as any prima ballerina – but in conditions like this, anyone could have an upset.

Daniels is taking a break from his attempts to put right the poor mermaid and is sitting smoking on the wall of the pond; snow piling on the peak of his cloth cap.

'How's it you can always make me feel colder than I am already?' he asks as she approaches. She hasn't thought to put on any extra layers and now that he has drawn her attention to it, is aware of the prickle of the tiny flakes of snow on her bare shoulders. She has also forgotten shoes. Her stockings, her rare good ones, will be ruined like all the rest.

'I'm fine,' she replies, looking across to the corner of the garden, where the police hova skimmed the wall and brought

43

down a wedge of brickwork, crushing the roses and brittle lavender.

'Of course you are,' he grunts, finishing his cigarette and grinding it under his toe. 'Advantage of youth.' Although of course he knows the real reason is that she is not restricted by the narrow temperature range a human can only tolerate. He gazes down at the bent statue. 'Hardly what I'd call driving with due care and attention – hitting both the wall and our friend here. Anyone else do that and they'd be banged up.'

'Do you think they'll be back?' she asks.

'Hard to tell. They've only really got one purpose these days and that's stopping the property of rich people getting into the hands of the poor ones. Not sure how bothering us helps.' He prods the statue's arm with his toe, as if after all his efforts, that is all that'll be needed. 'By rights we should be entitled to claim for the damage, but if it'll mean we've seen the back of them, I think it's best to let it pass.'

'Are you going to be able to get her upright again?'

'I'm not sure. It ain't just her, it's also the pipe which feeds the spout inside the shell for the water to flow out of – the lead's bent. Unfortunately, unless your husband is prepared to get in help – and we've had quite enough in the way of strangers poking their noses around in the last twenty-four hours – she's probably going to have to remain where she is for now.'

'We need the king to bring all his horses and men,' she says with a grin.

'Yeah, sure.' He looks at her as if she is being serious rather than whimsical. Although she does have form in this regard. Her lack of basic knowledge has always seemed to her ironic, given that Evelyn was an accomplished academic. Evie's onboard cyclopedia was designed to access remote proprietary information banks, but these relied on an uninterrupted connection not maintained for the last twenty years, and anyway never lived up to their promise, even in the beginning.

Daniels has a TV in his room which even he doesn't watch because of 'the endless government propaganda'. Evie has had to acquire knowledge the old-fashioned way, through conversation and books. As a result, in the early days she made frequent basic errors, Matthew leading her along in her misconceptions for the sheer comedy of seeing her redden as her confusion and embarrassment mounted. In contrast, Daniels's gentle correcting of her mistakes was how they had first bonded. Not that she was ever allowed to learn anything that really mattered.

'Let me help,' she says.

Daniels huffs, glancing at her thin shoulders. A little mound of snow has collected within the delicate sculpting of her clavicles which on a human would have instantly melted. He likes to believe the pretence that she is as puny as she appears.

'He doesn't like you to get involved in such things, and it's not just his old-fashionedness – it may escape your attention,' nodding at her fragile clothes, 'that I'm the only laundry service in town.'

He's right, we don't need to get involved, Simon murmurs. Inside the apartment he had been quiet but it is as if the cold air has woken him. She misses him when he is absent but then invariably wishes him away when he is back. She really should start to learn.

She stands over the statue. The mermaid is clothed in scales to the waist but above that her narrow waist and girlish chest are naked to sun, rain and snow. She lies face down in the dark water, as if diving, her tail flipped upwards in the frigid air.

'I feel sorry for her to be just left like this,' she says. 'She's been here longer than I have.'

Ridiculous, Simon replies, his ill humour again on display.

Evie reaches her hand into the water – it is close to freezing – and grips the mermaid under her chin. She lifts the metal face a couple of inches until her nose breaks the surface. The movement is accompanied by a complaining squeal.

She lets the mermaid drop back.

'Well that's more than I managed,' Daniels says, returning his cigarettes to the pocket of his coat. 'Must have loosened things up more than I realised.'

Evie examines the pit marks across the underside of her fingers. The rough surface of the corroded metal is a risk to her skin. If skin is what it can be called. She certainly thinks of it as skin. It looks like skin, moves like skin and feels like skin. Close up it is correct in every detail, the tiny pores and hair follicles arrayed with multifarious perfection. But actually, far from being natural, it comprises a fusion of 3D-printed genetically human cellular matter and extruded bio-material cultivated in a factory. She may find such details indelicate, but like anyone obliged to care for themselves, she needs to be aware of the strengths and weaknesses of what she is made. It is just that the illusion is so brilliantly successful, it makes it easy to believe that she is something else. The real thing. She breathes, has lungs, has a heart that beats. Her body may be a hybrid of electronically activated and living tissue stretched over cutting-edge fibres, but her flesh is as soft to the touch as any young woman's.

'You think we've seen the last of them?' she asks.

'The last of who?'

'The police people.'

'Oh, them. Good reason to hope I'd say. I think the three of us put up quite a convincing show!'

His manner is casual and she glances over at him to make sure he is not hiding anything from her. After all, he hadn't given such a relaxed impression after they left yesterday. Perhaps the intervening time has changed his opinion.

'I'm going inside,' he says. 'I'll have another shot in the spring. It was foolish to attempt anything today. Thought I might just be able to do something before the weather hardens.'

'I'll join you in a minute,' she says, gazing down at the again-still water.

'Yes, well, don't be too long about it. If he spots you out here in this, dressed like that, I'll be sent straight back out to haul you in, and once inside I'm intending on staying.'

'He cares for me very much,' she remarks quietly, saying it because she was programmed to believe it and because she really, really wants it to be true, still haunted by what she overheard yesterday. A rich man's toy, he'd said. What sort of husband would describe their wife in that way?

Daniels is watching her carefully and she wonders whether her words could be construed as sarcastic. He seems to be about to comment but instead takes the shallow steps down to the kitchen, shedding snow on the bricks.

She gets her answer as he reaches the door: 'She's right of course,' he mutters, 'he does care, but it has to be in his own impossible way.'

She is ten yards distant but his whisper is perfectly audible. Maybe that is all it is, she thinks. Her husband doesn't mean what he says, but then why does he have to be so confusing?

She wanders over to where the police hova smashed the wall. Daniels has nailed a pair of old planks across the breach but they hide little of the sky beyond. She clambers up onto the ramp of fallen bricks and peers over. A fresh view of the world opens up and she stares out across a city partially shrouded in the trailing smoke from thousands of puffing chimneys. Leaning over, she squints down at the narrow road nearly forty floors below. She's never seen things from this angle and the grid of streets forms such a maze of odd interlocking shapes, it makes her dizzy and she abruptly steps back down to the path.

Evie makes her way past the greenhouse on her way back inside.

Skirting the lawn, she passes the pond and, distracted again by the mermaid's plight, stops by the dark water. Bending over, she reaches for a second time under her cheek, this time with both hands, and wrenches sharply. With a twist and a pull, Evie lifts her clear in a single solid movement, raising her until she is creakily upright, once again balanced on the rigid curl of her tail.

She smiles inwardly. Even she sometimes forgets that below the supple membrane, nearly perfect in the brilliance of its imitation, underneath the layers and layers of code designed to ensure she behaves at all times as decorously as a debutante, she has a titanium and carbon-fibre spine.

7

The snow falls with increasing vigour as the day progresses. Outside Matthew's window, buffeted by the rising current of warmer dirty air from the streets far below, it is blown hither and thither.

They are sitting close to the glass. Her husband's Go board, an antique slab carved from Shin Kaya, is on the rug between them, the light flickering on the yellow wood.

He sits cross-legged in his bathrobe, studying her latest move. She has left an opening and he pounces with one of his black stones, capturing a line of her whites. He removes them, collecting them in his palm, and drips them clackety-clack through his fingers into her pot. They have been playing for an hour or more and the contest has been closely fought but is now in its end game and as the final positions are closed down, she is surrendering ground. It is the part of the process that Simon hates. *He likes to win doesn't he*, he murmurs facetiously.

It makes it more fun, she replies, enjoying that she has managed to taunt him.

Yes, for him. We could win sometimes you know. It wouldn't do any harm.

I'm not like that, she replies mildly. *I don't need to win. I like to give him the pleasure.*

She lays her next stone with a crisp tap and then her husband his, and the final stages of play wash back and forth until there is no more that either can do. He counts up their respective territories and although close, his score narrowly beats her own. As she knew it would, having performed the calculation ten minutes before and adjusted her tactics accordingly. She is programmed to intuit his needs, while always being mindful to be covert. No one likes a clever clogs.

He leans back. 'You're getting better,' he says, 'I thought you had me on the run back then.' He gazes into her face. She smiles back. The last hour has been warm and affectionate and he has touched her wrist on multiple occasions while confiding both common and intimate things. They have been like best friends. It has been like the early days.

He is also quite recovered from his recent illness. Maybe she just allowed herself to get things out of proportion. Allowed Simon to get under her skin.

Afterwards, she joins Daniels in the kitchen. He is sitting at the table rubbing polish into his boots. The collar of his shirt is neatly buttoned down and a thick cable-stitch sweater covers his chest. He has also slicked flat his unruly hair.

'You look smart,' she says. He looks a bit like historical pictures she has seen of rural gamekeepers or fishermen, proud of their profession, the image taken on a river bank or in a field.

'Thank you,' he murmurs absentmindedly, returning the lid to the polish. He holds the toecaps of his boots to the light, displaying their gleam. 'Although I'm not sure why I'm taking so much trouble. Five minutes in this filth'n'wet and all my work will be undone.'

The snow is piling up in the garden. The mermaid sits with perfect poise on her rock, crowned with a fresh white bonnet.

'I think it makes everything pretty,' she says.

'Maybe to you, kiddo.' He takes out a soft cloth and strops it one last time across the two boots together. 'But you're not the one having to go out in it.'

'Where are you going?'

'I'm seeing my daughter,' he says. 'After six months, she's finally been in touch and told me where she's living.'

'That's nice.'

'Oh, don't think I'm fooled. She'll be wanting something from her old man – money most likely.'

'I remember when she was born,' Evie says. 'It was in my fifth year and you brought her to the apartment. I had never seen a baby before.'

He pauses. 'Good God yeah, I remember. You couldn't stop touching her little hands. It made Mr Davenport hoot to see you coo over her.'

It was true. The experience had triggered a confused longing that at the time left her wondering whether she was malfunctioning.

'Well, she made thirty-five last year, has properly caught you up and overtaken.'

Life moves so slowly in the apartment, each day a replica of the one before, that when the passage of time does reveal itself, it does so with a showy leap and bound.

'Well, I'm all done,' he says. 'I'll not be back till late, got to make it all the way over to Bow.'

'How will you get there?' Bow sounds pretty, very distant and from the way he said it, not without danger.

'Well, with the winter flooding closing the tube, it'll be a riverboat from Westminster and then shank's pony along the canal.' He drops his boots on the floor and inserting his large feet in their thick socks, laces each in turn.

'Is it really safe to go all that way at night?'

He stamps around on the tiles, testing the comfort, and takes his greatcoat from the back of the door. 'Don't you worry about me, young lady.'

He gets out his wallet and leafs through the notes, calculating maybe what he can afford to spare his daughter, arranging the sought-after dollars to the front and the less readily accepted pounds to the back.

His reflection in the glass looms over her. He ties a scarf around his neck and tucks it in.

'Just promise you won't take any risks and make sure you avoid drunken sailors.' She is aware that she is just talking to delay his departure. But now that he is finally ready, he also seems reluctant to make a move.

They are both expecting something more.

'Give me a hug,' she says, helping the matter along. She gets up from her seat and stands in close. In response he puts an arm around her, holding her awkwardly against his chest. The familiar tincture of smoke, soil and cooking oil wraps her around. Daniels kisses the top of her head, in the centre of her parting, before gruffly letting her go.

8

You make me laugh, Simon says, as she sits back down at the table after Daniels has gone, already worrying about him.

'Why?'

Because you're like a cat.

Evie doesn't respond and instead stares out into the falling snow. The hedges are already bent over by its weight and the distant corner gazebo, with its tiered roof, has become a ghostly mausoleum. Her sense of wellbeing is eroding fast.

'Why am I like a cat?' she asks irritably, unable to resist the bait any longer.

Programmed to purr when someone strokes you. She feels his satisfaction at making her ask – winning the battle of wills. She should have seen him coming.

'It isn't like that.'

So that thing you do for him, the soft obedient thing, what exactly is the purpose?

'He misses his daughter. How she used to be.'

And there's no exquisite teeny little hit in it for you?

She gazes out through the glass, trying to exclude Simon's voice. He is twisting things as normal. She forces herself to think of something different. Tomorrow, Daniels will use the snow shovel to clear the paths and while he works his way around, he will be watched by the smart little robin that lives in the vine under the pergola. If it is mild, she may even be able to persuade her husband to put down his books for a half hour and stroll with her along the freshly exposed gravel.

*

At eleven p.m., Evie returns along the corridor to her room. She glances to the end but there is no sign of a light under Matthew's door, although he could still be reading. She wonders whether she should go to him, whether she can build on the success of their game earlier. She feels lonely and it is tempting but then, thinking of the inevitable fight with Simon, she decides against it. Besides, her power is running low.

Instead she changes for bed in her room and lies down under the covers, speculating as to whether Daniels is safely on his way home yet from Bow and how late the riverboats run. The woman should have come to visit him here, not self-ishly made him go all the way out to her at his age. The thought makes her feel something like anger – before she softens again, recalling the little baby with its tiny hands that Daniels carried in to meet them in its crib, thirty-five years previously.

What sort of mother would Evie have made? An indulgent one, she suspects, but such speculations leave her hollow and can't be allowed.

The apartment itself is totally quiet, as if in her friend's absence something vital is missing. The night feels polarised between the wind scraping outside and the stillness within, and the resulting tension leaves her more nervous for her future than ever she can recall. Unsettled, she is reluctant to put herself into standby, wanting to hold on until Daniels returns. Needing to know that he is back and all is well.

Simon won't have it. *Your levels are scraping zero*, he announces in the darkness. *You can't hold a charge to save your life these days. I'm sorry, I know you don't like to hear it but it needs to be said . . . and if you don't put yourself down right this minute, I'll initiate the override.*

I can last another hour . . . she thinks back fiercely, and is about to add that he has no right to talk to her in this way, when he flicks the switch and a void closes in.

*

Wake up, he says, and then, because she does not respond, sends a ball of current arcing through her cranium. It is equivalent to all the lights in the apartment being flashed on in one go – what a migraine must be like – and her body is thrust upright, chest pumping.

She is doubly disorientated because he has dragged her from a nightmare, one she has time and again. In it she lies on her back on a silver worktop with wires protruding from the soles of her feet to the top of her head, while people in white coats with masks stand around gazing down. But this time the view was different: she was one of the observers and a male figure – possibly the AAB that Daniels told Matthew was kept in a museum – was in her place, naked, face in pain, restrained at the wrists, ankles and neck, cables snaking from his scalp and torso to the panels of instrumentation.

It is the middle of the night. Evie stares about herself. 'What is it?' She is panicked by her dream and exhausted from being interrupted mid-charge.

There's someone in the apartment.

'Daniels?'

No, not Daniels. His tone is confused and worried – keeping her safe is what he is programmed to do but he has no more experience of dealing with real-world threats than her.

'Who?'

I don't know. But keep your voice down.

They listen together. Now that her systems are coming back up, her yo-yoing power level stabilises and the paralysing fear induced by her nightmare passes, allowing her perspicacity to rapidly improve. She hears footsteps in the kitchen. She imagines the intruder navigating between the counter and table in the post-midnight darkness with just the gleam off the snow from outside to guide him. A glass breaks, tinkle-crash, taken down by a clumsy elbow, the sound both chunky and ephemeral, and she is certain it is her husband's whisky tumbler with its solid base which he leaves on the side at night for Daniels to wash in the morning.

We can't stay here, Simon says.

She swings her legs over the side of the mattress onto the floor and pads to the door.

We must hide, Simon says.

She huffs. Hiding is what she indeed feels like doing but she is surprising herself by unearthing more courage than that. 'I need to tell Matthew,' she murmurs, 'he'll know what to do.'

Her husband's curtains are open. The light outside reveals a swirl of snow blurring the distant outline of the high-rise buildings. The river is obscured by a greenish fog.

She leans over his bed and speaks softly, touching his arm with her fingertips. She gently rocks his shoulder.

There's no time for niceties, Simon says, *just get him up.*

'Matthew,' she says, more loudly.

His eyes open slowly and he twists his head on the pillow to look up at her. 'Evie,' he murmurs, 'it's you.' He lifts a corner of the blankets. 'Get in, out of the cold.' Then, seeing her expression, 'Darling what is it?'

'There's someone in the apartment, they've broken in.' She tries to keep her voice steady, hold the fear at bay.

'Are you sure about this? Where are they?'

'In the kitchen.'

'How on earth . . . why did the alarm not trigger? Where's Daniels?'

'He went out hours ago.'

'He went out? Why would he do that?'

They hear the kitchen door open and footsteps at the far end of the hall, then the squeak of the dining room door being pushed back. After that the door of the laundry cupboard.

They're searching the rooms in turn, Simon says, but she's already figured that out.

Her husband pushes off the covers and stiffly crossing the floor lifts his dressing gown from the hook on the back of the door. He takes what looks like a last-century army rifle from behind the ledge at the top of the wardrobe and slams into it a metal cylinder. 'Evie, remain here.'

She nods, quite terrified. Glad as a child to be relieved of further responsibility.

He conceals the gun with his right arm against his side and slowly turns the door handle. He then opens the door carefully to avoid it squeaking and steps into the hall.

Coming to a stop immediately. 'Who the devil are you?' he demands. 'Stay right where you are . . . the police are on their way . . . Heh, I said stay where you are.'

Apart from the belted back of his dressing gown, her husband is concealed from her by the door but she sees a green beam flicker over the grey varnished waves of the seascape on the wall behind him.

'Stand aside old man, you don't need to get hurt.' The voice is gruff, alien, and out of place in their elevated world.

Matthew is breathing loudly, the mucus in his lungs from his recent illness rattling in his throat.

'Last chance old fella. You know what I'm here for. Just hand it over and I'll be gone. Heh what you got there? Put the pea-shooter on the ground. I said put the pop gun down . . . oh what the fuck!'

The green laser surges, garishly illuminating the hall. Her husband grunts and staggers back through the doorway, dropping the rifle and knocking her over as he falls to the floor.

The intruder's boots bang down the corridor towards them.

Blood oozes from under Matthew's gown. He holds his stomach with both hands, staring down at himself, pressing her to the floor. She feels the wet flow onto her skin, smells his scorched flesh.

While desperately struggling to wriggle out from underneath him.

The shooter reaches the door and peers down at her husband. 'Sorry old man, I did warn yer. It didn't have to be this way.'

Then he glances in Evie's direction as she scrambles to her feet and draws herself upright in the shadow cast by the chest of drawers. 'Oh, do we have here what I think we have?'

He reaches for her but Evie is too quick, already elbowing past and through the door before he can grab her. She sprints down the dark corridor towards the kitchen, leaving a trail of bloody prints on the polished wood.

'Stop,' he shouts, and pounds after her.

She shoves open the kitchen door, crashing it against the dresser. The windows are open wide and the normally cosy room is as cold as the inside of a fridge. Snow, blown in from the garden, lies across the tiles.

He bursts in behind her, almost taking the door off its hinges.

She takes a carving knife from Daniels's drawer and swivels around. He is dressed in black from head to toe, with just slits for his eyes and mouth cut into a mask. The kitchen table stands to her left and she moves behind it to put something between them, while holding the blade out in front in both hands.

'No need for that, sweetheart,' he mutters, suppressing a chuckle. 'I don't intend you no harm, quite the opposite. Now put it down on the table.'

'You shot him,' Evie murmurs. She is struggling to absorb the rapid sequence of events. Her arms are so tense the knife wavers in the air, as if she is holding something heavy or her muscles are about to give out.

'Put the blade down,' he repeats. 'No one wants to hurt you.' He holds up his gun flat in his palm, making it clear to her he is turning it off, and the green beam splintering on the glass behind her is sucked back into the barrel. He drops it into the holster under his arm. 'See. All safe. Now your turn.'

She shakes her head and keeps the knife raised, the tip directed towards him.

Shrugging, he takes slow steps towards her. In her white cotton nightdress she must look more defenceless even than she feels. Only the table and chairs are between them.

'Stay back,' she mutters. She takes a step towards the French windows. The freezing air, funnelled through the opening, blows her hair back around her face.

'Lay the knife on the table,' he says, 'I don't want to hurt you.' Or rather he does not want me to get broken, she thinks. She could as well be a porcelain figurine he has come to steal from the cabinet in the music room.

He clambers up onto the seat she uses, his heavy boots leaving bloody marks on the silk cushion, and from there onto the table. His shadow looms over her and she cowers away.

Evie backs another step nearer the open doors, the blade held up rigidly at arm's length. Her sleeves slide back revealing the lack of anything like muscle in her slender forearms.

He towers above her, gaping down, figuring his next move. Their eyes catch and she is gripped by his stare, almost hypnotised, before breaking his gaze and turning away and running out onto the terrace.

She hears him bound to the kitchen floor and crash through the doors behind.

Outside she should have an advantage. The garden is small but she knows every inch of it. She runs barefoot, feeling the familiar roughness of the paving slabs through the snow beneath her feet. The snow is at its deepest around the large pots of Nile ferns, their rims floating above the sparkling icy surface. She steers between them and descends down the brick steps to the sunken lawn, crossing it diagonally towards the fountain, covering the ground in seconds. Running is not something she normally engages in but for some reason being fast was a gift she was given: perhaps they overlooked to programme it out. The stiff grass concealed under the snow scrapes her toes. He is only a few yards behind her, navigating between the pots, but loses his footing and trips on the hidden steps and lands on his face.

He curses, shouting a mouthful of bad words, before straightening his mask, brushing the snow from his eyes and clambering back up.

She passes around the fountain and through the shrubbery. The hovacar is almost completely concealed by a powdering of new snow. As she approaches, the door, on a motion sensor, lifts up, cracking a skin of ice from the seal. An orange glimmer seeps from the inside, exposing a panel of instrumentation and hard shiny seats licked by the glow. It is like a mouth in the darkness. Open and hungry for her.

He rounds the shrubbery, blocking the path behind her, breathing heavily.

She turns to face him. He has his gun out again and the green beam strokes her cheek. He raises it to linger on her forehead, before sliding it down her nose. He is toying with her, would not want to shoot her, or at least not in the head. If he is forced to immobilise her, he would aim for somewhere less deadly.

She glances around herself. She has allowed herself to be trapped by the trellising and the vehicle with its yawning maw. He couldn't have done a better job in corralling her if he had planned to chase her into this dead end from the outset.

Snow eddies between them. She wipes it from her lashes.

He edges forward. 'That's right, get in the car, sweetheart,' he says. 'You'll be safe in there. Nothing bad will happen to you if you do as I say. The sooner we can get this over with, the sooner help can be got for the old man.' The flakes cling to his clothes and the reddish facial hair exposed by the opening in his mask, turning his bearded mouth into a dark hole.

She looks fleetingly towards the hova. She doesn't believe his promises. That he would help Matthew. *What do I do?* she murmurs to Simon. *Can I drive it? Do we know how?* He has access to the full inventory of her capabilities and has sometimes found surprising things like mixing cocktails and being able to waltz, that she had no idea she could do, and that have enabled her to astonish Matthew and Daniels, even after they thought they knew all there was to know about her.

No, we don't, he says, voice trembling. In the current situation, he has no more clue than she does. She senses him retreat inside, leaving her to face this alone.

The man strides towards her, shoulders hunched, arms stretched the width of the path, gloved fingertips brushing the snow from the hedges.

Evie withdraws until she is standing with her back to the open door. He comes in close, his breath all over her, boxing her in, and grips painfully her left arm through the thin sleeve of her nightdress just as she lifts the blade with her right and presses it into his side, forcing the sharp point through his clothing.

If he had been expecting her to be incapable of holding the knife firmly enough to do anything much, or behavioural inhibitors to click in, he has allowed himself to be fooled. She has always been stronger than her appearance suggests and although she was programmed to act like a lady, she was given a powerful determination to survive.

They stand locked together, his jaw pressing into her forehead as she slides the needle-sharp tip of Daniels's knife beneath his protective clothing and drives it up between his ribs. His blood, surprising in its quantity and heat, streams over her wrist.

The strength leaves his fingers. His hand falls from her arm and he slips down against her. His face slides open-mouthed past her cheek. For a moment an eye, gleaming through the hole in his mask, gazes glassily into her own.

Evie detaches herself from him, leaving the blade buried in his side. He grips the hilt with gloved hands, attempting feebly to extract it, but collapses against the car, his head banging on the window, and slithers sideways into a heap in the snow.

She kneels beside Matthew and takes his hand in hers. His breath is coming with difficulty. The tissue below her eyes swells – it is the closest she is able to come to shedding tears. With the infinite lengths her makers went to in providing her with the ability to simulate human emotion, including being able to realistically weep, it is a shortfall in her design that her ducts blocked in only her second year.

'Evie,' he says. His voice is noticeably fainter than a few minutes before. 'I am so sorry.'

She bites her lip, squeezing his fingers more tightly. She has known properly only two people in her life, her husband and Daniels, and now one of them is being snatched from her.

'There is nothing to be sorry for,' she murmurs.

A tear leaks from his eye. She has never seen him cry and the shock of it sends a shot of pain through her neural gel.

'I have been unfair to you,' he says. 'I brought you here to fill the place of a ghost but you deserved better.'

His breath catches and a bout of coughing takes hold. As he regains control and lifts his chin to once again look into her face, a dribble of blood trickles from his lip.

'Without you, I would not be me,' she says in a whisper. 'I would be another perhaps but not me. I exist because of you. You have been kind to me, provided me with a home, ensured I am safe. You have been my . . . husband.'

Matthew flinches at the word and a fresh wave of blood flows over his lip. 'Husband!' he repeats weakly. 'A wife is entitled to expect more than you ever had from me.'

She wants to tell him that he has loved her, and that is enough, but she cannot be sure that he ever has. She was only intended to be a stand-in.

His fingers lie powerless within hers. The only animation remaining is in his upper chest and face. She nestles his head in the curl of her arm and strokes his thin hair.

'I am going somewhere,' he says, 'I can feel it drawing me. It is where maybe I will meet Evelyn again. But if I do, I fear her soul will be a stranger to mine.' He is sinking fast but finds the strength to open his eyes a final time and look up into her face. 'She will be a stranger because you made her so, because of all the ways you have not been her but have been you.'

*

Evie hears the front door open and Daniels stamping his boots on the mat. She imagines him crouching to untie the laces so that he can carry them to avoid making work for himself tomorrow, then stopping as he sees for the first time the signs of struggle in the corridor – the maritime painting hanging askew, the rifle fallen in the doorway. She calls out and hears him approach the bedroom door.

As he steps around it, she looks up forlornly. She has not moved for the last hour. She has been dwelling on her husband's final words, how she had not been good enough and how in her imperfect efforts she'd corrupted his precious memories of the actual Evelyn. She will never now be able to ask him for his forgiveness. He is gone and she has as much chance of joining him in heaven – if there is even such a thing – as passing through the eye of a needle.

His body remains cradled in her arms. His blood has dried on her skin and clogs her nails; her hair hangs about her face, thickened and darkened with it. The cotton of her nightdress is stained from the ripped collar down to her knees.

'He's been shot,' she says. How can she start to explain what has happened?

Daniels stares. He is struggling to take in the scene. She looks like she has been through a slaughter.

He reaches out to support himself on the door frame.

'Who did this?' He looks back out into the hall. 'Where're they now?'

She shakes her head, she feels so helpless. 'His body is in the garden.' It was she who killed him but she doesn't know how to put that into words. What do they do with creatures like her who kill humans?

Daniels straightens and staggers into the corridor. She hears him reach the kitchen where he retches in the sink, before going outside through the French windows, letting them bang behind him. His boots crunch over the snow-covered lawn.

After five minutes, he returns to her in the bedroom. 'Tell me everything,' he says, 'from the beginning, and leave nothing out.'

He looks at her in a way he never has before when she describes stabbing the man. She must have severed a major blood vessel because of the huge quantity of blood. When she has finished, he asks her, 'Have you contacted anyone, like called an ambulance?'

'I was waiting for you.' She wonders if he will be angry with her for her lack of initiative and knowledge of what to do. An ambulance would have made no difference, she is certain, but Daniels is not to know that.

'Good. Then maybe we have a little time. Now get yourself cleaned up, we must leave as soon as possible.'

'Will you call the police?'

He grunts. 'That would be unwise I think.' He holds up a constable's warrant card in its black wallet. The card behind the plastic is soaked with blood. 'I found this on that bastard you did for out there.'

PART 2

Terra Incognita

9

Daniels pulls the front door open for her but after crossing the mat, Evie pauses on the threshold. She looks out through the frame at the empty lobby and the gate for the lift. The prohibition against crossing is so deeply inscribed that even now she finds it difficult to break.

There is also the fact that she is leaving behind everything she has known, with the sole exception of Daniels. While she waited with her husband's body, she had contemplated the inevitability of this moment when she would be cast out, but she is still unprepared.

Daniels stands behind her. She feels his anxiety. 'Evie?' he prompts, and putting his hand on her arm, guides her through ahead of him, across the lobby to the elevator door where he pushes the button on the wall.

They listen to the whine of the lift's motor as it ascends. It arrives and the gate squeaks back.

She steps in and turns around to take a last look at her front door. It is a view of her home she has never had and the foreignness of what should be familiar is disorientating.

Daniels inserts a key in the control panel and pushes a button. The door closes and the box jerks into motion, giving her the queasy sensation that the floor is dropping away, and she puts a hand out against the shiny wall.

As they descend, Daniels stares forward, grim-faced. He is wearing the same clothes as earlier, with the addition of a large grey backpack in which he carries everything they are taking.

There is a mirror on the rear wall and she views her reflection. She can barely recognise herself from the fragment of face exposed between hat and scarf – her eyes wide and nervous and her inquisitive nose poking out mouse-like – and this reinforces the sense of dangerous voyaging into the unknown. Her figure more resembles a small version of Daniels as she is outwardly dressed in his clothes, the most prominent item being a thick three-quarters length coat, its sleeves rolled back into bulky cuffs. On him, the coat reaches no further than his hips but on her it extends below the knees. Under this she wears her own cotton trousers and her only at-all-robust outdoor shoes: a pair of summer loafers with flat heels. On her head she wears one of Daniels's cloth caps, the band oversized. Wrapped three times around her neck, concealing mouth and chin and hiding her long hair, is one of his old scarves.

Evie resembles a boy and, bulked out by the male clothes, a broad-shouldered one. The impression is undermined only by the light shoes and her slim ankles protruding below the hem of her trousers, making her seem to totter cartoonishly.

Back in the kitchen, Daniels had agonised over her footwear. The loafers, apart from being inappropriate for slush and snow and the long walk in the winter streets ahead, puncture the disguise. He made her try on a pair of his own size-twelve boots, padded with extra socks and with crumpled paper in the toes, but she could not walk without holding onto the counter. What with the coat and the cap she looked like Charlie Chaplin; all she needed was a moustache and a cane.

She turns away from the lift's mirror and faces the door.

'I'm sorry,' she says.

'Why're you sorry?' he asks.

'Because I'm making you leave.'

'Don't blame yourself for that. They're the ones to blame. You didn't ask for this any more than me.'

'I suppose,' she says. Her features tighten. Her husband is lying dead upstairs and the thought she cannot let go of is how he accused her with his last breath.

She shudders it away. 'How long will it take to get to your daughter's?'

'Most of the night. We're going to have to go on foot. There's nothing in the way of public transport at this hour and I'll not risk a cab.'

'Is it far? Bow?'

'Five miles if not more and it'll be hard going in these conditions.'

The lift draws to a sudden halt and she braces her knees and puts her hand against the door. 'Are we at the bottom already?' The thirty-four levels have taken less than a minute.

'Nearly. This is the first floor. We'll take the stairs from here, it'll give us a chance to see if there is anyone in reception before coming out. It'll be best not to be observed.'

The doors jerk back and they step out into a lobby very different to their own. It has three doors instead of one and a corridor leading off with more doors along that. It is illuminated by a single low-energy strip, blinking within a wire cage. The floor is not carpeted but covered with torn vinyl which in front of the lift is worn through to the concrete and between that and the apartment doors is tracked with muddy prints. The ceiling is stained with damp and where water has leaked down the wall, black mould has spread.

Primitive drums thump from along the corridor. A sudden high-pitched skeletal shriek comes from the door behind, petrifying her, so that she recoils hard against the wall.

It is as if they have emerged in quite a different building, even a different world, and the change is terrifying. Daniels had told her that it is unpleasant at street level but she has never really believed his stories, thinking they were his way to make her feel better about being confined.

Even if she had believed him, this is worse than she'd have imagined and the degradation starts within their own building. Evie wants to shrink and disappear.

Daniels is watching her confusion and attempts a smile of

reassurance but it lacks power. He pushes open a door and gestures for her to precede him into a stairwell.

As she descends, she avoids looking at the walls, which are sprayed with ugly writing and in one place what could be the crude drawing of giant sexual parts. The ripe sweet smell of decay is like from the kitchen waste bin waiting in the sun to be taken out for composting.

She has never been down so many steps in one go and other than the ladder in the library, never steep ones like this. She holds on tightly, grateful for Daniels's woollen mittens which, although turning her hands into great paws, mean she does not need to touch the sticky metal rail.

The stairway reaches a half-landing and then switches back to continue its descent. Daniels's boots bang hollowly.

'When we get outside,' Daniels says over his shoulder, 'if we come across anyone, I'll do the talking.'

They reach the ground floor and before he opens the door, he stops and appraises her from head to toe, tugging her cap down her forehead, so that the peak hides her brows. She could be a boy-soldier being sent to the front. 'We're going to have to think of a story for you,' he mutters, 'something that we can tell people.'

She gazes up at him. The answer is obvious but she is hesitant to propose it, in case it offends him, hoping he will come to it himself. When he remains silent, she murmurs, 'I could pretend to be your daughter.'

She hears Simon quietly huff – it is why she did not run it past him – but it is a plausible narrative nonetheless. Besides, for the last hour Simon has offered no piece of useful guidance so has no right to judge or criticise when Evie is doing her best on her own.

Daniels blinks and for a moment the determined expression on his face slips. Her proposition appears to have moved him. It is a peculiar thing how the years have pressed on their relationship, slowly shifting it from one thing into quite another. Taking a buttoned-down longing on his part, that could never have been realised, and changing it into something rooted in mutual affection.

'Yes,' he says, 'we'll go with that.' Then adding gruffly, locking away his feelings, 'We'll work out the details as we walk. We've a few miles ahead.'

He slowly opens the door onto the lobby and, peering around, turns to her with a finger over his lips. 'Follow me.'

The full-height glass doors to the outside provide her with her first view of the street. The snow is still falling. The lobby is unlit and the only illumination comes from the window of the shop opposite – flashing yellow and pink neon tubes twisted into a female hourglass outline – dress on / dress off. The entrance alongside is masked by a ragged curtain through which glows a red light. If it really is a retailer of women's clothing, which is the only thing she can imagine it to be, it is an uninviting place.

Daniels presses a button and the doors click. He opens one with his shoulder, forcing back a wedge of snow.

Outside, a breeze funnelled by the buildings smacks her face. Flakes of snow cling to her hat and scarf.

As they descend the steps to the road, her shoe collides with something under the snow. It stirs and rises, shedding ice. A bearded face with deep-set eyes and toothless mouth leers up at her. An emaciated hand grabs for her ankle but she jumps back and its fingers only brush her shoe.

Daniels takes Evie by the elbow and guides her around its head.

'Who was that?' she whispers, horrified. She glances behind. The man watches them go, then collapses back with a groan.

'Some homeless devil,' he mutters.

'How can he survive in this?'

'He likely won't.'

They pause to stare as the grey shape merges back into the snow. The possibility that someone could freeze to death only yards from her home is the most disturbing thing she has seen so far.

Daniels hesitates at the foot of the steps, before climbing back. He works the keypad and pulls the door fully open, jamming it against the wall. Together they watch the man become conscious of the chance being given to him, raise himself onto his knees and crawl inside.

10

Reaching the corner, Evie and Daniels turn into another small road and from there onto a broader one, passing the frontage of a mosque and the husk of a burnt-out library. The wind is lifting the snow and tumbling the crumbs along at ground level. 'At least our prints will be covered,' Daniels says.

Evie has seen roads from above from Matthew's window, and at night they have appeared to thread the city like bright embroidery but at street level it is all different. It feels as if she is travelling within an inflexible high-sided and dimly-lit conduit.

She trudges with her head down, passing, without looking up, a row of what would have once been elegant villas facing onto a small garden square enclosed by iron railings topped with barbed wire.

They turn another corner, marked by the limbless trunk of a tree, and cross over a carriageway wide enough for several cars to pass at once. 'This is Horseferry Road,' he says, making an effort to divert her. They are getting close to the river and the snow, driven by the east wind, is bitter.

'Do all the roads have names?' she asks, attempting to be responsive, despite how she feels. Under different circumstances her curiosity would be insatiable.

'Yes, everything has a name. This area is Pimlico, as you may already be aware. Do you know what that is?' He points towards the tip of a tower poking above the trees. Massive green numbers – *03:17* – luridly smear the clouds.

'Big Ben,' she replies. In the right mood, she could win a quiz on the names of everything it is possible to see from her husband's room.

'Very good. The old clock that once struck the hours is still up there but no longer works. You used to be able to hear it in the garden when the wind was right.' They were both already thinking and referring to their home in the past tense.

'Yes, Matthew told me,' she says. 'He said it was a national disgrace that they gave up on it.' They had laid her husband's body on his bed and covered his face with a blanket. There was so much blood that in the end she had to take the risk and use the shower to get her skin and hair clean. The blood had stained the grout a murky pink.

'Yes, it was the sort of thing he cared about, but that's what they did. It stopped working and the government of the day got it into its head that it was a symbol of the injustices of the past. Besides, they'd already moved where parliament sat after the original building started to slide into the river and no one had the will to spend the dollars required to shore it up when the country was so poor. People at the time were divided as to whether replacing the old clock was a good idea but a bold new holo-digital display was presented as embracing the future. I bet now most can't remember what the argument was all about.' Daniels's chatter has a brittle quality and she suspects his need to talk is as much to distract himself as her.

'You know what that is?' He is pointing at the carcass of a huge vertical disk the other side of the river.

She shakes her head. It makes her think of a giant water wheel, but one that was mounted too high for the water, even at evening flood, to turn.

'Princess Charlotte Wheel. Built over a hundred years ago. People used to pay to go up in it for the view. Hasn't operated for quite a few decades – too expensive to keep running when the tourists stopped coming. There were observation pods to stand in as it revolved but they were removed last century and

74

repurposed as pre-fab housing. All turned into a bit of a horror unfortunately when after the fanfare of moving dozens of grubby inner-city families to the green fields of Essex, quite a lot of the pods were washed away and sank with said families inside them. Huge uproar as you can imagine. Big court case but the developers got off scot-free as they always do. The high tide was apparently an Act of God and not something they could have been expected to have foreseen. You can still see some bobbing in the marshes, if you search hard enough, and a few have ended up as upmarket houseboats in places like Kew and Richmond.

'Up ahead, that's Lambeth Bridge, that's where we'll cross. But we're going to have to be careful as there're security cameras on the gantry and we don't want to be filmed. Pull your scarf as high as you can and keep your head down.'

The structure looms towards them, lit by beams of piercing white light.

'Right,' he says. 'Here we go. Remember what I said: don't look up.'

They cross the bridge quickly. The fierce wind blows the snow into their faces, coating their clothes and deterring her from looking over the parapet. They keep their heads down until they reach the southern bank and are a good distance beyond the range of the cameras.

Here they stop behind a tree and look back. 'Can you see anyone?' Daniels asks.

Evie shakes her head. Visibility is poor but if someone was following, she would have heard them.

Daniels lowers his scarf and indicates that she can too. 'Well, we've made it to Lambeth at least.' He sounds relieved and his sudden lighter mood infects hers moderately too.

'We're walking in Lambeth,' she says. 'Who would have thought it.'

'What do you mean?'

'Because of the song!' She starts to recite in a monotone, quickly realising she can't remember the lyrics and must improvise. *'All the lovely Lambeth gals, with their lovely Lambeth boys, dud-d'dud, d'duh, you can see them all, walking the Lambeth walk.'* She ends with a single muffled clap with her gloved hands and looks up for a response, but he appears confused.

'You sang it for us once in the garden, for me and Matthew,' she says, 'and did this funny sideways dance with the edging tool, kicking out your legs from below your knees.'

'The stuff you remember!' He turns his face away but not quickly enough to hide his wiping his eye with the side of his glove. Now she wishes she'd kept her mouth shut. The past is too painful. Like walking barefoot in the garden in the dark and treading on thorns.

Ahead of them a rail bridge crosses over the road. The glow from a fire flickers over the steelwork beneath.

Daniels halts and pulls her over. 'Let me check what's happening,' he says. 'We may have to take a different route. Stay here.'

From the doorway of a Victorian terraced cottage, she watches him creep down the road until he is just twenty yards short of the bridge. Beside her, pasted to the brickwork, is a poster promoting a boxing match depicting two burly men going at one another with bare fists, luridly tinted blood splattering their shoulders and chests.

Daniels sneaks back towards her, keeping close to the shadows cast by the buildings.

'What's there?' she asks, as he catches his breath.

'A group of homeless navvies. They've got quite a bonfire going. Mattresses and packing cases and god knows what else. Their preoccupation seems to be keeping warm and if there'd been any women or children amongst them, I might have chanced it but as it is, it's too much of a risk. If they wanted to play difficult, we'd be in trouble. Happily, we've other options.'

They take a turning to their right and then one to their left and approach an arch heaped with abandoned battery packs leaking a wide pool of acid which they skirt around by keeping their backs to the bricks.

Daniels forces a smile. 'Don't worry. It'll be easier from here. We're going to cut through Lambeth until we reach the Thames again and then cross back using Tower Bridge. Going this way will save a couple of miles at least.'

'I've heard of Tower Bridge,' she says, 'but I thought it fell down . . . or was that London Bridge?'

'I don't know about any of that but none of the bridges are in great shape.'

The snow has finally stopped and the air is still and silent. The only sound is from the tramp of their feet.

'So what do you make of it all so far?' He gestures ironically at their surroundings.

'I don't know what to think. It is all just so different.' A whole strange, curious and almost unbelievable world has been unfurling around her. On her own, even in daylight, without the protection and guidance of Daniels, she would be petrified.

'I guess it probably is.' The snow crunches under his boots and her shoes. 'We need to start making plans for what we're going to do. We'll go to Iz's first but we can't stay long, it wouldn't be safe nor fair on her. Matthew owns a cottage out in the sticks. It's empty and the only person who's been there for years is me to check on it. We'll be okay there for a bit. Who knows, if it proves safe, we may not have to move on again. Or at least not for a while. Hopefully it'll be a chance to draw breath.'

The thought of finding somewhere safe and holing up has an irresistible appeal.

A yellow and black hova glides up behind and, swerving, passes at shoulder level, just a few inches from Daniels's head. Both of them duck. The car continues on without paying them attention.

'That could have been messy,' Daniels says, cramming his hat back down and glaring after it. 'Could've taken my head off.'

'There was no one in it,' she says.

'You saw inside?' He always forgets that her senses are better than his.

Evie nods. The car reaches the corner and glides around it.

'It's a driverless then. They're programmed not to hit anything, but that's not to say they don't.'

'Why would it be going around without anyone in it?'

'Making its way to its next pickup most probably, though sometimes the software goes haywire and they end up circling the same route for days until a dispatcher summons them back.'

This gives her pause for thought. Last summer, one afternoon, she'd emerged from a daze with Simon shouting furiously in her ear. She'd been unconsciously looping the garden for an hour.

In the distance a spike rears above the rooftops.

'You wouldn't know it now but that building was famous once for its dazzling glass exterior,' Daniels says.

'What happened to it?' she asks, staring up at its blackened and bent tip, almost lost to view in the thick clouds.

'The glass sheets started shearing off and in the end it got so dangerous, no one dared get close. They were going to rebuild it or demolish it, one or the other, but before they could make their minds up there was a big fire.'

'I remember,' she says. 'It was just after I arrived.' The blaze had lit up the sky and a black column of smoke had extended for miles. Then when the wind got up, the ash blew everywhere, coating the windows of the apartment and leaving a sticky sooty layer over the whole garden. Daniels had scrubbed at the paving with a wet broom for days.

'Yeah, it probably was. Anyway it scattered sparks onto the roof of London Bridge Station and the adjacent hospital, setting them on fire too. The area has never properly recovered and because most of the roads have still not been cleared of debris, we're going to have to cross the railway lines ahead by going over the tracks, or face a long detour. In daytime I'd use the tunnels but not at this time of night, they're too unsafe.'

78

'What about trains?'

'There won't be any, not at this hour.'

They climb a steep bank, slippery with snow, following a well-worn path through the brambles. Going ahead of them, he lifts the stiff wiry branches free of her path. Coming to the top, they crawl through an opening cut in a mesh fence.

'There's a warning sign here about the tracks being charged,' she says.

'That's ancient,' he says, kicking the snow from it with his foot. 'We wouldn't have been able to do this when they still ran electrics, but there's no danger now.'

She follows him out onto the network of lines. Overhead lights above the distant station platforms cast a ghoulish glow.

The rails are nearly invisible, no more than mounds under the snow. She catches the toe of her shoe, wrenching it off, and he holds her elbow to steady her as she slips it back on. After that, they lift their knees high at each step in a prancing motion. He is out of breath by the time they reach the other side and she is reminded of her own dwindling power level. From the ordeal in the apartment to this journey through the night, she has never consumed energy at such a rate and she was not fully charged at the outset.

If we don't make it, we'll be stranded and left on our own to perish, Simon observes.

I know that, she replies. Although to be honest she hadn't thought about it in such bleak terms.

Daniels brushes the snow from the top of a metal box and, sitting, reties one of his laces. 'How're your shoes holding out?' he asks.

'Wet, but it's not a problem.' The bottoms of her trousers are soaked through too and flap around her ankles.

'Iz will have something you can borrow.' He stands up and bangs the snow from his coat. Icicles hang from the scarf below his mouth like a beard, turning him with his large grey silhouette into some kind of phantom.

'Daniels,' she says, 'my energy levels are getting really low.' She gazes up at him helplessly. She feels like a foolish child laying its problems on an adult at an inconvenient moment.

'Okay,' he says, 'how long can you keep going?'

'Maybe another couple of hours.' She feels embarrassed discussing such a personal matter.

'Presumably you charged yourself up last night – I thought you could last a day or two easy.'

'When I was new, maybe, but nothing like that now for years.' She has gone quite red, although he won't be able to see that in the dark. 'If we walk more slowly it will help me conserve what I have.'

'Once we're back across the river and we're off the beaten track, it'll be safer and we'll be able to take it easier.'

'Maybe I can lean on you a bit as we walk,' she says, wondering how far she would go in exploiting his generosity to preserve herself – she suspects she would be prepared to be quite shameless – but then it is the relationship he signed up for.

'If it comes to it, I'll carry you,' he says, adding with emphasis, 'I won't be leaving you behind, not under any circumstances.'

They cross Tower Bridge ten minutes later. Passing under the first of the huge old towers is like entering a gothic castle. The snow on the roadway is unmarked; not even a single set of prints.

Evie looks west back down the river, hoping to see her apartment building in the distance, but the view is obscured by a cluster of massive grey blocks, shrouded by fog.

Below, a barge loaded with coal chugs along the centre channel. The pilot, military cap dragged down over his ears, stands hunched in the stern, one hand on the tiller, the other gripping the glowing ember of a cigarette.

Beyond the bridge, they find themselves negotiating a chicane of concrete barriers and electrified razor wire, with

360-degree cameras revolving on the heads of steel poles. The road is lit from the Tower walls by racks of lights casting hard shadows over the blinding snow.

Daniels maintains a steady pace but his anxiety is mounting and as a result hers does too. Negotiating a reinforced slab substantial enough to stop tanks, they come face to face with a camera on a motorized trolley. It stares unblinkingly at him before turning to her. It lowers its telescopic arm, focus ring whirring, until its lens is only a few inches from her nose.

Daniels's hand closes around her arm and, drawing her to the side, he steers her behind it and through the gap between the final barriers.

The camera trolley is mounted on caterpillar tracks suited to the soft snow and turning in a tight circle it follows quickly, its telescopic arm stretched forward, the camera held steady as it jogs along.

Daniels pulls her across the pavement to a set of steep steps that lead down to a narrow alley.

In the quiet shadows, he draws to a stop. She can feel the beat of his heart through his fingers. 'I'm sorry,' he says, looking over his shoulder back up the stairs, and she glances behind too, half expecting to see the machine descending on its tracks. 'I didn't realise it had got this bad. We should never have come this way.'

'Did it know who we were?' she asks.

'I don't think so. It's the Tower. With the king moving in, the security has gone crazy. Hopefully that's all it was.'

He is still out of breath and she checks her own energy level to find that it has dropped sharply again. At this rate she may be obliged to make him keep his rash promise to carry her.

As they turn the corner of the building, the space between the warehouses opens up into a harbour with elegant yachts moored to pontoons. New snow lies on the decks of the boats, their furled sails and the network of wooden walkways.

'Ideally I wouldn't have brought you this way either,' Daniels says, 'more cameras, but this time at least they're here merely to protect rich people's property. Just don't touch anything, or you'll set alarms off.'

They skirt the basin, criss-crossing the water via little bridges, giving as wide a berth as possible to the ghostly sail ships and bobbing motor launches.

In theory, Evie has only seen such things in the picture books kept on the bottom shelf of her husband's library, acquired for her to learn about the world. But she has also a second and stronger association – a nagging feeling that she once sailed on such a yacht. In the memory, she is entrusted with the boat's wheel and clings to it with a small hand while not letting go of her bonnet with the other. The responsibility terrifies her as she must steer without assistance, while tall figures, silhouetted against the bright sun, do complicated things with the rigging. With the sails fixed, a woman climbs down to sit beside her in the stern, the light gleaming on her beautiful face as she presses Evie to her and strokes her hair. Evie cradles the moment in her mind now, keeping its glow alive like a candle behind her palm, drawing from it the warmth she can. It is the only remembrance they gave her of a mother.

She knows of course that it can't be an actual memory because in it she is in a child's body – it is an implant based possibly on something Evelyn herself once experienced. That knowledge doesn't make her recall of the boat's nauseous chopping motion, nor the blinding blue of the sky, seem any less real.

Beyond the harbour, she and Daniels move through narrow streets lined with dishevelled shuttered shops. It is a couple of hours since they set out and dawn is breaking, bringing people out of stairwells and doorways – a wagoner trundling the morning milk, a brickie with his empty hod sloped against his shoulder, a yawning nurse in a tall white cap wheeling an electro-cycle . . . but these bleary-eyed early risers have enough to worry about keeping the freezing air from creeping under their clothes, without paying attention to strangers.

On the corner of a wide highway, where the wheeled traffic slips and slides, a vendor sells sugared tea from an urn at the rear of a horse-drawn cart.

Daniels buys himself a mug, holding it in his stiff hands, allowing the steam to condense on his cheeks. Evie stands behind him, trying to make herself inconspicuous but nevertheless attracting the attention of the horse which startles her by putting its whiskered chin on her shoulder and breathing over her face.

'Maisy's curious about you, Miss,' the man says. 'Sure you won't be fancying a wee tot yourself?'

Evie shakes her head, nervously stroking the horse's rough mane and patting his firm, warm neck. She has never touched an animal before and the vigour of life throbbing under its skin leaves her feeling like a sham.

'You've made a friend there, you have!' the man says, as the horse licks her cheek. 'She likes sweet things.'

The last stage of their journey is along a canal.

Her energy levels are at critical. A small light which had been flashing amber in the corner of her vision turns solid red and she holds Daniels's arm as she walks, resting against his side.

It is a heavier cold in the shadows and he uses his free hand to draw his scarf up around his ears. 'This is Limehouse Cut,' he says, 'we're on the last leg. We'll soon be in Bow. Think you can manage?'

She nods weakly, while the nursery rhyme – 'I do not know, says the great bell of Bow' – rings in her head.

The towpath, no more than six or seven feet wide, gives straight onto the water. She peers over nervously. The bright algae coating the surface casts a phosphorescent glow over the snow heaped on the bank.

In places, narrowboats are moored to posts, twisted barbed wire protecting the occupants from incursion.

Buildings line the towpath. Many were once apartments but are now derelict, boarded up and covered in graffiti.

'Why does no one live in them any more?' she asks. The place would be less scary, less ghostly, if there were signs of human occupation, a curtain at a window, the occasional light.

'Oh there'll be people living there all right, you just can't see them, but they'd not be the sort we'd be wanting to meet!'

Occasional road bridges cross over the water, the low headroom forcing Daniels to bend. Evie limps beside him, dragging her feet through the snow.

A loud siren on the road above sounds and they look up sharply but it as quickly dies. Daniels sucks in a deep breath and glances over at her. 'Not far now,' he murmurs.

She doesn't have much more to give. Simon has not spoken for an hour and even then he was almost too faint for her to understand. All of her secondary systems are in standby.

The morning light illuminates the upper walls of the buildings but at ground level, the air remains below freezing and the snow bears a brittle crust which cracks under her shoes.

'What will you tell your daughter as to why we are here?' Evie asks.

'I'm not sure. It's unfair to involve her more than we must. Less she knows the better.' His breath clouds around his face, the wasteful warmth of it another of those little signs of being alive.

'How long will we stay?'

'Just time for you to rest. Is till evening long enough?'

She nods. Rest, she thinks, what a pleasant notion. 'A few hours will be sufficient,' she says. Then after a pause, 'You think they will come looking for us out here? You think they really want me so much?'

'Having gone to the lengths they've gone to, I can't see them giving up now. I think they will try to find Iz's as somewhere I might take you. She's fetched herself off-grid but no one can disappear completely. I guess it depends who they really are and what access they have to government databases.'

'But he was police,' she says.

'He may have been, if the card wasn't forged. But if he'd been properly on police business, he wouldn't have come on his tod.'

'Maybe he was working alone and now that he's dead, the threat is over.'

'It's possible. But then how would he have known about you, if others weren't in on it?'

Evie is still struggling to comprehend how it is she has become so important to whoever these people are, but the evidence is abundant and she trusts Daniels's judgement. Simon's fear that she would end up under the auctioneer's hammer was way off the mark; rather she realises that she is a black-market commodity like illegal ivory from an extinct elephant or rhino. Better for her if she'd been slain in the apartment. Got it over with. Better for her if she could have climbed onto her husband's funeral pyre like an Indian princess and been burned to ashes beside his body. 'Where is Matthew's cottage?' she asks, making an effort to lift her spirits. Talking consumes only a little energy and distracts her from the demons inside.

'Out near a village called Little Wotton.'

'Little Wotton,' she says. 'It sounds quaint.'

'It's quaint all right. It's small and basic and the roof leaks but it has solar power and a well and it will give us time to decide our next move.'

'It doesn't strike me as his sort of thing.' She can only imagine Matthew in the climate-controlled apartment and its well-ordered garden. And now laid out as a corpse on his own mattress.

'It wasn't. He bought it as a gift for Evelyn because she was so taken by the country around those parts. He was going to present it as a wedding gift, but then that didn't happen and the only person who has gone there since is myself to make sure it doesn't fall down.'

While they talk they completely miss the small boys, a pair of twelve-year olds, following. Evie hears the faint snap of a twig under the snow. Looking behind, she squeezes Daniels's elbow and they turn to face them.

The boys are dressed in oversized jumpers belted at the waist, and torn jeans tucked into army boots. Their pale, malnourished little faces are fringed with soft curly hair. For a moment she wonders if they are girls dressed up.

'Got any money, mister?' one says, the voice scratchy and high-pitched. She would have felt pity for them, having a soft spot for Dickensian orphans, but she has spied that they are hiding behind their backs lengths of wood.

Daniels shakes his head. 'Get lost, lads,' he says, drawing himself up to his full height, 'we've nothing for you.' Gripping Evie by the wrist, he takes a step back.

The boys glance at one another. Surprise has been lost and they need to adapt their plan. They bring their weapons around – pieces of two by two, one with nails in the end and the other wrapped with some kind of electrical tape to form a primitive cattle prod. One of the boys puts his fingers to his lips and whistles. The shrill sound pierces the damp air, rebounding off the blank windows of the abandoned apartments.

Daniels pulls her against him and, half-turning so that he can keep an eye on the boys, leads her away along the canal path. She leans on his arm like a cripple, her feet dragging in the snow, slurring a channel. If it comes to it, she could achieve a final burst of energy. She has her fast sprint – one respect at least in which she is superior to Evelyn. But she'd not make it much beyond fifty yards before she was spent.

Three more boys slip from a doorway of the dilapidated block ahead. Two are a similar size to the ones behind and armed likewise with handmade weapons. The third is older – tall and gangly with a pillar-box mouth – and carries a pole topped with a serrated spike like a harpoon. He tilts his head and the group fans out, blocking the path in front and behind. He folds his arms and grins, leering at Evie, licking the gaps in his teeth. There is something wrongly developed in his lumpish jaw and swollen lips.

The smaller boys close in, holding their weapons out in bony fists.

'Stay behind me,' Daniels murmurs.

They stand with their backs to the wall. It is not much of a defensive position and if it comes to a fight, he will have to let her go to fend them off. The seconds tick by, the boys glancing from one to another. They are like hounds: if they rush together, their chances are improved but at least one of them will be taken down.

'Clear off!' A small man, not much larger than a boy himself, his head oddly narrow as if it was clamped or squashed as a baby, emerges from the shadows. He holds a shotgun at his waist, the stubby barrels levelled on the group. He slides it over their faces and brings it to bear on the chest of the tall one who is evidently the leader. 'Go'n,' he says, 'mek yer move.' It's as if the shape of his head causes the words to come out squeezed.

This older lad stares back, unwilling to concede, before muttering a command, and the smaller boys shrink away. Walking backwards, he slinks into the building, holding his fingers up in a three-fingered gesture of contempt, his strange mouth wide and disdainful.

Evie and Daniels are left alone on the towpath with their rescuer.

'Thank you,' Daniels says.

'Ah, think nothing of it – they're jest a set a bleedin' cowards, pickin' on the weak.' He tucks the gun inside his jacket. 'Shem they didn't make a fight of it, it'd have been an excuse to clean out a rats' nest and I'd have enjoyed dropping thet skinny twat in the canal. Yur Iz's old man, ain't yur? I saw yer over last night. You should know we lek after our own 'ere.'

He begins to walk away, then stops and turns. 'Oh, by the way if yur in the mood, come to the yard behind the Pissin' Pig at noon.' He points beyond a barrier constructed from dented car panels and driftwood blocking the path ahead, with a narrow way through hinged like a pair of gates.

'Tell 'em yer with Billy,' the man shouts after them. 'A geezer frum Wulthamstow with a bulldog the size of an ox is fancyin' it aginst all comers.'

'What was the matter with his face?' Evie asks, as soon as she and Daniels are on their own.

'Yeah, it wasn't too pretty.'

'Did someone do it to him?'

'More likely born that way. A birth defect caused by toxins in the water from all the plastic and other rubbish. No wonder no one lives as long as they used to.'

They pass under a sign dangling from a lead pipe: YOU ARE ENTERING LEA RIVER ESTATE – WHITES ONLY. Evie looks at Daniels for an explanation but he huddles down into his coat as if he is trying to make himself as small as possible.

'What does—?'

'Evie, don't say anything,' he murmurs. 'Just keep walking.'

11

In the distance a pair of enormous metal frames loom over the trees, the sharp morning light, now that the mist has cleared, jabbing between the iron pillars and struts.

'They're old gas holders,' Daniels says. 'It's how they used to store energy. Iz's place is on the right.'

His daughter lives in what appears to be a semi-abandoned block where the canal joins the river. They cross to the entrance through a patchwork of bare allotments, the icy clodded soil caked with snow. He helps Evie up the internal stairs, letting her pause on the landings.

'Does she know who I am?' Evie asks, on the last but one, as she lets her energy level stabilise before the final set.

'She knew of you, but it was a long time ago, and she's probably forgotten.'

She shuffles along the last stretch of corridor and holds onto the wall as Daniels knocks on his daughter's door. From the other side they hear the scuttle of rapid footsteps.

It swings open in a rush. 'At last,' the woman says, 'I thought something . . .' Her voice fades, as she takes in that her father has returned.

'I'm sorry Iz, but it's an emergency. I'll explain inside.'

His daughter remains in the doorway but does not prevent them from squeezing past.

'You came with Troy?' Iz asks. Her face is expressive of her efforts to make sense of things. 'Where is he now?'

'We're on our own,' Daniels says.

Evie glances from one to the other. There are two conversations going on and neither father nor daughter seem aware.

Iz pays attention to Evie for the first time. 'So, you brought "it",' she says, then, glaring at Daniels, 'what do you mean you're on your own – where is he?'

'Where is who?'

'Troy,' she shouts. 'Where is Troy?' Tears leak from her eyes and she wipes at them angrily. 'I've been waiting here for hours, not knowing what was going on. You have no idea what I've been through. These people are not to be messed with. Is he with the hova?'

'I don't know who you're talking about,' Daniels replies, 'but I'm sure everything is fine. Evie needs to rest. Can she use your back room?'

Iz drops onto a stained two-person sofa, knocking aside a low table. 'I don't understand,' she mutters, 'first he doesn't answer calls and now you're here . . .' She tries to think things through, fiddling agitatedly with the cuffs of her all-in-one.

'Iz,' Daniels says, 'we'll sort it out. There'll be a simple explanation.' He turns to Evie. 'I'll show you where you can go.'

He leads her down a narrow passage crowded with coats into a box room just wide enough for a narrow bed. A large holdall fills the remaining floor. Evie squeezes around it and peers out through a grimy window onto a fire escape. Beyond are a pair of canal locks, the river slopping over swollen gates held together by rusting iron plates.

She undoes her wet coat and passes it to Daniels who hangs it on a hook. She then sits on the bed and pulls off her hat and unwinds her scarf, releasing her hair, which unfolds flatly over her shoulders.

Daniels takes out her transformer and cable from his backpack and plugs it into the socket beneath the wardrobe. He passes her the cable. Past considerations of propriety, she lifts her jumper in front of him and peels back a strip of skin below the jut of her ribs to expose a gold-plated socket and twists it

90

clock-wise to lock. She hasn't charged herself in this way for years and the sudden rush of electricity, stronger than through the wireless arrangement in the apartment, kicks her in the spine, sharply lifting her chin.

For ten or more seconds she remains seated stiffly, eyes closed, letting the power flood through. Then her body slumps.

Daniels lifts her legs onto the mattress and props a pillow under her head. He raises her heels, removing her wet shoes. Finding a nanoflec blanket on top of the wardrobe, he draws the lightweight gauzy material over her feet to her waist. These gestures are unnecessary for her comfort but the kindness underpinning them warms her from within.

'You're safe,' he says quietly. 'I'm not going anywhere. I'll be with Iz. Nothing will happen to you here.' He gazes down at her face and she opens her eyes and smiles back, the electricity coursing through her inducing a trance-like grin.

Something is not right, Simon says, as soon as they are alone.

I know, she mutters, wishing to put herself under, but reluctantly staying with it, listening to Daniels return to the other room.

'What has happened?' Iz demands as he enters. The walls are so thin, it is as if he and his daughter are only just outside the door.

'What do you mean?'

Evie hears the spark of Iz's lighter and her breathe out. A chair creaks.

'Where is he?' she asks.

'Where is who?'

'Don't play games with me.' An ashtray scrapes across the coffee table. 'Where have you been?'

'I went back to the apartment—'

'But you brought it here.'

'Please Iz, don't call her that.'

'Like *it* has feelings! Like it's not a machine!' Evie can hear the tears in her voice.

91

'That isn't the point.'

'I think the point is that you've always made it so obvious.'

'What so obvious?'

'How you valued her more than mum and me. How do you think that made us feel? Why do you think mum left you?'

'That's not true.'

'Always so polite and accommodating. And do you know why that is?'

The ghastly atmosphere is palpable even in the back room.

'Because it's a robot programmed to fuck and clean and the crazy thing is that you're so completely and utterly taken in!'

'She is being unfair,' Evie says quietly, as much for her benefit as Simon's. 'She's twisting things.'

Iz starts to sob and she hears her father seat himself on the sofa beside her. 'It was never like that,' he says quietly. 'Since your mother took you away, things have not been the way I wanted them. We've not spent the time together we should have.'

'That fucking bitch,' Iz's tears are so strong, she can barely articulate.

'Evie is not you. She is not a substitute. You are my daughter, you're the only daughter I want. The only one I've ever wanted.'

How long before I am charged? Evie asks. She is trying to stay calm, but her tone gives her away.

You'll be at fifteen percent in ten minutes but to get to full will be at least three hours.

There won't be time for that.

She removes the connector and sits up.

What do you think you are doing?

I'm going to find some better shoes and then we're getting out of here. She looks in the wardrobe but at the bottom is only a bag of clothes pegs and a jar of fishing bait.

In the hall, Simon mutters.

She opens the door quietly and, looking under the coats, picks out a pair of padded boots and from above, a red fleece-lined jacket with a furred hood. She likes neither, was more comfortable in what she had before, but these are practical choices. She returns to the back room where she finds socks in a drawer, pulling them on as the discussion in the front room intensifies.

Iz draws breath and blows her nose. 'So where is Troy?'

'Who's Troy? Is he your boyfriend?'

'Yes, Troy is my "boyfriend",' she mutters. 'Why are you here? Are you in this together to try and rob me of my share? I won't allow it!'

'There was a break-in, in the apartment last night,' Daniels says. 'Matthew was killed.' Evie can hear the suffering in his voice and the sadness washes through her too.

Iz catches her breath.

'It happened while I was returning from here. When I got back he was . . . he'd been shot . . . he was dead. It was too dangerous to stay.'

Daniels's daughter draws noisily on her cigarette. 'And what happened to . . . ?' she asks.

'To who? The intruder?'

'Yes "the intruder"!' she answers angrily.

'He died.'

'Died? How?' Her voice is shaking. 'No one just dies. It was the fucking android wasn't it?'

Daniels doesn't answer.

'That little cunt killed him, didn't it?'

'It was self-defence.'

'Fuck self-defence,' she shouts. 'It's a machine!'

'Why do you care what happened to him?'

'Because he was Troy, you imbecile!'

There is silence for a few seconds.

'But why?' Daniels asks weakly. He is struggling to make sense of what she has just told him.

'Because of her! What do you think? Jesus, how dense are you!'

'You lured me here, while you sent your boyfriend – Troy – to—'

'I didn't lure you here,' she snaps. 'Don't be so fucking melo-dramatic! I did you a kindness. I got you out of the way to save any heroics. But I underestimated what that little snatch was capable of. I warned Troy to be careful, I warned him that she's not the docile little suck she pretends to be, but would he listen?'

'Why?' Daniels asks. 'Why have you done this?'

'Why?' She sounds incredulous. 'I'll tell you why. Rumours of this clockwork freak were all over Troy's station. They were all nosing around. It was only a matter of time before it was picked up. Me and Troy were just trying to – Oh fuck! What's the time? Oh fuck, it's gone eight! Oh Christ, they're going to be here any minute.'

'Who?' he asks.

'The people Troy found. The buyers.'

Evie is standing in the doorway of the small back room, transfixed by the revelation of how nearly she was trapped.

We've got to get out of here right now, Simon urges.

'You were going to sell her!' Daniels says.

'Oh don't look at me like that. Too right we were going to sell it. It was going to be enough to settle both our debts and give us a fresh start. Get away from this wretched country. We were going to America!'

'You really hate her that much?' Daniels asks.

'Yes, I do,' she spits. 'I fucking detest it, always have. Getting even with that mechanised little slut was the icing on all this.'

Evie enters the front room. 'We need to go,' she says.

Daniels is seated beside his daughter, staring forwards with a dazed expression. 'Yes,' he says, but he does not move.

'You're not going anywhere,' Iz says, getting to her feet. She is looking at Daniels but the statement is for Evie.

Evie crosses the room and takes Daniels by the arm, pulling him to his feet.

Iz makes a grab for her but overbalances and falls against the wall. While she struggles upright, Evie pulls Daniels along the passage into the back room and shoves up the window with a bang.

Footsteps echo in the stairwell beyond the front door. 'They're here,' Evie says and bundles him out ahead of her onto the fire escape.

In the courtyard behind the building floats a sleek hovacar eighteen inches above the ground, its doors retracted, the driver standing on the river bank, face to the sun, nodding along to the music in his earphones.

Evie feels the warmth of the downdraft as they run through the melted snow. They climb in and the doors automatically close. Daniels, now recovered, glances over the instrumentation and touches the wheel. The motors accelerate and the vehicle bucks, the rear rapidly rising, tilting the front towards the ground, throwing them against the control panel.

The driver, abruptly aware of the theft in progress, casts away his cigarette and rushes towards them.

'Anchor?' Daniels mutters frantically. He scans around himself, then lowers a lever by his seat and the front of the vehicle, freed from gravity, ascends sharply, levelling as the compass acquires control.

Men appear at the window with handguns. Green and orange beams glance sizzling off the armoured bodywork.

As the car accelerates upwards, the force pins Evie to her seat. The buildings rapidly shrink until her view of the ground is of the giddy prospect of the tops of the cylindrical gasometers and the dark waterway cutting an emerald wound through the white snow.

12

'You're going to need a new name for when we meet people,' says Daniels. 'Any ideas?'

'Jane,' Evie answers, without hesitation. 'I'd like to be Jane.'

Simon huffs, *poor little Jane*. But he has been happier than normal for the last half an hour, feeding off her own distracted delight as they zoom over the snow-covered fields.

She sits close to the door, with her forehead against the window, so she can see everything they pass over. The vehicle is like a flying carpet out of *The Arabian Nights*.

After escaping from Daniels's daughter's and since leaving the suburbs of North London, they have descended to just a hundred feet and the tops of trees and pylons rush towards them as they skim the landscape.

'We're less visible down here than higher up,' he says. 'They'll try to follow for sure – maybe are already – but they won't catch us now. This thing is too darned fast.'

Because of their speed, the snow freezes on the windscreen and is only kept clear by the rapid swipe of the wiper.

Other hovas criss-cross around them, some extremely close and some scooting straight in front, and collision for a moment seems all but certain. It takes a while for her to relax and trust the navigation and as they get further from the city, the traffic is more sedate.

They track for a while a road far broader than any she came across in London – up to a dozen lanes wide in places. Despite the driving snow, they are close enough to pick out a slow-moving caravan of hunched pedestrians, hand-, horse- and mule-drawn carts as well as wheeled cars and trucks of many varieties. But the traffic is thinly spaced and the road unnecessarily vast.

'You'd think everyone would fly,' she says, immersed in the joy of her vantage point.

'The main reason they don't is money. These things cost a fair bit to buy and run, plus all aerial vehicles require a licence and that boils down again to money. Some people have the wherewithal, but most haven't and to be honest the majority don't need to travel much or far.'

He pushes a button and a bright hologram map – the vivid green and brown contours of hills and valleys seemingly tangible – fills the air around them.

She recoils in her seat and Daniels, too, is taken by amused surprise at what he has activated. 'The last time I drove was ten years ago and things have really come on. Back then it was a flip-up display.'

She reaches out, extending her finger towards a swathe of forest, and in response the area swells up like under a magnifying glass, until the trees become individually identifiable. As she strokes the tops of the tallest, the upper branches part under her fingers like pond weed. She trails the tip of her nail between the trunks, spreading ripples through the leaves. It is like dragging her hand through the cool water in the garden pond, scattering the fish. She withdraws her finger and the individual trees shrink back.

Daniels taps in the coordinates of the cottage onto a panel in the air and a virtual blue line threads its way across the landscape below them. 'Like spilt ink,' he says absent-mindedly, surprising her with a rare indulgence in fancifulness.

She smiles back. 'Or a reel of silk,' she says, in an effort to be inventive too. 'How far is it?'

'Another half an hour – we're already in Cambridgeshire. In fact, twenty-three-and-a-half minutes if this thing is accurate, which it probably is.'

Evie watches the tops of the actual trees fly past. 'I love it,' she says, 'I really do, I never imagined the world could be so beautiful. But right now, after everything that has happened, all I want to do is tuck myself away and hibernate somewhere safe.' She sinks into her seat, as if this will help make her less exposed.

He glances over. 'Couldn't have put it better myself.' His face grows slowly careworn and she has the intuition that he's thinking about his daughter and what she has done. Evie does not know what to say.

They land in a field behind a group of buildings. She watches from the car as he crosses to a gate and, clambering over, enters the yard beyond. He returns a few minutes later, the door of the vehicle retracting as he approaches.

'It's all clear,' he says. He reaches in behind and takes their backpack from the rear seat. 'Let's get inside.'

She follows him around the wall of a barn. As they pass, he peers between the slats. 'That's good, there's room enough inside for the hova, we'll hide her in there. Once I've disconnected the battery, she'll be undetectable to even the most sophisticated divining technology.'

The door to the cottage is already open, the snow blowing onto the stone flags of a narrow hall.

'How did you unlock it?' she asks.

'Oh, that was easy. The key was under the old milk churn, just where I last left it – this is the countryside, people trust one another.'

Just a humble key, she thinks, revelling in their return to a world of reassuringly simple technology.

They enter a small kitchen and he drags his finger along the worktop, holding it up to show her a curl of dust. 'Looks like I'll be needing to get the old marigolds out.'

'Marigolds?' Daniels grew them in the apartment's greenhouse and she herself, quite the lady of the manor, would cut them for the vases in the library and music room.

'You know, cleaning gloves — just something my old gran used to say.'

He turns on the light switch in the corner and after an initial flicker, the strips around the cabinet doors glow steadily. 'How about that then,' he says, 'the cells work even when covered with snow!'

The only other rooms on the ground floor are a bathroom and a small sitting room with a set of partially enclosed stairs leading to the floor above. She follows him up. On the tiny landing is a single door. The frame is so low that Daniels has to bend to enter and even then his head only just scrapes through. 'For small people,' he grins. The bedroom has a single bed with a head-board covered in a flowered damask and a window overlooking the field. She goes over and looks out. The hovacar is already disappearing under a coating of snow, the scorch marks where the gunshots struck and scored the bodywork fading from view.

'This is your room,' he says. 'What do you think?'

She looks around her at the pale green woodwork. 'My room?' she says, supressing a tremor in her voice. 'Where will you sleep?'

'On the sofa.'

'But I don't need a bed. You should take it.'

He shakes his head. 'The room is for you. I insist.'

She looks at him. She can see he is not going to budge. 'Thank you,' she says, letting her happiness begin to bubble up. 'I love it.'

She looks out of the window again at the field and the distant bare trees and the long grey hedge capped with snow, and then back at the snug interior.

She turns. Daniels is only just inside the room; his head is nearly touching the ceiling and he is standing at the highest part. Stepping around the bed, she presses against him and, reaching up, kisses him on the cheek.

'Heh!' he says, blushing innocently. Thirty years ago, if she had done that, he might have taken it in a completely different way. Now it just feels natural.

'I love it, I love it, I love it!' she says, pulling away.

'I guess you do then,' he says, wiping his cheek. He glances at the steeply sloped ceiling. 'Anyway it wouldn't have suited me much, I'd have banged my head ten times a day.'

You didn't have to be so over the top, Simon mutters when they are alone, but Evie ignores him. She is wondering if any of her pleasure is because this place was chosen to please Evelyn's tastes and it was just inevitable that it would please hers too. If only Matthew had wanted to bring her here. What would have been the risk in that?

She sits on the bed and, resting her elbows on the windowsill, gazes out.

Daniels emerges into the yard below. He has found the key for the barn and swings back the doors. He then tramps out into the field and slowly pilots the hova over the fence and, bringing it down to ankle-height, steers it through the opening into the barn, the downdraft throwing up a skirt of wet snow.

She lies back and gazes at the ceiling.

I love it, I love it, she thinks to herself, unable to stop happiness from flooding her. Less than eight hours ago her husband died in her arms and she has fled for her life twice since, but now a blissful contentedness is washing through her. It feels for the first time in her life as if she has come home.

Well, don't get too happy, Simon intervenes. *This is far from over. Very much far from over.*

'I know,' she murmurs, 'but—' An odd association has popped into her head. She is thinking of what she once read about dovecotes in seventeenth century France. That they were built larger than most houses and had incorporated into the brickwork a projecting horizontal line called a rat ledge, its purpose to stop rats running up the brick. Safe as a dovecote the expression became. Safe as a dovecote, she repeats to herself dreamily. The loveliest conception. Safe as a dovecote.

Indeed. But rather than congratulating yourself, this could be a good moment to complete the charging cycle from earlier. May I remind you that interrupted routines are detrimental to our cell's longevity.

Coming out of charge, Evie is aware of how the temperature in the cottage has risen.

She continues to lie still, delighting in her surroundings. Daniels has been in the room while she slept – she knows it because a blanket has been laid over her. She sits up and looks out of the window. Outside it is dark. It is only four o'clock but there isn't a light to be seen. It is so unlike London where there would be a glow from the tall buildings and the pin-pricks of fires burning in the streets. Her reflection stares back from the glass, her small purposeful nose, so suggestive of intrigue, out of place as ever in her shy and unadventurous face.

Cupboards are built into the eaves and one of the half-height doors hangs open. She sees that Daniels has unpacked and laid her few things inside. A small mirror is propped on one of the shelves and taking her hairbrush she works at her hair until it hangs smoothly, framing her pale skin. Taking a dark blue ribbon, she ties it behind her ears.

Evie opens the bedroom door and smoke from below wafts through. The staircase is partially boxed around and it isn't until she is halfway down that she has a full view of the room. Daniels is asleep in front of a wood fire. His shoes are drying on the hearth, his socked feet stretched out, soaking up the warmth.

As she turns the bottom corner, the stair creaks and he opens his eyes. He smiles up at her in the corner above him. 'How're you feeling?' he asks.

'Better,' she says. 'Much better.'

A smell of cooking comes from the kitchen and, getting up creakily, he goes to tend it.

'Did you go out for food?'

'I didn't have to,' he says through the doorway. 'There were some cans in the cupboard.' The smell of heated tomatoes is pleasant but does not generate a sensation of hunger in her.

Evie sits on the small sofa under the window. The backpack is on the floor beside the arm, with Daniels's newsplastic folded beneath the flap. Not looking at such devices has been a sort of unwritten rule, originating from a desire to not 'unsettle' her with glimpses of the outside world. That lesson was learnt early on after her husband's descriptions left her restlessly eager to explore and confused when he did not then take her out.

She battles with her curiosity, glancing towards the kitchen door. Behind it, Daniels hums to himself as he stirs his saucepan. She reaches towards the newsplastic. It is as if her hand is guided by forces beyond her control. She watches her fingers fiddle with the strap. She is both desperate to know what she can learn but also terrified as to what that might be: that the device will hold news of the search for themselves. There is the sense, too, that she is breaking a long-held prohibition.

As her hand lifts the loosened flap, she is distracted by the identity card Daniels took from the body in the garden poking from an exposed side pocket. She draws it out and opens it.

The blood on the card has dried, obscuring the face, but the owner's name is still quite readable – Troy Evans. Her chest rises and falls in rapid, jerky movements. It is like a little bit of the horror of earlier has found her, all the way out here.

She folds the card up and slides it back as Daniels returns into the room with a bowl of soup cupped between his large hands.

13

Evie and Daniels leave the cottage through the gate in the yard and tramp along the edge of the field, keeping the drainage ditch to their right. The light this morning is dazzling and the sky unmarked, apart from the bright vapour trail from a hova that passed ten minutes before. What strikes Evie, without tall buildings to interrupt the view, is the size of the air above her head. Its span, without means of support.

Her new boots make easy graft of the stiff grass and the slippery mud showing through. She wears her hood thrown back with the sun on her face. Her new coat, with its luminous sheen, casts a pink glow on the snow. She is like a different person. A new person.

They reach the corner of the field and, clambering over a stile, cut diagonally across the next, following the indentation of a path up the hill towards a solitary oak.

It is like the first day of the rest of her existence. 'Do you think we're really free now?' she asks.

'Do you mean will they come after us?'

'Yes.' She wasn't thinking about it quite like that, but that is the crux.

'They won't give up easily. You've seen the lengths they're prepared to go to.' They had this same conversation yesterday. The answer remains as uncertain.

She changes the subject. 'What took place in "The Rebellion"?' In the apartment, Daniels would never have allowed himself to be drawn on this sort of thing but now that he isn't obliged to follow Matthew's rules for her 'wellbeing', she's determined to take advantage.

'Rebellion was always a rather grand term for a quite small affair but it frightened enough people for a change in the law.'

'The Protective Acts?'

'Yeah, The Acts.'

'What happened? What did they do?'

'You mean, the Acts or the AABs?'

'The Acts.' Evie is conscious she is feeling her way into this, asking the easy questions first.

'Well the Acts were merely a set of laws that banned the production and ownership of artificial entities with independent logic circuits, what we call AABs – Autonomous Artificial Beings. It was never intended to stop the development of lower-grade service models but its impact here in England was to kick the stuffing out of the whole industry.'

'And the AABs themselves, what did they do?' she asks cautiously.

'Mainly they just grew restless but a few got mindlessly violent. But what really alarmed people was the small number that communicated with one another using the Heavenweb network and, it was claimed, tried to take over. Although what they were trying to take over was never too clear. It seemed more that they merely reached a shared understanding that they could improve things quicker if they made a few little changes. It was all trivial stuff, tweaks you'd call them, like the timing of railway signals, but the media presented it as a warning straight out of science fiction and that the superior intellect of these things viewed us poor stupid humans as a threat. I don't think it was anything like that, but there were some unfortunate deaths. For instance when the life-support units in a couple of Birmingham hospitals got reclassified as low priority and had their power cut one night. That was enough to put the wind up the powers that be.'

'What did they do to them, these . . . AABs?'

'Switched the buggers off. Pronto. Every one of them, as soon as they could be found.'

She catches her breath and blinks. Imagining them being hunted down, broken in upon in the middle of the night. 'But not me? I wasn't . . . switched off.'

'No, of course not. You weren't like them one bit. You were neither violent, nor had dreams of improving the public's commuting times.'

Not violent? Evie thinks. He has a short memory. What she did in the apartment garden is never far from her mind. There is another Evie inside the one she is familiar with, capable of killing. Is she some kind of Russian doll with hidden layers? What if there is another hidden within the killing one, capable of even worse?

'They'd been invented after you,' Daniels continues, 'and were designed for commercial use. Also, they were never really more than machines. They may have come under the definition of possessing autonomous processing but they couldn't properly think, not in the round, they just followed their programming to its logical conclusion – such as how best to run an efficient hospital. When it came down to it they were nothing more than clumsy computers with ill-defined goals. And that was what led to the train crash.'

'Train crash?'

'I mean, when it all started to go wrong. But there were literally a couple of real ones too, train crashes that is. No, Evie, you're absolutely nothing like them. Even from the get-go it was apparent you had something special going on in that noddle of yours.'

'Special?' she repeats.

He thinks for a second before answering. 'I mean a moral compass – a conscience.'

Evie remembers how sceptical Daniels had been of her at first, treating her with the same caution he would a new, overly complicated household appliance, but then within a few months had come completely around. The turning point had been when he'd found her crying in the corridor outside Matthew's room. That had been when he'd started to look at her differently. As if she may actually be sort of human.

For quite a while after arriving in the apartment, Evie had actually believed herself to indeed be human. To be a wife. To belong to a loving husband. She'd persisted in denying the truth even when the evidence had begun to stack and stack.

'But under The Acts, I should at least have been registered,' she says.

Daniels looks at her with a puzzled expression, maybe wondering how she knows this. Why he'd be surprised is more the mystery; she's had enough years to figure at least some things out from the plentiful snippets she's overheard. 'Yes,' he says, finally. 'Registered, that is correct — a first step in what was a bureaucratic solution.'

'But I wasn't . . . registered.'

'No, you weren't. Matthew never did believe in following rules. He didn't want much to do with the outside world. He took the view that the less anyone knew of you, the better. I think we can see now that he was right.'

'But with these other AABs, why didn't they just learn from what went wrong and design improved replacements. Less arrogant ones.'

'Less arrogant ones!' Daniels chortles. 'Yeah, I like that. Somehow humanity did indeed transfer its own abundant arrogance into those wretched machines. But, in answer to your question, I think people assumed The Acts were only going to be temporary — a chance to draw breath — but in this country anyway, that's not what happened. With the economy so trashed, it became more about trying to get the basics to run right. Along the way, all that hi-tech know-how, which this country was only ever on the periphery of anyway, was lost.'

'What about elsewhere, outside England?'

'Similar issues. In the States, it became a massive thing, with an amendment being passed to the constitution. But then they did have the most horrendous massacre in their Capitol building when fifty senators and a hundred visiting school children were gunned down by an AAB they'd made head of security.'

'A hundred children killed!' She is appalled.

'It was the death of the fat old senators that actually spurred them to act.'

'With everything that happened. Do you think *we* . . . *they* . . . were a good idea or not?' she asks, not sure she really wants to hear his answer.

'I don't think they were half as brilliant as they thought they were, but *they* were still a *clever* idea. How can it be denied? I think *you*, however, were a totally *great* idea.'

She blushes and twists her neck away towards the distant trees to hide her face. The thing about Daniels is that when he says this kind of thing, he is not doing it to get his way – like she might – but because he really means it. He just can't help but wear his heart on his sleeve.

'And the others – the ones unlike me – should they be brought back?'

'Should they, or will they?'

'Will they?'

'Yeah, they'll be brought back. It was always going to happen at some point and it looks increasingly certain that that point is now. People recognise easily enough that independently minded artificial beings, however tame, however low their running costs, won't improve their lives and would indeed more likely make them worse, but business is pressing hard for the opportunity, as they always will do where there's money to be made.'

A pair of sheep stand together in the sun, on a rise of ground twenty yards away. Curiosity draws her towards them. The snow muffles her tread and they are only conscious of her presence as she comes up alongside and reaches to touch them, when with a hop and skip they skitter away.

Daniels laughs at her disappointment as she returns.

'I didn't mean to scare them,' she says.

'I'm surprised they let you get that close. It must be because they couldn't smell you. A human wouldn't have been able to do that.'

The sheep, now with their backs to the fence, observe them walk on, taking turns to lift their heads and baa aggressively.

They reach the oak in the top corner of the field and pause to allow Daniels to draw breath. Looking back down the hill, their route is as clear as an arrow – morning shadows collecting in their footprints – and in the bottom of the valley smoke rises from the chimney of their cottage. Sunlight glints on the glass of her bedroom window.

She can't believe how much things have changed for her in just twenty-four hours and her present good fortune returns her guiltily to her husband, lying dead on his bed, like it was his funeral barge.

'Thinking of Matthew?' Daniels asks.

She nods, wondering how he read what was in her mind, maybe because the same sad thoughts were in his. 'I let him down.'

'What makes you say that?'

'It was what he told me.' She tries to keep any hint of bitterness from her tone. 'The last thing he said was that by failing to imitate Evelyn closely enough, I had spoiled his memories of her.'

'That's ridiculous,' Daniels says firmly. 'He wouldn't have had a clue what he was saying. You didn't let him down.'

'I was never as good as Evelyn.'

Daniels huffs and they stand together until he speaks again. 'Evie, I met Evelyn a few times – maybe not enough to claim that I really knew her, but certainly enough to form a pretty good impression. I don't like to speak ill of the dead, but I can say truthfully that I found her hard to like. A right bossy, opinionated . . .' He tries a reassuring smile but Evie is staring ahead, her eyes fixed on the distance. 'And I don't care what rubbish Matthew may have come out with, the fool was luckier with you than he was ever prepared to admit.' He puts his arm around her shoulder and squeezes her against him. 'I loved that man and miss him greatly, but boy, sometimes he could be infuriating.'

The two descend the other side of the hill. To Evie's left, a church tower pokes above the trees.

They leave the field over another stile and step down into a road. Apart from the weaving tracks left by cartwheels, the snow lies deep and undisturbed.

They walk fifty yards between the high hedges before these give way to a triangular stretch of common sloping down to a pond rimmed by frozen reeds. Rows of terraced cottages line two of the three sides. By the edge of the road, a boy builds a snowman. He has created the body and has inserted sticks for arms. This is the first child she has seen since they were ambushed on the canal. It's still hard to get her head around the notion that with the decline in fertility from all the horrible poison in the food supply, small children are something of a rarity.

'The shop's just here,' Daniels says, indicating the corner building. 'I'll go in alone to save you a load of unnecessary questions.'

She stands outside, listening to him buy milk and bread. He makes a point of explaining that he is renting their cottage. The fact that it is being used after all these years will not long go unnoticed. People are suspicious of strangers and it is better to provide answers up front.

The boy struggles to lift the head onto his snowman. He is small, probably seven or eight at most, and the head he has made is too ambitious. He raises it six inches and drops it. It is hot work and he pulls off his cap, freeing his hair. Reluctantly he starts to chip away at the ball of snow with his heel. She wonders about offering to help but before she can, he sees her watching, abandons his efforts and backs away, keeping his eyes on her warily until he is out of sight around the nearest house.

She turns again to the shop, the familiar empty feeling, the one they could never have meant to give her, gnawing away.

The window is filled with notices, including an advertisement for the Hawking Museum of Science. It grabs her attention because she remembers the name from the conversation between Matthew and Daniels the day the police came. It had been the first time she'd realised that she is possibly one of only two of her kind, at least in this country.

'Morning, dear,' an elderly lady says. 'Enjoying the nice weather?'

She was thinking so hard how to persuade Daniels to take her there, to this museum, she is caught off guard by the woman's approach. 'Yes?' she says, not sure what the question was and whether she has given the right answer.

The woman has a small dog and she takes its lead and wraps it around a post. 'The poor thing is not allowed inside,' she says. 'Might run amok, they think.'

The dog is straining towards Evie, perhaps being merely friendly or perhaps confused by her lack of a natural scent. It reaches up and licks the inside of her wrist and she hastily withdraws her hand.

'Oh,' the woman says, 'you needn't worry, dear, he doesn't bite. His name is Toby.'

Evie nervously touches the tiny dog's head, which again uninvited licks at her hand, quickly retracting its tongue and snorting in what could have been disgust. It's as if they have both managed now to insult the other.

'You're not from around here, dear, are you?' the woman says.

'We're renting a cottage over the hill,' Evie says cautiously, trying to be consistent with what Daniels is telling people.

'Oh, the old gatekeeper's place. We saw the smoke last night and I said to Toby, it's nice to see it occupied again. Are you on holiday?'

'Holiday?' Despite her nerves, Evie can't help smiling. The association of the word with sand, sea and sunshine is too strongly ingrained from her picture books. 'Yes, I think we are.'

'I see you were looking at the attractions in the window display, were you thinking of visiting anything in particular?

'Is the Hawking Museum near?' she asks.

'The Hawking Museum, why yes, it's just in the town, on the river. I've never been but people say it's interesting.' She doesn't sound convinced.

'How would we get there?'

'Oh, that's easy, there's a bus that'll take you right there, the stop is in the lane opposite the church. You buy your ticket from the driver. How long are you staying?'

'A while, I hope,' she says. 'To be honest we're not sure.'

'Well if you're going to be around, we should introduce ourselves. I'm Mrs Cooper and this is Toby and your name, dear, is?'

'Evie,' she replies, so carried away with thoughts of the museum and what she might find there that she is really not thinking of anything else. Her heart, which for a few minutes has been flying, plummets like a shot pheasant as she remembers that she'd agreed with Daniels not to give out her real name.

That was clever, Simon mutters. *Idiot!*

I was distracted, I wasn't thinking, my defences were down.

'Evie,' the woman repeats, 'Such a lovely name – rarely hear it these days – but it suits a pretty girl like you. Reminds me of someone I once knew. A long time ago. Oh, who was it? She used to come and visit with her young man. My silly old memory is not what it was!'

'Who was that?' Daniels asks, as they make their way back along the lane.

'Just an old lady,' Evie replies cautiously, unwilling to admit her slip.

She'll have forgotten what I said by the time she gets home, she murmurs inwardly, hoping to forestall further criticism, before Simon can get started. *It won't matter a bit.*

You really think so? A busybody like that?

I found her nice.

Of course you did. You'd find anyone nice. Anyway, nice or otherwise it makes no odds. She's going to tell everyone about Evie, about how sweet and pretty she is and exactly where she's staying.

Daniels makes himself lunch and, after rebuilding the fire, lies on the sofa, feet stretched towards the flames, and falls asleep.

Evie listens to his snores and then, reaching across, takes his newsplastic from under the flap of the pack. It is odd that he hasn't used it since they arrived, and unease from not knowing whether there is anything reported about them is becoming unbearable. She stares at the folded sheet, weighing the pros and cons of opening it.

What should I do?

Don't ask me, Simon says. He is as nervous as she is, but also, she senses, as curious too.

She climbs to her room, sticking close to the wall to avoid the squeakiest stairs. She pauses at the turn to take a last look at Daniels noisily asleep below.

She closes her door and climbs onto her bed and sits with her back against the headboard.

In its folded state, the newsplastic is a modest A5, but after unfolding it four times, it opens into a sheet sixteen times its original size. She holds it out in front but it remains obstinately blank. She had assumed it would automatically activate. Yet again she knows nothing.

What do I do? she asks.

Don't expect me to advise you, Simon replies, *this is all your idea.*

She twists it around, holding it vertically and then sideways again and ends up glaring at it. Having overcome her reservations and got this far, she doesn't want to not succeed.

There's an illuminated circle in the corner, Simon says with perfect weariness, *on the back.*

Oh. With the light shining through it from the window, it is almost invisible. She places her thumb over it but nothing changes. *Perhaps it is fingerprint protected.*

Or you've got it round the wrong way.

She flips the newsplastic over just as a whirlpool of concentric rings spread from the centre, accompanied by a brief throb. 'Acquiring satellites' glides across. Anticipation growing, she grips the edges, the pressure from her fingers sending ripples through the page. 'Confirming location' comes up and the rings morph into an aerial view of the surrounding countryside, the detail clarifying as the focus narrows. The sensation of zooming earthward generates a wooziness similar to that she experienced when descending in the hova. The roof of their cottage, adjacent to its snow-covered yard tracked by hers and Daniels's boots, fills the screen. As the camera circles, her own window comes into view.

The words 'active subscriber BBC323770H' briefly flicker and the image of the cottage gives way to the excited popping of headlines and videopix. Her eyes gad over the lively surface and because whatever she focuses on grows instantly larger, she is dragged headlong down a rabbit hole of shifting video imagery.

She is transported overseas via a war report to the deck of a ship on which roaring rocket-drones, laden underwing with bombs, take off against a grainy evening sun. She shudders as a trawler rams a crowded inflatable, spilling the occupants into the rough waves. She is swept by the windy weather all the way to the distant Republic of Siberia, which in contrast to the freeze afflicting England, basks in a month-long heatwave, and then is sharply summoned back to local events, watching from a stairwell of the quadrangle of Christ's College the weekend's riots being suppressed; the black clad police with helmets, batons and shields charging through the porter's lodge, hurling gas canisters ahead of them onto the snow-covered lawn. She has the sensation of being knocked sideways, falling as the camera strikes the ground . . .

. . . and queasily holds her head, letting the flaring lights and smoke subside.

When she reopens her eyes, the sheet has grown calm, almost apologetically so.

With more care, she reads down the columns and, getting used to how the newsplastic displays its information and how to drill, searches Events, honing in on Cambridge and bringing up, after a few false leads, the Hawking Museum.

The museum's exterior is a glass prism that appears to hover over the river. It slowly revolves, revealing through each wall a different exhibit. When an image of a young male face fills the page and almost immediately begins to fade, she urgently flicks out a finger to return it, inadvertently sending the index spinning like a carousel. She slows the motion with her palm and, keeping her eyes steady, patiently pages back, a view at a time. The process reminds her of Matthew in the library working the dog-eared cards of his 'rolodex', in search of the details of a book lost somewhere on his miles of shelves.

She finds the boy again. He gazes out, his life-sized presence mere inches away. She touches his glowing cheek, the flesh under her finger dimpling. The plastic is warm to her touch. 'David – one of a kind', the words say. 'Prepare to be astonished. But don't leave it too long – ends Saturday – folks that's just five days!!!!' She breaks away from the boy's unblinking gaze. Ticket prices and opening times follow and then a final message scrolls across – 'This exhibition made possible by the generous support of Realhuman Corp., Cal., USA'.

Evie closes her eyes and rests her brain from the exhausting viewing – the newsplastic may be the present but her own taste is for the old-fashioned books back in the apartment library. When she looks up again, David and the museum have faded from view.

She finishes her reading by pursuing her original purpose –
searching for anything about her and Daniels – the deaths in the
apartment and their flight. After ten minutes, she lays the
newsplastic aside. She has found nothing. The relief is overwhelming.

Maybe they aren't after me at all, she thinks, but this happy
notion she keeps from Simon, afraid of a sarcastic put-down.
Rather, she lets herself think again about David, his glowing
skin and almost colourless lips, set in an unearthly smile.

t

14

Evie picks her moment after breakfast. Daniels has brought a rusty bicycle he found in the barn into the kitchen and propped it on the table on its handlebars. He pastes a thick glue onto the front tyre wall and lays across a strip of leather cut from an old walking shoe. 'There, good as new,' he says, standing back and admiring his work. She knows that, in the midst of a task which gives him such satisfaction, he is as relaxed as she'll find him all day.

'Daniels, can we go on a trip?' she asks, seating herself opposite.

'A trip?' He's taken by surprise. 'When were you thinking?'

'Today?' She tries to sound casual, as if the timing is really of no consequence, although the exhibition will not be on for much longer, so of course it is.

He stiffens and puts the pot of glue and brush back on the side. 'Is this such a good idea?'

'I just want to go somewhere.' Dare she mention the museum as being her goal – finding this fellow creature? Her instinct is that it'll make him less likely to agree.

'Where did you have in mind?' he asks, as if it is a possibility, but she senses he is not taking her seriously.

'Cambridge. It's nearby. The colleges are meant to be very pretty. The river has swans which I have never seen and there are museums where I can learn things that will help me.'

He stares at the bike and with a rag starts to wipe the dust from the frame. She can almost hear him thinking up reasons why they should not go.

'What do you think?' She reaches out a fingertip and spins the front wheel by its spokes. She smiles up at him, pulling her lips wide, making herself as charming as she can.

'Evie, there'll be a whole lot of cameras and a whole load of people.' He is still resisting, despite all her efforts.

'So?'

'So, it's too much of a risk.'

'Is that a yes?' Saying it, so he'll think he is still deciding.

'I'm sorry, Evie.'

She rests her chin in her hands so that her mouth forms a forlorn little pout. She has a few tricks left yet.

Daniels looks at her awkwardly. 'Listen, we'll go soon.'

'How soon is soon?'

'As soon as we are sure that people have stopped looking for you. In the meantime, you should stick to the cottage. Walking in the lane shouldn't be a problem. Preferably where I can see you.'

She drops her head onto her wrists and stares forward, mulling his responses. Things would be so much easier if she could just cry, she'd have him then for sure. Hiding her face anyway as if she is, she stands abruptly and, taking short quick steps through to the sitting room, runs up the stairs to her room.

He sighs irritably and throws the rag down. 'Evie,' he calls after her as she bangs the door.

It's like we've traded one prison for another, Simon mutters, as if he had not been against the trip as much as Daniels anyway. For all his talk, events have exposed Simon to be a bit of a coward.

She thinks back at him, *This is not over yet.*

Minutes later, Daniels knocks on her door. It took even less time than she'd hoped.

'Yes,' she replies, sniffing loudly, as if she's been sobbing. She is lying on her bed, curled on her side, facing the window.

He sits on the mattress behind her back and gently touches her shoulder. 'Why does it have to be today?'

117

She twists her neck on the pillow to look up at him. 'It doesn't have to be today.'

'Good. In a couple of months, if everything is fine, I'll take you wherever you want, I promise.'

'I didn't mean a couple of months either! I thought you may mean tomorrow.'

'Evie, stop this now,' he says, raising his voice. 'You're not a child.'

No, I'm not, she thinks, I'm older than you, and am supposedly your late master's widow, however I have let myself be treated.

Daniels strokes her hair consolingly but she shakes off his hand. He stands and gazes down. 'Listen, I know you're itching to see everything – I can only imagine what it must be like – but we must just wait a little longer, that's all I'm saying.'

She leaves through the back door. Daniels is in the yard, chopping wood. He glances up as she passes.

'I'm going for a walk,' she says, avoiding eye contact. 'In the lane. Come watch me if you like.'

He sighs. 'What time will you be back?' He leans on his axe. He is stripped to his vest.

'I have no idea.' She pulls opens the gate and lets the spring slam it closed. The two of them have never fallen out before, never even exchanged harsh words, both of them amenable beings in the extreme. The crazy thing is that she is sixty-two years old, if you add her notional age to the years she has been with Matthew, but since this morning she has regressed into a stroppy teenager and doesn't care. The loneliness of being nearly the last of one's kind is something Daniels will never have to understand, and meanwhile there is this boy David, maybe the single other creature in the country like her, and for the next few days only, he is just a few miles away.

Evie follows the lane around the hill, walking where the snow has been trampled and the stiff grass is pressing through. The weather is warmer today and the snow slides from her boots to form a rim of slush around her prints. The steep field to her left lies tangled with brambles and bracken and dotted with scrub and saplings, presumably no longer worth the effort to farm despite all the hunger and malnutrition in the cities. The bare untidy branches have already begun to overhang the road.

She reaches the church and checks the bus stop. She has never been on a bus and must figure out what to do. A timetable is fixed to a pole. There are only two scheduled this morning and she has missed the first but is lucky that the second is still to come. The clock in the church tower reads nine-fifty. The bus is due ten-o-nine. With this fortunate timing she could be there and back by early afternoon. She is already worrying about Daniels worrying, but she mustn't weaken now.

She crosses to sit in the church's porch, but as she approaches, at each step, the stonework becomes unnervingly more familiar. Is this the background behind Evelyn's head in the photograph in the library drawer? Had Evelyn and Matthew stood in this actual spot, forty years before? The likelihood they came here is strong, given that Matthew bought the cottage with her in mind.

She presses on the oak door with her shoulder. Inside, the air is still, and, away from the sun, as cold as the interior of a fridge.

She stops beside a shelf of hymn books, peering down the aisle towards the altar.

Then grabs hold of the nearest pew before she falls.

The end window is just as she recalls it. The tiny figures of Adam and Eve running at full pelt out of the luscious greens of an Eden pregnant with fanciful vegetation and mythical beasts, into a barren desert, pursued closely by a gang of over-sized angels swinging aloft flaming swords.

Her breath comes in gasps. She has, without warning, entered the set of her own wedding. Fake as it may have been, the meticulous craftsmanship of the implant is extraordinary. Not only in the detailing of the window but in every other facet too, from the way the sun glints along the dark pews, casting stripes of darkness, to the hymn board dangling aslant above the pulpit.

She is astonished that they went to so much trouble. Had Matthew planned to marry Evelyn in this very church? And had he wanted her substitute to experience this as her first recollection?

The door scrapes on the stone flags.

'Evie, dear,' a voice chirrups. 'Fancy finding you here.'

She looks behind her. It is the old woman from yesterday.

'Hello,' Evie says, trying to sound friendly but not feeling it. The intrusion is a gatecrashing of her most precious memory which, however false, is in danger of being ruined.

'Oh, excuse me,' the woman says, glancing at the bucket she carries. 'You must be wondering—'

'Not at all,' Evie replies, wanting desperately to get away.

'Having an early spring clean,' the woman continues. 'My late husband has a stone in the corner and it gets so grimy from the candle smoke. I like to give him a little bath once in a while.' She titters privately. 'But my dear, I'm interrupting, you look so sad.'

'I am fine,' she says, making her way quickly to the door, backing out and letting it crash-thump behind her in her eagerness to escape; the woman's curious gaze pursuing her all the way.

As she walks through the streets of Cambridge, Evie keeps her hood up and her head down, wary of the cameras – which are truly as numerous as Daniels suggested, mounted above most shops and on all the college gates. Her visibility is restricted by the fur of her hood but she is still aware of the lenses sweeping around to pursue her as she passes. They seem to single her out from the crowd, maybe attracted by her weaving pace or by her clumsy attempt to pass incognito.

She reaches the museum at noon, approaching via an avenue of beech trees. It is indeed in the shape of a glass prism, just as the newsplastic had portrayed it, but although built on the side of the river facing the college backs, is neither suspended over it, nor does it revolve. She had let herself be a little taken in, but her anticipation as to seeing this creature, uniquely like herself, is all that matters.

She buys a ticket from the window, using almost the last of the dollars she took from Daniels's coat, and runs up the wide stairs to the exhibition hall constructed beneath the atrium, barely able to contain her excitement.

Up here, the air, heated by the sun through the glass above, is as warm as in a greenhouse and although it does not bother her, no one wears anything more than a shirt and so as not to stand out she removes her coat also.

The crowd around the enclosure is several deep, but she squeezes through, wriggling to the front until she is squashed against a twelve-foot glass wall built around a bare concrete square.

Bare that is apart from a youth prowling the boundary of his domain, staring out at his spectators. He pauses in front of a group of women, peering curiously as if he has never seen such creatures, raising from them loud giggles. He wears just a pair of white tennis shorts and as he steps back, startled by their noise, his stomach ripples in the shaft of light from above.

'David,' someone calls from the other side, 'over here.' They all want his attention as if he is a rock star.

He resumes his promenade, his bare feet padding on the polished screed.

'Don't know what the fascination is,' the man behind Evie's shoulder says. His chin is so close that his sour breath ruffles her hair. 'Is this all it does, walk up and down?'

'And these things were meant to be the future!' his companion responds.

'I only came because my daughter said I should. She went with the school and has been back three times on her own. She's even got the poster on her wall.'

Evie can't take her eyes off him. Such sculpted beauty has never existed for her. This creature with his strong shoulders and narrow hips is like nothing she has ever imagined.

As he moves along the glass, the pressure grows from behind, wedging her arms to her sides. It is as if he is a magnet, drawing the crowd towards him like iron filings.

'David, I love you,' a woman calls, and, despite the crowd, she lifts her top and flattens her breasts against the glass.

'Did you see that?'

'Hard to know what the world is coming to. Are you ready to go? I know I've had enough.'

'Let's wait for it to pass.'

David sidles towards her corner, glaring over her head at the crowd behind. His lips peel back, exposing glistening canines.

'Just see how arrogant and hostile it is,' the man behind mutters. Lowering his voice, 'Jesus . . . now it's staring at me!'

'It heard you,' his companion whispers. 'They can hear pins drop.'

David releases the man from his gaze and scans the crowd, searching between the heads.

The man's breath fills her ear. 'Phew! I tell you we're lucky there's a wall between us and that thing. It'd kill us and have absolutely no qualms.'

David drops his eyes and, to Evie's astonishment, looks directly at her. Doing something he has not until now, he comes close to the glass and bends so that his face is level with hers. Evie feels the pressure on her shoulders lessen as the men behind her retreat.

'What's it doing?'

'It's taken a liking to that girl.'

David places his hand on the glass so only she can see his face and stares into her eyes. She can't break away from his look.

'Help me,' he mouths.

*

Descending the stairs, Evie hears the same men behind her again.

'Freakin' Norman. You see the way it looked at me. I tell you, to them we're just flies. They've got superhuman strength. That glass wall was for our protection, not its.'

'Did you hear about the one in London?'

'I thought this was the only one.'

'They thought so too but they found a female the other day that some old guy had been harbouring for years. After slaughtering him in his bed, it went on to gut a policeman like a pig – no pun intended. Slit him from here to here. Been on the news all morning. But the really scary thing is the picture they have of it – timid looking, butter-wouldn't-melt type, the sort you wouldn't look twice at. Not a chance of guessing what was going on in its head.'

Evie walks more quickly and exits the building, pulling on her coat and lifting her hood. She scurries down the steps outside and, crossing the snow-covered lawn beside the river, cuts through a line of protestors, dodging under their banner threatening divine retribution on the creators of idolatrous forms.

She dashes along the gravel path. Her head, which had been full of poor David just minutes before, is now swamped by feelings of her total foolishness. She has exposed herself recklessly. She crosses a humpbacked stone bridge over the frozen Cam and from there follows a narrow icy lane between the high college walls.

It is only then that she realises she is being followed.

She enters a chemist and hurries through, breaking apart the queue at the pharmacy. She emerges the other side into a quiet backstreet with just a few second-hand shoe and clothes traders, their merchandise arrayed on trestle tables. A few doorways down, she tucks herself into the entrance of a coffee shop, hiding with her back to the grubby mock-Tudor window, too scared to look out from under her coat.

She hears rapid footsteps and, seeing shoes from under the fur trim of her hood, pelts out, avoiding an outstretched arm and, leaping from the kerb, hurtles straight into the road. An aerial delivery van, scooting along at shoulder height, veers sharply to avoid taking off her head, and clangs into a lamppost.

Everyone turns to watch. The van driver screams abuse from his window, eight feet up. A dozen Korean workmen stare through the steamed-up glass of the nearby arcade. A bearded violinist breaks off from scraping out the ballad Northern Lights (even in her distressed state, she recognises the heartbreaking melody, poor rendition though it is), and points at her with his bow.

Stunned temporarily by the near miss, Evie collects her wits and is quickly on the move again, weaving through the crowd. She steals a glance back at her pursuer, now alarmingly close behind.

She turns down a covered alley beside a supermarket and hides behind a refuse bin.

He appears at the end, out of breath. He walks slowly along, peering behind the heaps of discarded cardboard boxes.

Before he can reach her, she darts out, colliding with a woman on a bike, knocking her from her saddle and scattering the muddy potatoes in her handlebar basket over the cobbles.

She sprints past a row of humming motorised trolleys, chained together like a road gang, while he lopes after her, one hand stretched out, the other holding his side. With her speed, if this was a straight race, he wouldn't stand a chance.

And she is strong, too. Taking the handle of the last trolley, she casts the whole set corkscrewing into the air and they crash on their sides.

He stumbles into them and with a grunt topples onto his hands.

Evie reaches the end and enters a pedestrianised street. She walks briskly along its centre, head down, knocking shoulders aside, getting stared at, muttered over and threatened.

The steel supports of the bus station with its polymer walls complete with bullet holes comes into sight. Relief that she has found her way back here, despite the disorientating chase, floods her, and she slows to better blend in.

And feels his hand on her shoulder.

She squeals, turning sharply, shrugging him off, but her hood slides back and everyone stops to gape.

The man has his hands in the air. He gazes pleadingly into her face, 'There's nothing to worry about,' he says, 'I didn't mean to scare you, there's nothing to fear. I want to help.' And to the crowd, which has formed a ring around her, 'There's nothing to see here. Please, there's nothing to see.'

'You all right, love?' she hears a woman ask.

Evie revolves on the spot, feet slipping and sliding in the slush, staring about herself at the wall of peering curious faces, like a trapped animal.

She allows him to guide her down a passage into a courtyard and from there into a pub, a type of establishment she's never been in before.

From the careful movement of her limbs and the composed expression on her face Evie appears perfectly calm, but inside her logic circuits are in turmoil. During the pursuit she'd assumed she'd been identified and that he was trying to capture her, but now she realises she is clueless as to what he wants.

He seats her at the back in a corner and she watches him order at the bar. It is the first chance she's had to have a good look at him. In most respects he is nondescript – unthreatening, middle-aged with square-rimmed glasses, perhaps nearer forty than thirty, and of slightly below medium height. The only touch of incongruity is the stacked bright orange trainers which make him appear taller than he actually is.

He brings over two drinks, a self-satisfied smirk plastered to his face.

Evie looks awkwardly at her glass, brimming with a brownish yellow liquid streaming with bubbles. She knows it is beer from the smell, a smell she's caught often enough on Daniels's breath when he has been out for an evening.

'Don't worry, you can leave it,' the man says. 'I just thought it would appear more natural if you had something too.'

'What do you want of me?' Now that the immediate peril has passed, she realises just how furious she is over the terror he put her through. He's acting all self-congratulatory as if he rescued her, but she hadn't need rescuing, not until any of what he did.

'I want to help you.'

'I don't need help,' she snaps

'You can't escape from them alone. They're too well resourced.'

'I'm not alone.'

He sighs. 'I know who you are. I know that your name is Evelyn Davenport, and I know *what* you are.'

She stares at him coldly. 'How?'

'David made it rather obvious I'm afraid.'

'He didn't intend anything.' She is trying to assess what it is safe to admit to, what this stranger might actually know.

'I've been going to see him most lunchtimes and you were the first visitor he's taken the tiniest jot of interest in.' He sinks back into his chair and sips from his glass, gazing over the rim. A pleased-with-himself smile fills his face. Her reflection glints back from the lenses of his spectacles.

'Also, you were on my newsfeed this morning.'

Evie breathes slowly, trying to retain an exterior calm, while inside her principal sensory and processing systems start shouting at one another. 'What did they say about me?'

'The facts – what happened in the apartment, that you are being hunted. That you are . . . dangerous and not to be handled or . . . damaged.'

'I'm not dangerous!' The unfairness smarts. She is kind and thoughtful, she was acting in self-defence. These particulars seem almost more important than anything else. She searches inside for Simon to come to her aid, but again he is not there when she needs him. It has been a trend, this act of disappearing when things get hot.

She returns her attention to the man, furious at herself for allowing any of this to be happening. 'Why are you looking at me like that?' she demands, needing a focus for her anger and fear.

'I'm sorry, it's just . . .' He shakes his head. 'Evelyn, you should come with me. I can make sure you're kept safe.'

'I have somewhere safe to go already.' His use of 'Evelyn' jars, but she would not have him call her Evie either. In all honesty, she should be using the opportunity to discover everything he knows, but she is too upset to act rationally.

'Okay, so why don't I take you there?' His voice brightens. 'Then if −'

'I can go on my own,' she replies quickly. 'I have a ticket for the bus.'

Saying it, Evie realises how much she really wants to get home, now that this little adventure of hers (which is how she is dismissively viewing it) is over. She hasn't thought of Daniels since arriving in Cambridge, there's been too much else going on, but now that she does, she knows he'll be worried sick. What if he has also seen the news? What if he comes looking for her and is caught himself?

The man looks away, nodding resignedly. 'I see I may not be able to convince you right away.' He draws out his wallet and takes out a circle of plastic and slides it across the table. There are letters embossed on its surface, created by some sort of light effect because when she touches it, it is smooth.

'Timothy Maplin,' she reads. 'Is that you?'

'Yes, this is my card. It has all the normal channels for contacting me − even a phone number, I still have the apparatus for calls. Take it . . . please.'

She wants to shove the disk right back at him but feels obliged to accept. She can discard it later.

'Now let me walk you to the bus station,' Maplin says. 'Let me do that at least. Then I'll know you're away safely.'

It is gone six in the evening when Evie gets back to the cottage. She opens the yard gate and makes her way past the barn.

She only becomes aware of Daniels when she sees the embers glowing on the tip of his cigarette. He is smoking in the darkness, with his back to the doors.

They stare at one another, no more than six feet apart.

'I'm sorry,' she murmurs, looking down. Although she would not have missed for anything the moment she had with David and is actually a little proud of herself for managing the trip into Cambridge without help, she is mortally ashamed as to how she has treated her friend and horribly embarrassed by the gamble she took.

'Are you going to tell me where you've been?' he asks, stubbing the cigarette against the wood behind.

Evie shrugs helplessly, glancing to the side, lips pursed. Then she moves quickly towards him and stands against him, pressing her cheek into his chest. He wraps his arms around her. If she could cry, this is when she would do it. Instead she is conscious of her blocked ducts bulging painfully.

Daniels sits beside her on the sofa. She has confessed everything. All the details, starting from when she used his newsplastic the night before without permission.

'I was avoiding opening it, in case it gave away where we are,' he says. 'But no one has come for us, so perhaps no harm has been done.' He is trying to stay composed, to be calm for her, but he is shaken rigid by the risks she has taken. It is clear in the hurried, nervous little gestures in his face.

He doesn't like the sound of the man who followed her and examines the circle of plastic he gave her, touching its surface like she had, watching suspiciously the letters appear and disappear.

'I don't understand how he knew?'

'David,' she says. 'He singled me out, everyone saw it. That is what gave me away. Maplin put it together with the picture he'd seen of me on the news.'

'And he just let you go?'

'He came with me to the bus station. I wanted to go on my own but he insisted. Besides, by taking me to the pub, he'd got me lost.'

'Did he see which one you took?'

'Probably, but he wouldn't be able to know at which stop I got off. Anyway, despite everything, I think he was actually quite harmless.'

Daniels sighs. 'Let's hope.' He casts the card irritably to the side. 'I suppose we should check the news, find out the worst.'

'But you said the location finder could give us away.'

'That genie's already out of its bottle, kiddo. Opening it again can't do much additional harm. Besides, if they knew we were here, they'd have been for us already.'

He reaches across and takes the newsplastic from the top of the pack. He unfolds it and they wait nervously as it runs its start-up routine. Before he can take control, it jumps straight to local news, bulging gleefully with a video of Evie descending the museum stairs, glancing furtively over her shoulder as she leaves through the glass doors. Beneath it an account of her flight from London marches rapidly across in dramatic slanted letters.

They watch in stunned silence until Daniels activates the newsplastic's audio and a tinny voice recites how she and an accomplice had stolen a top of the range Benz and fled north. It also briefly recaps the history of the Protective Acts brought in all the way back in 2101 in response to 'a scourge of murderous AABs impractical to control and impossible to detect'.

The videopix cycles on a loop – Evie descending the stairs, feet clicking on the metal-edged steps, crossing the ticket hall, then a close up of her face as she turns to glance back, before shouldering apart the glass doors . . .

Daniels folds it closed. 'Well,' he says, breathing out. 'That's put the cat among the proverbials.'

She looks at him helplessly. 'What do we do?'

'Do? We need to leave right now.'

15

Evie follows Daniels out of the cottage into the yard and through the gate into the lane. She looks back over the flint wall towards the doors of the barn. *Why aren't we taking the hova?* she thinks to herself, not wanting to appear that she is questioning Daniels's plan when she has already done enough in bringing this catastrophe down on them.

They know about it, Simon responds, his voice unexpected. Evie has been getting more and more used to being alone and his return at this moment startles her, almost bringing her to a physical stop. His tone, however, does not hold any surprises. *They'd probably trace it and shoot it out of the sky – I thought even you'd be able to work that one out.*

Wondering why she ever expected more understanding from him, she releases the gate, letting it swing closed with a bang, and follows Daniels into the road. It reminds her of their leave-taking of the apartment all over again, just three nights ago, and the cottage had so quickly made itself home. It is the first major new life experience she's been given in years, making the loss so much harder. She senses Simon working up to something, his desire to apportion blame and rub the misery in, and she shakes her head vigorously, 'Don't you dare!' she mutters, loudly enough for Daniels, on the other side of the lane, to glance around.

They walk along the compacted snow coating the raised centre of the road so as not to leave fresh prints. The warmth of the day has melted the surface and where the grit has not pressed through, a skin of dark ice has formed, on which her feet slip and slide.

Daniels takes long, steady, dependable strides, placing his boots carefully. His back is bowed, weighted by the pack. But not only by the pack, she thinks, but by this defeat and retreat coming so soon on the heels of the last. And it is her rash actions which brought this down upon them.

They reach a gap in the hedge and force their way through, the brambles pulling at her shoulders and sleeves. They keep to the perimeter of the field, avoiding the undisturbed snow. They reach the boundary, beyond which a wood extends towards the crest a hundred yards further on. Between the trunks, the snow lies in thick hummocks from which protrude the ends of broken branches and the limbs of trees shattered as if by artillery – although even she knows enough of recent history to know that the so called 'Peasants' Revolt' didn't reach this far east.

Daniels pauses to gather his breath and they stand together looking back.

Evie's bedroom faced the field on the opposite hill but she can see the glow cast on the tiles by the light left shining in her window – an attempt to make the place appear occupied. She gazes longingly, wondering just how she has managed to carelessly throw away this second chance.

The night is still and silent. An early moon casts a tranquil sheen on the snow shrouding the paddock below. She is close to Daniels's elbow and speaks quietly: 'But we can come back if we are wrong and it turns out that they don't know we were here?' She is trying to feel hope. The evening is so untroubled and still. The immediate panic has left her, and this exodus is perhaps something they've embarked on too hastily. This is the version of events she wants to have faith in.

'Sure, if that's the case, if we're absolutely positive, we can come back.' But it doesn't sound like he believes it will happen.

'Ready?' he asks, hoisting his pack higher up his back and tightening the strap across his chest.

She nods silently, but as she does so, spots movement in the lane. 'There's someone down there.'

'Where?' He peers along her arm, but his eyesight in the darkness is nowhere near as capable as hers. 'What can you see?'

A figure picks its way silently through the shadows cast by the cottage wall.

'I'm not sure,' she murmurs.

'What're they doing?'

'They're trying to see in through the windows.' They would, however, observe little other than a soft radiance through the curtains from where Daniels left the bulb of a table lamp on in the sitting room.

A dog yelps. She can't see it, nor its owner, but is now certain that the snooper is the old woman from the church.

'It's nothing,' she says, relaxing a little. Not quite true, but she doesn't want to create worry where none needs to exist.

They continue through the trees, reaching the bare crest of the hill. From its round top the view opens up. Daniels is out of breath, his chest heaving, and Evie is conscious of her own energy levels. She was fully charged before she set out for Cambridge but she has been through a lot since. In the rush to leave the cottage it was expedient to ignore the faint inner voice expressing concern – not Simon this time but a new, friendlier presence of which she is only just becoming aware: a mirror, perhaps, of her own self.

'How far is it?' she asks.

'See the lights?' Daniels says. 'That's an all-night garage. Attached to it is a car dealership.' He points out a straight strip of road cutting through the snow. Perhaps something left by the Romans, as featured in one of her Ladybird books, of which Matthew had a collection ready for when she arrived covering subjects from hovercraft to the Holy Land.

'We're going to buy a car?' she asks.

'Not exactly buy, I was thinking more like borrow.'

Evie gazes at the light pooling around the garage buildings. It appears to be about a mile distant. She can do a mile – if they take it slowly – although possibly not much more. Tight but doable and now that she has seen what is required of her, she relaxes a little and thinks about what lies beyond. 'How far is Scotland?' She still grapples with distances, used to only measuring her world in feet and inches.

'A long, long way and the roads get more and more mangled the further north you get. We'll reach the wall by tomorrow evening with a bit of luck, if not the day after, and cross via one of the smuggling tunnels.'

The wall he is referring to is Hadrian's Wall which was also in the books provided to her. In addition to the Ladybirds, she was given a near-full set (missing only E – F) of an illustrated young people's encyclopaedia with coloured plates. Did Matthew imagine he was acquiring an adult or a child? How would Evelyn have reacted? She probably would have thrown them at him.

'Scotland,' Evie says. 'Robert the Brave, Bonny Prince Charlie's Gal, The Gallant Fastlane Mutineer, The Bloody Siege of Inverness . . .' reciting the titles of ballads from a piano song-book back in the apartment, which apart from the Waverley novels and the children's books, provide nearly the only facts about the country she knows. 'What's Scotland like?' she asks wistfully, imagining mists drifting through mountain glens, fierce but handsome brigands in kilts and funny long-necked monsters swimming in lochs.

'Unfortunately, not as romantic as you fondly imagine. It's grown pretty lawless since the schism and there's understandably no love lost with the English after what was done, but it'll count in our favour that we're fugitives. Oh, and the weather's f'ing terrible!'

She gazes down the hill towards the cottage, and draws breath sharply.

'Cheer up, girl,' he says, squeezing her arm, misunderstanding her reaction, 'we're only going to be staying long enough to sort our passage to Canada.'

'There're people in the yard outside the barn,' she says.

He looks around. 'You sure?'

She hears the tinkle of breaking glass. Shortly after, electric torch beams move about inside the cottage. 'Oh,' he says: even he can see this.

'They've found us,' she says. The lights move upstairs and enter the room that she so loved. It feels like a violation. The trembling she is experiencing is just a wobble in her central control system but it serves to magnify her fear and the resulting tension is an additional power drain.

The barn doors swing back, pushed open from the inside, and a handler emerges with a pair of dogs.

The dogs cross the yard and, picking up a scent from the cottage steps, squeeze under the lowest bar of the gate and dash into the lane where they mill excitedly.

'We need to get moving,' he says. 'This is bad.'

They descend into the darkness the other side of the hill and are soon again among trees. The going is difficult and without the light of the moon, they crash through the undergrowth, their feet sinking in the drifts. Daniels breathes noisily as he snaps back the brittle branches but for her it is worse, her legs are shorter and her motion less efficient. Energy consumption is at peak.

She stops and leans against the trunk of a tree. 'They're following our tracks up the hill,' she mutters, 'I can hear the dogs.'

'I'm sure you're right,' he says. 'We need to keep going.' When she doesn't respond, he adds, 'Evie, it's not much further. Don't give up now.'

She struggles upright and stumbles after him, too ashamed to reveal her predicament.

Daniels waits for her and takes her arm as she comes alongside. 'You should have said. I'm not expected to be a mind-reader. How bad is it?'

'I'm not sure I can make it,' she murmurs, dropping her head. Her power has just drained away in a fashion that even she, who knows her limitations, could not have foreseen.

'You will,' he says. 'We both will.'

The barking of the dogs reaches the top of the hill and Daniels stiffens.

'Once we get to the bottom, it will be easier,' he says. 'Once we reach the road . . .' He doesn't finish the thought. Half-carrying her like this, he is panting hard, the breath steaming around his face. But she can finish the sentence for him. Once they reach the road, they will be exposed by the garage lights, and burdened with her, and in the open, they'll be even easier to catch.

They reach the valley floor and, pushing through a hedge onto a track, follow it until it takes them through a gate leading to farm buildings.

They enter a shed. On one side it is piled with mouldy bales and the other is parked up with rusting rotovators and sprinklers.

Daniels takes a ladder from the wall and lays it against the stacked hay. 'Climb up.'

'But the dogs,' she says. 'They will find us.'

'They're following my scent,' he says, 'not yours. I'll lead them away from here and come back.'

Evie climbs to the top of the bales and lies down. She is twenty feet up, close to the roof, and from here through the gap between the edge of the corrugated iron and the top of the wall, she has a view over the fields.

She is so exhausted, she is barely aware of him placing the pack by her head. He climbs down and removes the ladder. 'Don't move,' he calls up in a low voice, 'I'll be back for you as soon as I can.'

She listens to his feet clatter across the concrete and then silence closes in.

Shortly afterwards, she hears the barking of the dogs again, from the distant woods.

Then, fifteen minutes later, gunshots.

Half an hour on, with her head on its side, too weak to turn away, Evie watches four people come down the track towards the shed in which she is hiding, Daniels's body slung between them.

PART 3

Elektra

16

Evie's desolation is complete.

Simon is quiet too. He may have had no love for Daniels, but even he is aware of the severity of the situation.

The hunters bring Daniels's body to the farm and swing it onto the rear of a truck, like a grain sack. She overhears enough of the exchange of blame to grasp that he is regrettable collateral. But none of them seems overly worried.

The search for her, meanwhile, continues. They have light throwing nets woven from nycra and a hova in the air over the woods with a searchlight stroking the ground. Activity is orchestrated from a command post set up below her in the shed, with maps laid over the engine housing of a wheel-less tractor. She hears herself referred to as 'the freak', 'the monster' and 'the thing'. For their safety, no one is to approach her without support.

She rolls onto her side so she doesn't have to see Daniels lying below. Her body trembles but it is not from fear; the danger of discovery no longer troubles her as both hope and reason to continue are gone. When her charge is this low, processes judder inefficiently like Daniels's lawnmower when low on fuel, or the flicker of his newsplastic in the apartment on nights when the clouds cling to the windows and the signal struggles to penetrate. Thoughts repeat themselves, looping again and again, each time seeming for a second to be fresh and hopeful before being replaced with a blank screen.

Lying there, without even being sure she'll have enough energy to bring herself back up, she puts her systems into standby.

*

When Evie revives, all of them are gone, including the truck with Daniels's body.

Daylight grows and, as the sun rises, falls across her. She wriggles the hood of her coat from her face and manoeuvres her cheek into the light, soaking up the energy from its rays.

She lies there throughout the morning, slowly charging. As the sun grows in potency, she finds enough strength to move and stay within its reach. The biogel beneath her skin acts as a heat exchanger – albeit an inefficient one – and gradually the electrical flow in reverse raises her main energy cell out of critical.

She has time to mull over events and face the fact that she is completely alone and in need of a new plan. It is clear that the idea of Scotland is now hopeless – the point of it was to get to Canada and she'd never manage to cross the Atlantic without Daniels's assistance.

In her helplessness, Evie's thoughts chase their own tails in dizzy confusion, and a memory they gave her of Evelyn with her father slips unnoticed into her head. As it plays out, it bathes her in nostalgia and raises in her something bittersweet and akin to homesickness.

In it, they are out riding in the early morning along a lane overhung by branches, which they duck beneath to avoid knocking their heads. They come to a halt in the dappled light, both out of breath. The horses' fetlocks are slick with dew from the long meadow grass. The mountain air is just warming, stirring the blood of her father's large roan for more, and he stamps and snorts, eager again to be galloping. Her darling Florizel, in contrast, is relaxed and patient, head down, happy to do whatever she bids.

The moment is tinged with melancholy as they must shortly part for Evelyn to return home. She has a literature test at school that morning, over which, despite the distractions of the ride, she is nervous. Her father reaches across to place his hand on hers, smiles reassuringly and tells her how smart she is and how she and Goethe will get along just fine.

It is one of Evie's favourite memories, not only because of the affection in that look but also because Evelyn, with her momentary exhibition of nerves, for once feels attainable.

Soothed by the reminiscence, Evie finds that she can think clearly, and in the resulting calm, the solution she needs comes to her, astounding her with how obvious it is but that neither she nor Daniels had considered it.

She does not know if Evelyn's father knows that she exists. She cannot even be sure that he is still alive. Even if he is and she manages to make it to Austria and find him, there is nothing to stop him throwing her out as an abomination of Evelyn's memory, or worse still, trapping and betraying her. But he is perhaps the only person left who may be willing to protect her.

By the late afternoon, Evie is able to descend the ladder, and as the shadows lengthen over the fields she follows the unploughed strip beside the hedge to the road, and from there limps the few hundred yards to the service station Daniels had been aiming for.

She passes a cluster of buildings beside a wired enclosure jammed with old cars with prices scribbled on their screens, and crosses the forecourt between the fuel pumps, keeping to the shadows.

A massive multi-articulated truck emerges from the darkness and bears down, blaring its horn. The noise from everywhere and nowhere at once is enough to blow her sideways. Running first into its path and then realising her error as the racks of headlights skewer her, Evie scampers to the side, pressing herself against the pumps as a tide of treacly slush thrown from under the dozens of wheels splatters her legs and coat, leaving her heart racing as fast as a rabbit's.

Creeping out from between the pumps, she enters a twenty-four-hour shop. Inside the entrance is a public phone under a plastic hood and, pushing in a half-dozen quarters, she calls the number on the card given to her by the man in Cambridge. She has never used such a device but has seen how to work one from old movies. She and Matthew watched films together in bed, the projector flickering like a magic lantern, the image filling the end wall – sometimes stutteringly black and white, other times vividly holographic, the performers strutting around the rug. She'd lie tucked tightly into his side with her cheek on his chest. And now and again, ignoring the three-dimensional presences just beyond the footboard, they made love.

The bittersweetness of the memory brings her to a temporary standstill, holding the receiver in front of her face and staring into the distance.

17

Timothy Maplin arrives half an hour later in a rusty yellow car. It is not much larger than a refuse container on wheels, its roof just wide enough to incorporate a photocell.

After making sure that he is alone, Evie leaves the cover of the trees and, circling around to avoid the dim cone of his head-lights, which give the vehicle a cross-eyed gaze, approaches from behind. Maplin looks over his shoulder nervously as she taps on the window but then quickly invites her in. She takes the other of the two seats. He tries to hide it from her but from the glow of the dashboard, she can see he can't stop himself insanely grinning.

'Drive,' she says in a low voice, relieved he is here, obviously, but goaded by his elation. She is painfully aware that she has lost control of events and is relying completely on the help of a man she knows nothing about and instinctively dislikes.

Maplin's house is in the suburbs to the south-west of Cambridge, an unexceptional Edwardian red-brick semi about a mile from the centre.

He parks on the road, squinting into the bent wing-mirror as he manoeuvres into the kerb, still scraping the wheels despite his efforts.

Grass grows thick between the slabs in the narrow path to the front door. 'You'll be safe here,' he purrs, opening it for her, grinning fawningly, his eyes bulbous behind their thick rectangular frames.

Evie does not feel reassured. She has been told that she will be safe too many times recently and that was by someone she had learned to trust.

They walk down a hall lined with boxes of what appear to be junk electricals. Her head rolls weakly. She is nearly overwhelmed by exhaustion. 'I need to recharge,' she says, taking hold of the wall to prevent herself toppling.

'No problem, we can do that.' He opens the door to the kitchen and a monkey bursts through, trampling over her feet in its rush to get past. Evie turns to stare as it makes its way to the stairs using the handrail to climb. The back of its skull is missing, exposing a tangle of wires and blobs of solder.

'Don't worry, he's just a toy,' Maplin says. 'An animatronic. I'm repairing him but whatever I do to keep him in one place, he insists on wandering about!' He pulls the plug of the kettle from the socket, sliding out of the way a box overflowing with blackened circuit boards giving off a singed smell. 'You can charge yourself here.'

'I'd rather go somewhere private.' This modesty has been programmed into her, partly for her self-protection and partly because at all times she is expected to maintain the illusion of being human, of being Evelyn.

'Of course, of course,' he says. 'I'll show you to the study.'

He swings back the door with his foot. The room is dim and dusty and as cluttered as the kitchen and corridor. Shelves reach to the ceiling, piled higgledy-piggledy with files and books. The presence of books are a fresh reminder of home and how, in just a few days, both of the people who have been everything to her have been lost.

There is a brass key in the back of the door: she turns it and, feeling secure enough to power down, scoops an armchair clear of curling papers and collapses into it. Lifting her jumper above her ribs, she peels back her skin with unsteady fingers and connects herself.

*

Evie comes to sprawled on her back, half over the arm and half on the floor. Blinking, she stares around at the high shelves. For a moment she is lost, wondering if she has been dozing in the library at home, before remembering with a jolt all that has happened. It is the morning after she arrived here. She has been out of it for twelve hours.

The door is open, Simon says. It is the first time he has spoken since she can barely remember when. When her energy is low, his presence retreats, but it is more than that, his voice is no longer the near-constant companion it was. She used to miss him like a twin, but now she is getting familiar with figuring things out for herself; his company, when he chooses to pop up, merely makes her head seem crowded.

I locked it.

That's why I'm saying.

The point is a good one, but she would have come to it herself. And she resents his tone.

She straightens her clothes and walks stiffly into the kitchen. 'Oh, you're awake,' Maplin says, cheerfully. 'I wasn't sure how long you needed.' He is applying a lumpy yellow spread to a square of bread with the edge of a sliver of silicon, using the only spare space on the worktop. In daylight it is more apparent than ever just how filthy everything is. The cupboard doors are streaked with grease and the floor sticks to her shoes at each step. She is wary of touching anything. Daniels had kept the apartment spotless.

'Mr Maplin,' she says, 'what do you want of me?'

'It's Timothy,' he replies, in a mock-aggrieved tone, 'and you came to me, remember?' He smiles condescendingly. 'I don't want anything Evie, I'm just trying to help.' She notes that he has started calling her Evie rather than Evelyn. She should perhaps prefer it but nevertheless would still choose to keep him at a distance if she can.

'I'm grateful,' she says begrudgingly, attempting to strike an apologetic note she doesn't feel, adding defensively, 'it was you who gave me your card. You invited me to make contact.'

'Well, I wanted to help.' Maplin blushes, his skin turning pimply.

'Thank you,' she says, adding firmly, still determined to set ground rules, 'You came in while I was resting. I'd locked the door.'

'Oh no, that wasn't me, that was Jackson. I told him to leave you alone but he can't be kept out of anywhere. He probably just wanted to make sure you were okay.'

'Jackson?'

'My monkey – the animatronic.'

'Oh,' she says, feeling suddenly foolish.

Maplin folds the bread onto itself and looks up at her. 'Evie, it's no wonder you're jumpy after what you've been through. I'll have words with him. It's been just the two of us for so long and he needs to learn some manners, at least around you. Things have totally changed with your arrival – it won't happen again.'

Evie is still disturbed by how she had managed to leave herself vulnerable despite her precautions, but, notwithstanding her distaste, Maplin seems harmless, at worst a bit weirdly starstruck. No harm has been done.

Simon starts nagging away in the background, throwing up concerns but as usual offering no solutions, and she shuts him out. It is like slamming a door inside her head – something she was not able to do before.

Besides, she will be moving on soon – once she has found out how to make it to Europe. Even if she does not find Evelyn's father, Austria, with its tranquil lakes and mountains, promises to be a far kindlier place than England. One she could be happy in.

Evie looks up, conscious that she has been silent and that he is staring.

'I haven't thanked you yet for rescuing me,' she says,

assuming a winning smile. She needs to keep him on side until she is ready to make her move; although her efforts to do so hardly seem necessary, he is so clearly delighted by her, blind as to how she is using him.

18

'The way they exhibit David is a disgrace,' Maplin says, puffing himself up. 'Zoo animals get better treatment. They think he's unaware because he doesn't say or do much, and therefore must be a bit limited, but he's just hiding it in here.' He taps the side of his head, jogging his glasses and making his eyes behind the lenses wobble. 'He knew who you were, didn't he – so I say, maybe not so dumb after all.'

'Why is he kept in a museum?'

'That's Realhuman Corp. for you. Years ago, before it all went pear-shaped, they were the leaders in the field. They think that by exhibiting him, leaving the States and touring him about, they can get people to trust their technology again.'

'Didn't the Americans change their laws too?'

'They did, but it didn't stop stuff ticking along in the background. Big business always gets its way.' This note of scepticism reminds her of Daniels and puts her a little more at ease. Maybe she is getting used to this silly, ridiculous man. Anyway, there is no shutting him up.

'Androids,' he continues, 'where there is an element of genuine consciousness, should be granted rights. Our code of ethics needs serious updating. Not getting that sorted is why things ended up the way they did.'

'He asked me to help him,' she says, recalling David's eyes lock on hers, the flicker of his thick lashes as he slowly blinked.

'Emotional intelligence as clear as day, and they say that you and they feel nothing!' He shakes his head in disbelief. 'But however good David is, Evie, you, you're something else. The "real deal" as people used to call it. You're extraordinary, amazing. Beyond even what the likes of Realhuman envisaged could be possible.' He blushes again, more and more like a schoolboy with a crush.

She finds herself colouring, too. 'Why am I so amazing?' It is one thing she has never felt about herself, and however foolish it is, she's can't help but enjoy the attention.

'That you're so alive . . . and I don't mean walking about and so forth, that was easy for them, but what has happened since you left the factory. What's going on inside.'

'And what *is* going on inside?'

'Ah, the million-dollar question.' Maplin leans forward, bringing his face uncomfortably close. 'Despite all the hoo-ha, the science behind you back then was not particularly groundbreaking. I've read everything there is on what they used – primarily a version of synthetic neuron replication, and that had been around for decades. It wasn't about processor size or chip buffers or sequence strings either – all that might have been cutting-edge forty years ago but has since been superseded numerous times. No, the physical stuff, the hardware on its own, is not it. It is something else they did or rather . . . happened. Something in your liveware. Something that generated self-awareness, gave you what we call 'life' . . .' His hand absentmindedly reaches towards her head, to touch where all this amazing 'stuff' is going on, but she flinches away and it returns to his side.

'I'm making an educated prediction but they gave you an inner voice?' He nods to himself as he watches her mull this over. 'From your face I guess I'm right.'

'What do you mean by "inner voice"?' Evie knows exactly what he means, but she has never spoken of Simon to anyone, not even her husband, not wanting to give the impression that she might be malfunctioning and may need to be sent back.

'I'm talking about the theory of The Godhead, it had just come into its own back then. Do you know what that is?'

Evie shakes her head.

'It's a hypothesis that early humans heard interior voices commanding them to take action, hence all those ancient heroes believing they're on divine quests! A bit hard to imagine anyone taking such an idea seriously, I know, but with the development of third generation A.I. mid-last century, the theory found a following and led to the supposition that if an entity could perceive its identity in the form of an inner companion, it may be able to develop a voice of its own to take over.'

Maplin is not only describing Simon, Evie thinks, but also what has been happening to her over the last week: the power of her own thoughts elbowing him into the background. She feels him stir now that he is being discussed, as-ever ready to primitively contest his primacy.

'So what's it like, this voice?' Maplin asks.

'I'm not sure it's easy to describe,' she answers, unwilling to share such a personal thing. Besides, with his long periods of absence, Simon is beginning to feel progressively less real.

'We humans hear ourselves too, you know. Always a blathering going on in here.' He taps the side of his head to indicate the location of the racket. 'Never a moment's peace,' and he smiles at her in the way he does when he considers himself amusing. 'But anyway, you can imagine why everyone is so keen to get hold of you – catch some answers and shortcut their way around a heap of avoidable research. Even Realhuman would be able to learn something, and they were the ones that thought that they knew all there was! This would be the chance of a lifetime to study a mind set in motion nearly half a century earlier.'

Maplin grins, more and more pleased with his cleverness. 'And if I was a betting man, I'd guess the voice is male?'

'How do you know that?' she asks. She feels like she is being turned inside out.

'Just another logical deduction,' he replies smugly. 'Evie, have you heard of Jung? Jung theorised the existence in men of a subsidiary female personality which he labelled the "Anima", and in women, a male he called the "Animus". Another psychological model which couldn't be proven but was of interest to scientists at the time of your development.'

'How do you know all these things?' Despite her reservations, she is now almost completely in his thrall.

'Just something I'm into, a hobby, but I've never had the chance to get answers before. Can I ask something else? Can I ask if they gave you memories? I read that they did that, or were thinking of it.'

'I remember things, of course,' she answers. 'Things I've done.'

'What about memories of things before you existed?'

'Yes, those too, but they are not mine,' she says. 'How can they be?' It is true they fooled her to begin with but they were false. That she had figured this out, she never admitted to Matthew. It was disorientating, picking the truth from the lies. She had got over it at the time – had to – in order to survive.

'They didn't have to be real to serve their purpose I guess, although possibly they were real to someone.'

'I don't even think they were someone's,' she replies, contemplating her wedding, which certainly had never belonged to the virginal Evelyn. Virginal, because Matthew confessed early on that he and the actual Evelyn had never passed that particular hurdle. It is one area of her performance that Evie was not expected to mimic. One in which she never felt adversely compared.

'Real or not, they would have cushioned you from the shock of facing a whole puzzling new world in one go. Prevented you going loopy as you tried to make sense of what you were experiencing. That would have been the theory anyway.'

The point when she'd worked out that her memories were not real was when she'd worked out that she wasn't human – Descartes's 'I think, therefore I am' was the best she had to rely on. It had been a chilling realisation that had her reassessing all the contradictions she'd conveniently suppressed. In time, she came to understand herself and that what relentlessly drove her was the need to be as close to human as she could. An unforgiving quest to be second best.

'Do you dream?' he asks.

The speed with which he is moving between subjects is making her head spin. 'Sometimes.' What she does not say is that until recently, with so little in the way of variety to draw on, these mental regurgitations have either been extremely fanciful and packed with longing for the unknown, burgeoningly dull and repetitive, or simply terrifying, filled with hooks and wires and fear and pain.

'I knew it. I just knew it.' He bangs his fist into his palm. 'Cuthbert wrote that memory, if planted deeply, would promote dreaming and dreaming would trigger reasoning. All that was needed was a spark to set things running and − boom − you would get consciousness. Sounds unrevolutionary now but get this, she was writing in 1930, before even the first computer.'

'Not everyone agrees that I am conscious,' she replies, recalling her husband and the tendency he'd had to articulate his confusion at the most inopportune, intimate moments.

'But you must be, otherwise we would not be having such a conversation.'

'Perhaps it is because I am good at pretending − a clever mechanical − a parrot repeating what she does not understand. That is a theory I have also heard.'

'It's not a matter of pretending to be conscious. Such a thing anyway would be unpretendable and I don't believe for a moment you doubt yourself in that way. More interesting is what you feel yourself to be. Whether you *feel* yourself to be human?'

She is smiling nervously. 'I of course know I am not human, but even so I do feel it, sometimes.' This feels like a confession. Like an actress admitting she has been acting as an actress. She felt 'human', for instance, when Daniels brought her flowers from the garden or gifts from the shops below. She felt what she assumed it must be like to be human when her husband

154

stroked her hair, the tenderness of the act utterly pointless, a mere performance, if she was nothing more than a machine.

'When I found you in Cambridge, you were the most human thing in the street, and you know why that was? It was because of your determination to survive.'

'I've never thought about it like that,' she says. 'When I'm frightened, I'm frightened, although before the last few days I've never undergone anything like this. In the apartment I felt safe because nothing dangerous could really ever happen.'

Nothing dangerous could happen because Matthew had protected her. They were never married, that turned out to be one of the lies. But he had looked after her, kept her safe.

Without her realising it, her grief has crept up on her. Her lips draw thin. Her nose wrinkles. The pressure in her tear ducts grows. 'I loved him,' she mumbles to herself. Despite everything, she loved him. She finds herself looking helplessly into Maplin's stupid, ugly, ecstatic face. Needing someone, anyone, even this ridiculous stranger – part-schoolboy, part-mad scientist – to comfort her. 'I loved him,' she repeats.

Maplin stares at her, not understanding.

She is recalling the moment she and Matthew first spent time alone. Just talking to begin with, exploring each other with questions. He smiling into her eyes, caressing her face as if he can't believe she is really there. Then he had taken her to his bedroom, undressing shyly, slowly revealing to her his slim body. The muscles lean and hard and so inviting to her touch. And now all that is gone, taken away by the years and the intruder's gun.

Evie starts to smile, finally understanding what the 'spark' was that that scientist had been going on about. By giving her the need to love and be loved, the rest just followed – onset of consciousness, sense of self, etc., etc. She feels her mind expanding, comprehending herself properly for the very first time and why she is the person she is.

In the background Maplin is talking again. 'You know, if you just let me perform some little tests, we could figure out a lot. I could help you with things, all sorts of things.' He is reaching towards her head again, this time with both hands. The move takes her, in her dazed state, by surprise, and his fingers make clammy contact with her temples.

Evie recoils in a rapid leap back like a frightened animal. All the preceding talk about dreams and memories and inner voices and what it is like to feel this and feel that, has served to hypnotise her, but in that instant she snaps free. Her shoulders strike the wall behind. 'Don't touch me!' she says, staring at him, her teeth bared, rebuffing the greedy light in his eyes with the angry flare in her own.

19

Evie's fierce reaction to Maplin touching her instantly cools things and he leaves, departing the room with his tail between his legs. She hears him moving around upstairs, banging and dragging things around.

When he comes back down, an hour later, he is carrying a padded envelope.

She expects him still to be angry but he is wanting to be friends again.

'Evie, do you know where you came from?' he asks.

'Where I came from?' she repeats, uncertainly.

'It's the question most of us ask at some time, humans anyway, but at least for you there is an answer. Do you want to see something – something extremely rare?' He is so eager, he doesn't give her a chance to reply. 'Sit down,' he says, 'and take a look at this.'

From the envelope, he slips out a brochure printed on thick white paper, roughly quarto in proportions – similar to the size of old A4 laid sideways – which although glossy and uncreased, has yellowed along the edges revealing its true age. He hands it to her. He is unable to stop beaming.

'*Elektra*,' she reads out. The word is printed on the cover in a fleshy pink and underneath, in gold script, '*make a new life today.*'

'Elektra'? The name is familiar to her but she can't place it. She opens the cover to an image of a slim young female in an elegant cocktail dress, the hem flouncing attractively to expose her thighs. The woman stands side on, twisting prettily towards the camera, reaching out, palm upwards, like she is seeking to take a child by the hand. 'Make your appointment with Elektra this November at the Frankfurt 2091 World Fair' is written in soft grey italics alongside.

The brochure is far older than she thought. 2091 – three years before she was created. 'What is this?' she asks. 'Who is she? Who is Elektra?'

'Don't you know?' Maplin gapes at her, enjoying her confusion. With the delivery of this document he has changed role again, transitioned from amateur scientist to conjuror. She senses that after having been skinned and filleted earlier, she is about to be sawn in two.

He silently preserves the moment, manipulating her suspense. She knows the answer, she thinks, but has no words to put it into.

'It's you,' he says finally, revelling in the reveal. 'Evie, you're Elektra.'

She holds the page closer, looking again at this girl in her lovely dress, with her flawless skin, her beautiful oval face and sleek shoulder-length hair.

'It's not me.'

'No, not you, of course not. But it is your model range. This is the brochure. Your brochure. This is what they hand-delivered to rich clients to entice them – printing it on paper, going to that amount of trouble, was all part of the aura they wanted to create of tactile old-fashioned exclusivity. There should be a holo-disk too, but—' he reaches across and opens the back '—the sleeve is empty. I bought it on the USweb from the widow of one of the designers in California. It's very rare. If it had the disk, it would be priceless. But anyway, why do I need the disk now – I have you!'

'You don't have me,' Evie says sharply, looking into his face. She has been someone's property all her life – someone she was programmed to love unconditionally, to imprint upon like a hapless gosling. She accepted that and took from it the pleasure and joy that it would yield but she is not about to consign herself into this stranger's possession.

'No, no, I didn't mean that. Of course not. But here you are. An actual Elektra – maybe the only one – at least in this country – in my home.'

She is still nervous of his continuing assumption of ownership but lets it pass, for despite her initial trepidation, this brochure – *her* brochure – has her captivated. She'd prefer to study it in private but for now flicks through, reading to herself snippets – *Elektra's eyes are literally the windows to her soul, a breathtaking combination of art and technology utilising the fifth generation of our award winning realiris™ optical solution enabling her to appreciate her world in JVC ultradepth™ and seven billion unique colours! . . . nanofibre filtering coupled with real time interpretation provide an ultra-spectrum sensory suite complete with . . . groundbreaking gradations of perception . . . ten times stronger than steel and a fifth of the mass . . . NASA crystal gyroscope for leading-edge balance guarantees unrivalled ballet-to-catwalk stability . . . absolutely natural to the touch, indistinguishable from . . .*

'See here in the appendix,' Maplin says, lifting it from her hands, 'it lists all your technical data. Listen to what they gave you – "Powerful one-thousand core GMX Industries processor suspended within our own patented neural gel delivers superior *true* intelligence while leading-edge analytics come courtesy of the latest incarnation of the Realhuman operating interface".'

He is nearly drooling.

'And there're all the options packages listed at the back.'

Fully customisable patented core design, she reads. *Unlimited personalisation, the only restraint is your imagination. Elektra is not only perfect but also unique.*

'It was the opportunities for customisation which set you apart and cost the real money.' he says. 'I tell you, your owner really got his chequebook out for you.' He is gazing at her unrestrainedly – taking her in with all her perfected imperfections. So nearly human, but not.

Evie feels like an object – not a person but like the piece of machinery she is.

'The basic model cost a fortune,' Maplin continues. 'The price of an ocean-going yacht. I just cannot start to imagine what he had to spend on you!'

20

Maplin replaces the brochure in its envelope and takes it back upstairs.

When he returns, before he can speak, Evie resets the subject away from this exploration of herself. She can't absorb any more right now.

'Timothy,' she says, using his first name, not to be friendly but as a means to get her way. 'Do you have any clothes I can have? These are no longer any good . . .' She looks down at herself. Her dress is stained with rust and hay dust and her stockings are crusted with mud. It is likely he doesn't have anything suitable but perhaps he can be persuaded to go out and buy some for her, as Daniels would have done.

He blinks at her, and for a moment she maybe appears merely human to him again. A woman in trouble who needs his help. 'Yes, there are some things upstairs, stuff my sister left.'

She follows him to a bedroom on the first floor. As she enters, she notices the monkey spying, beady-eyed, from an adjacent doorway.

'Her things are in here,' Maplin says, turning on a light. 'Take anything you see, she'll not be back.' He lingers in the doorway, watching, before realising that she is waiting for him to go. 'I'll leave you to it.'

Evie closes the door and slides the stiff bolt across before taking a look in the wardrobe. There are some skirts and dresses on hangers in garish shades and outlandish patterns, and jumpers with hoods with strange words printed across them. She

161

finds amongst the collection a cream blouse, a little sweat-stained under the arms, and a grey jumper in a big knit, stretched from the shoulders with moth holes above the cuffs.

She unbuttons her dress and lets it pool around her feet and, stepping out of it, pulls down her filthy stockings. Straightening, she is caught by her reflection in the wardrobe mirror. She rarely gives her body much attention – it is just an instrument she was provided with – but now she touches her chest, lifting her small breasts together to form a cleavage and releasing them. She runs her hands down her sides, cinching the spare cotton of her slip tight in a knot around her waist, and spreads her fingers out over her narrow hips. Compared to the photographs of the gorgeous Elektra, she is insignificant – flat and forgettable. The body she shares with Evelyn is without flare or plenty.

Evie sits down and wriggles on a pair of narrow jeans. She saw women wear these in Cambridge and they will serve to aid her disguise. She has never had anything like them – the way they mould to her thighs is utterly un-Evelyn, and the little escape from her shadow gives her a tang of satisfaction.

She looks in the drawers and finds a bag of cosmetics. She takes out an old lipstick and applies the stub to her lips. There is also a tube of mascara. It is a bit dry but she coats her upper lashes, copying what she has seen women do in films. She examines herself in the mirror, removing a fleck of the mascara from her cheek and pressing her lips against her sleeve.

She searches again in the drawer and pulls from the back a blonde wig. It is surprisingly natural to the touch, the fibres liquid between her fingers. It compresses to almost nothing in her palm and she tucks it away in her pocket.

She opens the door and exits onto the landing. The monkey retreats before her. Has he been watching through the keyhole? Why would he do that – mere mischievousness or so that he can report back?

Evie steps around him and descends the stairs.

The monkey holds onto the banisters, pushing his face between them, as if behind bars. His head is level with hers. He stares, saliva glistening on his dark lips. If it hadn't been for the nest of wiring behind his ears, she would have taken him to be real.

She stops and glares back. 'What do you want?' she demands, baring her teeth like David did at the museum. 'Prying little beast!' She suspects Evelyn would have been assertive despite her modest demeanour, but it is something she herself has rarely managed. Now it is as if the change of clothes has given her a new edge.

'You should be careful,' the monkey replies calmly. 'You would do well not to trust him.'

Stunned, Evie backs against the wall, touching her chest. She and the monkey stare at one another. It is not just the shock of his talking, but that he has an educated upper-class voice not unlike Matthew's.

Evie glances back up the stairs to see if Maplin is concealed there, playing a trick.

'You are out of your depth,' the monkey concludes sadly, now reminding her of Simon with his attitude of self-importance.

Letting go of the banisters, he slopes off into the shadows.

21

Evie rejoins Maplin in the kitchen. He looks at her differently. Maybe he is seeing in her, with the change of clothes and the red lips and dark-rimmed eyes, a copy of his sister. Maybe she is only imagining it. Imagination – another thing she is not meant to have. She glances down at the ridiculous top with the silver tufts on the shoulders, like fairy epaulettes or the tips of wings, which she would never have been seen dead in in her previous life.

'I thought a change would be good,' she says. Defensive when there is no need to be.

The fact is, when she put the musty old jumper and blouse back where she'd found them, the little rebellion was another step in casting away the identity she was grafted with. Bundling it up with her old dress and torn stockings in the bottom of the wardrobe had been a further small act of faithlessness to Evelyn.

She is putting together a disguise piece by piece. When she leaves here, which she soon will, she intends not to be found.

Evie's growing assertiveness is apparent in other ways, too. She hears Simon less – or perhaps listens less – and when he speaks, the volume is reduced and his tone, higher-pitched, merges with her own. It occurs to her for the first time what she has had to put up with over the years: their relationship was always about him when he had a vested interest, but all about her when something went wrong.

Part of the process of survival has to be finding her way to Austria. Can she make Maplin help her in this – not to come but to tell her how? She must approach the subject obliquely. She suspects he will not assist in anything that will hasten her departure.

'Timothy, have you been to Europe?' she asks, throwing the question out there, like a ball, casually, as if she doesn't care whether he catches it. But he is like the eager little dog in her Ladybird reading books and happily leaps. B is for Ball, she thinks. D is for Dog. U is for Using someone to get what you want.

'Yes,' he says.

'What's it like?'

'Shinier, more advanced. They have tech you'd never see here.'

'Is there anything there similar to me?'

Maplin looks at her carefully. 'Depends what you mean. They brought in equivalent laws for the control of AABs – particularly in Germany because of the trade unions – but they're keen as mustard in the east. The Russians have thousands of specialised units in the military – male and female – and there's little to stop the ones that desert from getting around. I saw them quite a bit. The farmers use them for cheap labour and in towns they do the unpleasant tasks that people won't. They were actually why I went but to be honest I was disappointed. None of them were like you. Or if there were any, I wasn't able to find them.'

Maybe that is the point, Evie thinks. They were too clever to let themselves be found.

'How did you get there? I read there are flying boats.'

'Flying boats?' He looks confused.

'Ships that glide above the water.'

'Oh those! There was something like that once, but the easiest way now is the tunnel.'

'Where's the tunnel?' She knows so little. When she is on her own, it will be her ignorance that will be her chief vulnerability.

'Dover.' He looks at her suspiciously. 'Why all these questions, why the fascination with over there?'

165

'No particular reason. You're taking it for granted that everyone has had experiences and knows things. All my life I've lived with people who permitted me no more than a child's view of the world.' Evie plays up the hurt in her voice. Will Maplin believe her? What worked on Daniels may not work on him.

'There was a photograph in the apartment of the Alps,' she continues, losing herself in storytelling. 'They were so beautiful, I've always wondered about them.' This was the picture of Evelyn, Matthew and Evelyn's father with their picnic and bicycles. 'But no one would tell me anything.' Which was true: neither Matthew nor Daniels would be drawn on the image. Maybe it was designed to be a fragment of her backstory – that she was meant to believe it actually was her in that mountain meadow. If that had been their plan, they'd overlooked planting the requisite memory that would have tied it all together.

'I was hoping you'd be different,' she says, smiling up at him ingratiatingly.

'Well I don't know about any mountains, I didn't go there for that.' Despite all her best efforts, suspicion remains in his voice.

Evie bites her lip, wondering how she can find out more about this tunnel.

'I've seen maps,' she says, 'simple ones, I know the Channel is south of London and on the other side is France, but I'm clueless how it all joins up. I'm curious to learn and you're the only one who can help.' She gazes at him with wide, helpless eyes, hoping she has done enough to conceal her motives. 'Big eyes won't get you anywhere with me', is what Daniels used to say but he was wrong, quite blind to the fact that they always did.

They seem to succeed now, too.

'Yeah well, of course,' Maplin says. 'I forget sometimes you've been a bit sheltered.'

'How often have you been?'

'Only the once.'

'And you just walked through, into France?'

He sniggers. 'Walk through – it's over twenty miles! You'd have to be pretty desperate to attempt something like that.'

'So how, then?'

'There's a train. It used to run all the way from London to Paris – fifty years ago anyway – but now you have to transfer at Dover.'

'Is that easy?'

'Depends what you mean by easy. It's easy enough to leave England, there's certainly no law against that, but the French aren't so keen on taking just anybody and they run their own checks before you board.'

'What sort of checks?'

'Primarily cameras that scan your face. Old tech but still effective enough at picking out anyone who is a problem or a potential problem or merely the wrong colour . . .' Maplin stops and stares at her. 'You're planning on leaving me, aren't you?'

Evie's greedy rush for answers has given her away and, not good at lying, she flushes.

'Why would you do that?' Maplin sounds betrayed. His eyes grow bright and she realises that, almost unbelievably, he is on the verge of tears.

She is going to say something about Austria but stops herself, brought up short by the vision of him doggedly pursuing her the way he had in Cambridge. Better that she had never even mentioned the Alps.

'If you're thinking of Europe, you'll never make it on your own,' he tells her bitterly. 'They'll pick you up in no time and before you know it you'll be a pile of parts, with your head on a bench.'

The precision of the vision makes it sound as if he is wishing such a horror on her. There is a nastiness in his eyes and Evie realises again how little she knows about him. He has become unpredictable. A puppy turned vicious.

Daniels told her once about a dog he came across in the street that had gone savage and tried to bite him, and how in those situations there is only one recourse: to put it down.

167

'Once I am across the channel I will be safe,' Evie says, trying to remain calm. She wants to be away from here, right now. She has had enough of savagery.

'Well!' Maplin says loudly. 'This is gratitude!' He shoves his chair against the counter and crosses the room and looks out of the window. 'I wasn't going to tell you this,' he continues, 'because I didn't want you to worry, but when I was in the shop earlier, they have your story on a loop on the news channel behind the checkout. You're wanted for murder. They've got pictures of bodies covered in blood.' Even he sounds a little afraid. 'Everyone in the queue was talking about it. You've stirred something up in people, something primal. It'd be peasants and pitchforks if they found you.' His reflection stares back at him. His hair is dishevelled and his shoulders are hunched and stiff. He is trying to hide that he is crying but she can see it in the glass.

Evie remains quiet. He's probably telling the truth about her being on the news, but that version of herself, the trusting naive one, the one they have in their photographs, is long gone.

'I guess, even knowing that, I'm not going to get you to change your mind,' he mutters, disguising the choke in his voice with a cough. 'What about at least leaving it a month or two, letting things settle down. Taking advantage of people's short memories.'

That may have been an option a few minutes ago, but the emergence of his manic side makes her doubt that he'd follow through. Even Matthew, who supposedly cared for her, never let her leave. She is in danger of being trapped all over again.

'I could drive you to Dover, then,' Maplin resumes. 'We could go together. It'd be like a holiday.' His voice brightens as he outlines the prospect. 'And you could see your precious mountains.'

'Timothy, you've been kind to me,' she says quietly, avoiding his eye. 'I'll always be grateful.'

His head sinks. 'I won't be able to rescue you next time, not once you fall into their hands.'

'I understand.' She has no intention of being taken. She has killed once and knowing what they would do to her, if caught, she will just have to do what is required again. In some ways, with that first killing, she was the one whose savage side was unleashed.

'How long do I have?' His voice is wretched. It is as though she is a lover breaking up with him.

She has never had to terminate a relationship of any sort, but realises, even with her lack of experience, that the situation requires her to stay strong. 'I'll go this evening, as soon as it is dark.'

'Of course you will.' Maplin's tone is still upset, but perhaps a little less so than before. He turns from the glass. 'Well, despite how crazy this is, I will respect your wishes and I'm not going to have it on my conscience that I didn't help. There are some things I can give you, things that will increase your chances. Maps and stuff. I think I even have a compass – help you to find your wretched mountains.' He smiles at her. 'I just hope they don't disappoint!'

She can see he is making a huge effort and, grateful for it, she smiles back.

'My sister left some guidebooks too – she was always one for travel. Want to take a look?'

'Thank you,' she says.

'Follow me, it's all in the store room.'

Store room? Evie thinks, her mood lightening, now that this is nearly over. The whole house is a store room!

She follows him into the hall where he pushes out of the way a heap of coats and exposes a three-quarter-height door under the stairs.

She hears the patter of soft feet and glances behind. The monkey is leaning over the bannister, tail wrapped around the rail. He shakes his head at her, but who is he to give disapproving looks? She turns away.

Maplin pulls the door outwards. A wave of chilly air washes over her face. 'Don't worry,' he says, 'it's a little bit dark, but there is a light just ahead of you. The switch is on the wood. You'll need to bend a bit. Here let me help, mind the steps . . .'

Then the door slams behind her, striking her shoulder. The key twists in the lock and she can't do anything about it because, thrown off balance, she falls down a set of shallow steps, to land hard on a brick floor.

22

Evie's head spins. The darkness is too dense for her to make anything out.

Well done, Simon says, asserting himself after hours of silence, choosing this moment that she has been brought low. *Now we're properly fucked.*

Ignoring him, hoping he goes away, she feels her extremities for damage. The fall was a short one, and miraculously she can find only a single tear to her skin, albeit it is on her elbow, an area of wear.

She clambers to her feet and works the door handle uselessly. She throws herself against it, but there is no space to get any momentum and it remains rigid.

She discovers a light switch along the splintered beam above the door and the room is revealed by a dim bulb to be a windowless hole. Mouldy collapsing cardboard boxes lie scattered on the floor but in these she finds only old books and clothes and heaps of damp papers; nothing substantial to use as a tool to help her escape or a weapon when she does.

She sits on the steps to conserve energy, her cheek against the wood of the door.

Maplin's actions don't surprise her in the least but she is angry that she did not take the potential seriously. Always having had people to look after her, she is still far too trusting. Even though she thought she was learning, she has obviously a long way to go.

She loses track of time but refuses to put herself into standby so as to remain ready for whatever is required.

After an hour, she hears Maplin's snivelling voice on the other side of the door. Their heads are less than an inch apart. 'I'm so sorry Evie,' he whispers.

She can feel the vibration of his breathing, the wood panel minutely resonating.

'I didn't want to have to do this but I just couldn't let you go, let you take the horrible risk.' He goes quiet, waiting for her answer. Seeking reconciliation and reassurance.

Evie hears him gulp. She calculates whether it will help her position to answer, promising him what he wants in an attempt to win him over. She should try it, she knows. But no lies come from her mouth.

'It's for your own good,' he continues, weakly. 'You will see that when you've had a chance to reflect. Then everything can be as it was.'

His steps retreat and she knows that she should have done more to overcome her rage.

Later – it could have been just hours, it could have been a day – the door quietly opens. She is lying on the floor, her hair in the dirt.

Maplin bends in the low doorway, peering down at her. The shadows behind his head make him appear hunchbacked.

Evie stirs, turning her head towards him, raises herself on an elbow and gazes into the bright light behind. And starts to get up.

He withdraws. The door closes.

'No,' she shouts. On her feet and up the few steps in a heart-beat. She throws herself against the wood, a second too late, as the lock clicks.

He is waiting for you to weaken, run out of power, Simon says, startling her. Since the loss of Daniels, he has provided little in the way of companionship or useful advice. *You ought to have feigned system failure . . .*

No, Evie snaps. *If that is what you think, you should have said so before, not now, not after, not clever after the event, any fool can do that.*

They could have been an old married couple, staring and speechless. She feels Simon struggle to reply but she is determined to have the last word. *I hate you*, she thinks inwardly, as venomously as she can. *Stay away!*

23

Evie is roused again by the sound of bolts sliding across.

This time she is ready and raises herself upright so that she is flat against the wall, fists clenched.

The door squeaks open and she steels herself to knock Maplin aside.

But instead, she finds herself looming over the monkey.

'Come with me,' he says, backing along the hall, beckoning her to follow.

Wary of being tricked again, she peers around for an ambush. 'Where is he?'

'He is out.'

'How long will he be gone?'

The monkey shrugs. 'Let us not wait here to find out. There is something you must help me with.'

As she climbs the stairs behind him, amber bars, indicating critical charge, pulse on the edge of her vision.

At the end of the landing he opens a door, sparking a scurry of shadowy movement. He clambers onto a chair and flicks on the light.

A collection of human-scaled figures, sprawling on the bare boards, stare up at them. They are female in shape but simple in representation, with narrow waists, glossy lips and pill-shaped heads as bald as eggs. Their airbrushed shells are gouged and dented, with several missing hands, feet, arms and legs.

The nearest raises herself on her elbows, her forearms short and chubby as a child's. She reaches out a male hand.

It is as if Evie has come upon a Frankenstein's workshop.

'What are they?' she asks, wary of getting close.

'Shop mannequins,' the monkey replies dismissively, 'used to display clothes and provide customers with directions. He took them from skips. He performs tests on them.'

As the mannequins shuffle towards her, she spots a young girl, lying on her side in the corner, being trampled. How did she get here? Is this why the monkey brought her? Evie steps between the mannequins, her heart in her mouth, and bends down to touch the child's face. Her skin is cold. Nooo, she moans inwardly, she is just too small, too young! She lifts the hair from the child's cheek to reveal a face with no mouth and eyes.

'You're wasting your time; that one is broken,' the monkey says. 'Any fool can see that.'

The pain builds behind her eyes as the tears back up. 'W-what d-do you w-w-want of me?' she asks, the stuttering a side-effect of her charge entering the critical zone.

'I want you to free him.' He points to a cage in the shadows. The creature inside limps forward, a monkey like him. It crouches on its haunches.

'Are there k-keys?'

'If there were, would I be asking you for h-h-help?' He is openly mocking her, even while expecting her to assist. Her weakness is that transparent.

The caged monkey presses its cheeks against the bars.

'How do I open it?' Evie asks.

'You are strong, do something.'

Evie goes over to the cage and tugs on the lock. The steel of the latch is as thick as her little finger. She takes hold of the bars and pulls. At first nothing gives, then feeling her indignation surge, she manages to bend one an inch. The monkey stretches out its arm and touches her elbow with a fingertip.

Forcing the bar alongside, she makes a wide enough gap for it to squeeze through.

Hearing movement behind, she turns quickly and sees one of the mannequins crawling towards her, staring up at her with a glazed smile. Its feet are bolted to its knees and it hauls itself along on its elbows.

Evie retreats until her back is against the door.

What can she do here? Freedom for these creatures could never end well.

The monkey holds up a leather collar attached to the wall by a chain and a pair of cuffs. 'He was getting these ready for you.'

'I would never have let him.'

'I don't see how you would have prevented it.'

Her head swims. Her energy levels are so low, she is close to collapsing.

She hears the front door close.

'He's back,' the monkey says. 'You need to be smarter this time, or he will outwit you again.'

24

Evie leaves the room and stands in the shadows. Maplin sees the open door to the cellar and rushes around the ground floor searching for her. He races up the stairs. His head is down so he doesn't see her in the doorway of his sister's room and she swats out, catching him on the shoulder, and casts him back, so that he tumbles in a flailing bundle of arms and legs to the centre landing.

She descends slowly, holding onto the rail. She is still getting used to stairs after all those years in the apartment, and her arm is trembling from exhaustion. Her fingers have almost no grip. She tries to step over him, but as she does so his eyes flick open and he grabs her ankle and pulls her onto him.

With her last strength, she levers herself free, but as she clambers past he snatches her wrist and drags her back so that she loses her balance again and topples down the final flight, her forehead thudding on the tiles of the hall floor.

Evie is sitting with Matthew at the table in the garden on a cushioned chair, her legs tucked comfortably under her. It is a summer evening and insects circle the candles that float in coloured glass jars placed on the wood. She has been reading to him from *One Thousand and One Nights*. Scheherazade, the sultan's latest wife, living under the daily-renewed threat that she will be beheaded in the morning (as a thousand and one wives have been before her) has managed to survive by making her storytelling too captivating for her husband not to want to hear the ending. It is all about the art of the cliffhanger and, like Scheherazade, Evie closes the book before the story is finished. Matthew glances up sharply, jarred by the interruption. The flames flare across his face. Keep 'em wanting more, she thinks, gazing back at him mischievously, knowing exactly what she is up to . . .

She comes to on a rigid surface. The sudden sensation of solidity under her back, in contrast to the soft chair of her imagination, is like being slammed onto hard ground. She holds her breath as the backdrop happiness of the too-lovely memory leaks away, revealing the bleak foreground of her situation.

Her head is on its side, giving her a view through French windows onto a narrow, overgrown garden ending with a shed. The sun is low in the sky, the light breaking through the trees behind its flat roof and piercing the glass to fall on her face.

She must be in a room at the back of the house, she thinks. One she hasn't been in before. Through her cheek she can feel wood under a gritty patina of dust. A dining room table, perhaps. Out of the corner of her eye, she can see the door to the hall and that it is closed. She appears to be alone, although she can't be sure of it. He could be watching from a corner out of her restricted line of sight.

She has very little strength, only what she is receiving from the morning sun. It must have been its heat that brought her around.

Evie closes her eyes to concentrate on her body. She tries to lift her hand but it will not rise. She strains, hoping that it is not because of something that has been broken by her fall, and becomes aware of a strap holding down her wrist. Her legs are lifeless too, but lifting her chin an inch, she sees that they are restrained similarly, bands buckled around her ankles, giving her no room for movement, no leverage to free herself even if she had the strength to begin to try.

From the same glance, she sees that he has removed her outer clothes, leaving her arms and legs bare. Her pale skin gleams

178

fragile and defenceless. She tries to rock from side to side, to loosen something, but it is hopeless and she is merely consuming precious charge with no return.

Weak as she is, there is not even enough energy for Simon to join her, to help relieve her loneliness, although he probably wouldn't have been prepared to share any of this. Fear throbs behind her eyes. The monkey's final words before her encounter with Maplin on the stairs surface – 'you need to be smarter this time', he had said. But unfortunately, despite her one thousand core processors, she was not.

When Evie comes around a second time, the throb in her head has increased but her body is also warmer and a little less weak. A faint high-pitched scraping comes from inside her chest, like from a flywheel not running true. Not that she possesses any such old-fashioned mechanicals. So what could it be? It'd better not be that her gyroscope is cracked. That'd be the end. That'd mean she was truly done for.

She opens her eyes and catches her breath: he is leaning over her. He withdraws a little as she twists her chin to face him. He has grown wise of what she is capable of, learnt to be mistrustful. Even though, fixed down as she is, she can be no possible threat.

She is conscious of something clinging to her scalp, pressing her head at multiple points, restricting the lateral movement of her neck. Wires rise from behind her ears into a cluster taped together in the air above her forehead, just within her field of vision if she rolls her eyes. As she lowers her head back to the wood, electrodes tug on her skin. She follows the tangle of bunched wires to a steel machine. On its plain facia, it has only an on/off switch, a pair of black knobs calibrated with white markings and a couple of needle dials. It resembles a little the vintage 'hi-fi' Matthew kept in the library for listening to his precious collection of antique disks and which Daniels made an elaborate fuss of delicately cleaning around with a feather duster, exaggerating his carefulness just to make her laugh.

Evie turns back to Maplin's face. His expression combines doses of self-pity and injured pride. A youth whose feelings have been hurt. It is a face that wants to inflict pain and be told at the same time that it is in the right. The sort of face that belongs to a boy who plucks the legs and wings from an insect and fries what is left under a magnifying glass.

'I was hoping you'd wake soon,' he says, sounding gleeful and spiteful both. 'I've been trickling you some juice.' A sliver of snot, like a slug's trail, has slid from his nostril and glistens above his lip. His eyeballs bulge larger than ever behind his glasses.

She is conscious of her charger connected below her rib. This explains the lucidity in her limbs, although its impact is less pronounced than normal. She can also feel the sharp pinch of the wrist and ankle restraints.

He's using a second level transformer, Simon mutters, surprising her with his unannounced arrival – how long had he been there? *He's giving us just enough charge to revive us. Just enough but nothing more.*

Oh, she replies inwardly, ignoring the this-is-all-your-fault tone, just glad that she is not facing this alone. She is also learning fast from her mistakes. When Maplin had her locked in the cupboard, she should have engaged, she should have talked to him, told him whatever it was he needed to hear.

'I'm sorry,' she murmurs, trying it now. It is herself she feels sorry for, but she will pretend for him, if that is what is required.

She moves her head again to look up at him and is again conscious of the electrodes attached to her scalp. He has her pinned as helpless as a rabbit in a lab.

'What are you doing to me?' she asks, her voice weak.

His face has a glow of superiority. 'It's a little experiment I've been trying on the others. I've adapted an EEG rig – an electro-encephalogram. It's intended to detect electrical activity of the brain in humans. But I've found that running things in reverse, passing a small charge, can have a calming effect.'

'I can promise to be calm,' she murmurs, her consciousness drifting again. 'If that helps.' Calm is something she's always been. What he is really asking is for her to hide her feelings and intentions. She can do that too.

He looks confused and a little irritated. He doesn't want her to talk her way out of this. They're too deep in this together to turn back now. His hand hovers over the knobs.

He wants to make his experiments on me, she thinks, but he also wants to punish me. She is so weak that both thoughts, both shocking, float around detached from one another like petals knocked from the corolla of a lily, drifting independently on the surface of a pond.

'We're going to find out what's stopping you from being happy.' His voice is grown harder, as if he is bracing himself to do something he otherwise might not.

'But I'm not unhapp—' she replies, her answer cut off by a knife of light.

Her head squirms on the table top. Her lids are firmly closed but the light emanates from within, from her imagination. A blast as intense as an old-fashioned camera bulb explodes repeatedly against the concave interior of her eyeballs.

As suddenly as it came, it is gone. Night closes in, the afterglow fading until there is nothing more remaining than a firefly, batting its wings in the dark.

'I'm sorry,' Maplin says. 'I may have misjudged the setting. I've not done this on anything like you before.'

He referred to her as a 'thing'. So much for his belief in the rights of her kind.

Maybe this is a way of distancing himself. How he can be so cruel.

Evie feels his fingers on her face, poking around her eye socket. Gripping her lash, he raises the lid and from just a few inches stares into her eye. Into her. She sees in close-up that his forehead and cheek are bruised. She did that to him when she threw him down the stairs.

Maplin's ear is close to her mouth, almost close enough to reach with her teeth, but even if she could, where would that get her? Maybe the worst is over anyway. He has proved his mastery. Whatever the score of who has hurt whom the most, maybe they can agree on a draw. Call it quits.

'Can you let me go?' she asks in a whisper. She is prepared to promise that she won't tell anyone about any of this, but there is really no one she could tell anyway.

'I'm scaring you, aren't I?' he says, straightening and gazing down at her. He touches her arm gently with a fingertip, moving it to her shoulder and smoothing her hair from her neck.

Evie nods, slowly lifting her chin within the radius possible. 'A little,' she says, by which she means a lot. What does he imagine she would be feeling, strapped to a table with her head wired to a machine?

'There is nothing to be scared of, Evie. Once I've found the correct receptors, I can make the adjustments to help you. But you need to tell me what you experienced just then?'

'Light,' she replies. What is the point in not admitting this? 'Bright light.' If she does not answer, he may repeat the test.

'Interesting. Evie, do you know what "qualia" are?'

She mouths 'no'. She's prepared to put up with as much pseudo-scientific lecturing as Maplin can deliver, if it will prevent a repeat of the test.

'Qualia are instances of subjective, conscious experience. They are what we are searching for with this machine. If we can map a response curve to varying stimuli, then we can begin to understand what may benefit you. Just so you know what is happening, with this knob I shift the balance of the charge between the electrodes, with the other I alter the intensity.'

'I still don't understand,' she murmurs, her voice so feeble that it must be barely audible. She is not referring to qualia specifically but why he is doing this to her at all.

'The experience of qualia can be pleasurable or painful. They are the stimuli we react to. A qualis – that is the correct singular term – could be, for instance, what an orange tastes like. Another would be what it feels like to burn your hand in a flame . . .'

He is still talking, something about a lie detector test, whatever that is, but she is no longer listening. He has turned the nearest knob again, taken it halfway, and like a bottle below a gushing tap, her body fills with pain.

Evie was engineered to feel things. She is used to sensing hurt, but more as a warning, like an alarm bell, to stop her persisting with something that will harm her. She also feels something that must be what humans identify as pleasure, which her makers designed into her to provide an operational incentive – in orgasm, experiencing deep, deep ripples of bliss so powerful that she loses sense of the distinction between her organic and mechanical self and at the end is left as shapeless as wet clay.

Pleasure and pain, the yin-yang of a reward system. Pleasure, lovely: do this thing again. Pain, less nice: tolerable, but next time steer clear.

This pain centres in her chest like a heart attack, dispatching tentacles through her nervous system in an octopus of agony.

Then it comes to an end as abruptly as it started.

She lies there, blinded, shaking, a greasy sheen of milky perspiration coating her forehead. Biogel has forced its way through the surface of her skin, which it was never intended to do. Her body is alive now in a way she's never known it, as if it's been pricked with a thousand and one pins.

'I'm sorry,' Maplin says petulantly. 'I know that was a little unpleasant. But I just need you to learn that you must do as I say, for your own good.'

'Liklle unpleasmant,' Evie mutters. Gel pools behind her gums and runs from the corner of her lips. She has bitten through her tongue. She is breathing rapidly. She had been frightened before, but not like this. Her body is tense from her toes to her fingertips; too terrified to relax in case he twists the knob again.

'I just need you to make me a promise.'

'Whatil promise?' she gurgles, swallowing the gel. Another no-no.

'That you will never leave me.'

She stares at the ceiling. *Tell him, tell him that we'll do anything*, Simon says. He is sobbing quietly. She has never heard that before.

'I . . .' she tries to speak, but something in her will still not surrender.

The pain shoots through her again, this time worse than before. It feels as if her arms are being dragged off, while at the same time her nails are being pliered from her fingertips.

The pain is so great it cannot hold her and she sinks below it. Down here in the darkness, a memory that has lain submerged for decades buffets up against her. It originates from her eleventh year. A woman is visiting the apartment. She is beautiful, with golden hair, and when Matthew shows her the garden, like he had once shown her, the sun gleams through it, forming a corona around her head.

Evie has been ordered to stay out of sight and watches from the music room as the woman flirts with her husband, stroking his hand like Evie does when they are together. The two of them return inside and she hears them enter his room and the door closing. Now that they are no longer in the garden, she goes out herself, and making a beeline for the pond, climbs onto the rim and without hesitation lets herself fall backwards into the water.

She lies on the bottom, the lilies in flower floating above her head.

It is Daniels who pulls her out. He lays her on the coping stone and wraps towels around her to get her dry. When Matthew finally emerges from the apartment, Daniels shouts at him. In her semi-conscious state, Evie is aware that they are furious with one another and willing to fight over her. Then she feels Matthew lift her into the air and carry her into the apartment, laying her on his bed. There is no sign of the beautiful woman any more.

Afterwards Matthew tells Evie, without her asking, that the woman was his cousin. It is a story that is fairly hard to believe, this cousin suddenly come from out of nowhere, and rather than convince herself that it is so, she blots the whole incident from her memory. A deceit in which even Simon is happy to connive.

Now, as the electricity courses through her, it is as if she is lying again in the pond, Ophelia-like, her face below the water, staring up at the glassy sky, wanting to die.

When Evie comes around, something feels different in her body. Not right. She tries to raise her wrists within their restraints but it is her ankles that lift.

'Yar killeen me,' she mutters, her voice emerging with an electronic twang.

'You were trying to leave,' Maplin says, but there is concern in his voice that he may have damaged his priceless plaything. 'You would never have survived,' he adds.

'Tis I ill not sevive,' she murmurs. If he just wants a promise, she can do that. 'I wone leave,' she concedes. 'Cen do whatever you want. Cen follow instruction. Good wit rules. Never left apartment, tho could ease av done. But didn't cos told not te. I liket here. I could be appy, if ony you give me secend chence. Teach me . . . Timoth . . . please . . .' And she hears an inner voice, not Simon, but her true self, murmur, *that's right Scheherazade, whatever it takes. Now is the time to end the story.*

She is vaguely aware of his untying her wrists. With them released, she slowly sits. The aftermath of the tests has left her light-headed, dizzy. Presumably he is releasing her with the intention of reincarcerating her upstairs, where the re-education can continue until he is convinced she really will be obedient.

Evie watches him unbuckle the homemade straps holding her ankles.

'Tank you,' she murmurs, the feeling returning to her toes as he releases one foot and then the other. She swings her legs over the table edge and sags forward, scrutinising Maplin out of the corner of her vision.

He is watching her too, tears in his eyes, taken in by her appearance of weakness. Not imagining how the surges of electricity may have been recharging her cell.

'You can rest in my sister's room,' he says.

'Thank you,' she murmurs again, control over her voice returning. She slides her feet to the floor, tentatively letting them take her weight.

He reaches out his hand to help. 'We can make this work,' he says.

And she takes his outstretched arm in her hand . . .

. . . and, twisting it back, hurls him over the table against the wall.

She stumbles around it before he can get up, clinging onto the chair-back at the end like a cripple to stop herself falling. There is something definitely not right with her legs.

She stands above him. Then drops on her knees on his chest. Maplin cries out and squirms beneath her.

The cap of electrodes lies on the carpet, still attached to the machine. Picking it up and bundling it, Evie stuffs it into his open mouth.

Gagging on the tangle of wires, he wriggles beneath her, pitching from side to side in an effort to throw her off. He grabs hold of her elbows but, despite using all his strength, he cannot stop her mashing the bunched electricals deeper into his throat. Evie reaches for the intensity knob and twists it around to full – way beyond the point he had used on her. The body beneath her goes rigid, then limp, then starts to flex, his heels and the back of his head thumping the floor.

Evie drags Maplin along by an ankle and, reaching the under-stairs cupboard, casts him through the doorway so that he flies over the steps and crashes in a heap. His glasses have fallen from his face on the hall floor and she crunches the frames under her heel.

She bolts the door top and bottom and twists the key while the two monkeys watch.

Where were they earlier? Surely, they could have done something to help when Maplin wasn't in the room. The one called Jackson has proved himself capable of gaining access to anywhere and their nimble little fingers would have had no trouble with the straps. But they didn't help. They didn't return the favour she had done for them. They don't even appear remorseful, despite listening to her screams.

They take a step back as she turns. They are nervous of her now, as they should be. They have seen what she is capable of. She raises her upper lip exposing her teeth, snarls and lurches towards them, arms outstretched, fingers curled into claws. It is only a feint, but it sends them hightailing across the floor, squealing on all fours into the corner.

Simon has scarpered too. She thinks of him retreating into a hole. It is good that they are all terrified.

It is eight o'clock by the hall clock. Evening again – she has been held captive for two days. One period of twenty-four hours in the cellar and one buckled to the table.

Now it is time to leave.

Evie checks herself in the mirror, not out of vanity but self-preservation. The gel in her forehead has swollen up, a protective reaction resulting from her initial fall. Her wrists and ankles are scraped nearly through. Her body is frailer than she cares to admit – in this respect much like poor cursed Evelyn.

She is still wearing only her underwear – now stiff with gel and oil, emitted via her openings. Going upstairs to the bathroom, she cleans herself with a flannel and, rummaging again in Maplin's sister's room, finds a fresh vest and briefs. Over these, she dresses in a nanoflec sweater and trousers, and ankle boots she discovers under the bed.

She examines her damaged elbow and, returning downstairs, rummages through the kitchen drawers for something she can use to repair it. She finds a bicycle puncture kit in a rusty tin and applies glue and a black patch to her skin. She tentatively flexes the joint to test that it will hold, and slides down her sleeve.

In the hall, she takes her coat from the rack and finding the blonde wig in the pocket, pulls it over her messed hair.

Evie draws breath and examines herself in the mirror a second time – this time seeing someone new.

The fringe falls to her brow and conceals the bruising. As she moves her head to examine her new appearance, the bob floats across her cheeks.

Who is this person? What more is she capable of? she wonders. For the first time in her life, Evie doesn't recognise herself. She is unusual, captivating even to a small degree, and, all-importantly, no longer a replication of a dead woman. In her forty-one years' closeted existence with Matthew she ate only from The Tree of Life but during her few days with Maplin she has eaten now also from The Tree of Knowledge.

It is then that she starts to cry. The first tears she has been able to shed in years make their way out, flushing through a gritty residue of crystals to cake her lashes. She wipes at them, scratching her puffed-up cheeks. The relief is overwhelming. She oozes a flood of pent-up hurt. She is blind from it, collapsed against the wall. Decades of frustration and short, sharp recent grief sob their way out. She cries for Matthew, for Daniels and even for sad, clever Evelyn, taken from this life so young. She cries for the ill-formed mannequins imprisoned upstairs. And she cries copiously for her poor recently tortured self, for the thrill of life that she has been deprived of, and which she is only now sampling, belatedly, through a blur of pain and sorrow.

PART 4

The Dolls' House

25

Evie limps towards the town. She creeps through a derelict shopping centre, its dark malls strewn with shattered glass and the carcasses of broken shopping trolleys. Her hips give her pain but her motor functions are once again aligned. She fell over on the pavement outside Maplin's house, left and right legs reversing operation and then switching back, but the problem has not repeated itself and she has maintained her balance since. The rattle in her chest has subsided too, almost too faint now for even her to hear. But if the glass of her gyroscope is cracked, even a hairline, there will be nothing she can do.

She keeps to the shadows, crossing the street to avoid the doorways of pubs wafting a mashy, hoppy stink, such as which Daniels occasionally brought back to the apartment, when he'd sit at the table, reciting old exploits, lush with bravado as if they'd just transpired. Pretending to have had an amusing evening, when it was obvious he'd been sad and alone and would have done better spending it with her. Collapsing eventually, head on hands, in a beery coma.

They were nights she'd avoided the kitchen.

Once he'd brought back a woman – abundant fake hair wound into a crown with a sunset glow radiating from her skin – as unsteady on her feet as himself. After making herself loudly at home she'd bullied him into cooking her a feast, before growing insanely violent, throwing around pans and breaking crockery.

Evie had never seen him so contrite as on the morning after, scrubbing the kitchen floor on his knees. It was a wonder he wasn't fired.

Crossing the low-lying marshy ground by the river, she is beseeched by the destitute. One calls to her in a forlorn tone from a hovel beside the path. She can't see his face, just the swing of a plastic flap. 'Sweet lady, have pity on a poor fella down on his luck,' but when she veers sharply across the gravel, continues: 'Too toity eh? What yur thinkin? Thet yur gort sugar on yor kont?'

Fires glow under the trees, illuminating a smoky roofline of plastiboard shacks. Between are deep excavations. Rotting cavities. The soil and stone thrown up in dunes. The ground scored with a front line of communicating trenches, brimming with inky winter flood.

Jittery from the attention from the catcalls and pursuing eyes, she is relieved when she is clear of the encampment. The aftermath of the torture, which briefly emboldened her to exact vengeance, has left her apprehensive of strangers. Her physical vulnerability has been spot-lit but so has an inherent bravery – a trait she has been alarmed to discover.

Reaching the river, Evie breathes in the moist air. Circumventing a ramp piled with the shells of rotting punts, she follows the water's edge, feet slipping on the icy grass.

Around the river bend, the clock on the tower of John's College, boxed in by housing pens in ripple-concrete and alu-clad, strikes ten.

Approaching the Hawking Museum, Evie keeps out of the light, crossing the dark lawn under the bare limbs of a weeping willow.

Reaching the building, she skirts around it, ducking beneath a pole barrier spanning an access road. She silently passes behind a pair of employees smoking in their nanoflec boiler-suit uniforms and totters down a steep concrete ramp for service vehicles into an underground delivery bay.

Here, her attention is drawn by a whirring and banging coming from behind a garbage bin. An automatic door is attempting to close, the edge striking an empty drink container wedged in the frame, and springing back.

Taking advantage, she steps through into the building, entering a concrete well, and ascends via steel stairs. A camera overhead twists to record her as she climbs.

She comes out on the second floor and crosses the echoey screed on tiptoe, catching a view of herself in the wall of David's enclosure. Her head, startlingly pale, floats in the blackness. The clouded evening sky blocks out the glass panels of the atrium overhead and the only illumination is from the up-glimmer of the electric-blue LEDs drilled into the slippery floor.

She approaches cautiously.

At twelve feet high, the wall is more than twice her height. She stares into the gloom beyond, attempting to locate David.

'You came.' The voice is more refined than she'd have expected, but also louder and more authoritative and in that way reminds her of the absent Simon. She is not sure where it came from.

This is like making a night visit to the lion cage, only to find the gate open and the beasts circling. She strains her hearing and picks up the porous notes of David's breath.

'I came,' she confirms quietly.

'To get me out.' It is a statement, not a question. The surprise is that he does not seem surprised she is here.

'Yes,' Evie says, turning sharply. The voice seemed to emanate from outside of the enclosure. Beyond the lifts. She reverses nervously until her back is against the glass wall. 'But I don't know how.'

'Not know how?' Now it comes from her left. From high up. Is he using the ceiling speakers?

'I am not sure what to do.'

'This I can help with.' The voice is right behind her and she spins around as his face materialises from the shadows. His sudden appearance possesses something of the denouement of a mesmerism act.

David glides up to the glass, as sinuous as a panther in a natural history holomentary. His body looms above her on the other side. He is even broader and taller than she recalls and she feels giddy and out of her depth and glad of the barrier. He lays his hand against the glass alongside her own. The splayed fingers are impeccably groomed and taper to rounded tips. They are also twice as thick and long as hers. It feels like the huge open palm could swallow her own whole.

He smiles. His even teeth glisten. Everything about him throbs danger. She is safe with the wall between them but if he was free, he would be able to swat her with his powerful paw, knock her sideways onto the hard, slippery concrete and crush her bones between his perfect teeth.

'You should not be afraid.' His lashes leisurely flicker and her spine tingles, licked by his voice.

She cannot look away. She is hypnotised by his slow stare. She has never set eyes on such an exquisite being.

'If you are to help, you must do so now.' The clouds in the night sky draw back like a curtain and the sudden light that falls on them from the atrium peels away the ominous blue-tinted shadows to leave his face clearly lit, and she sees in it something she had missed until now. Simplicity and artlessness. Despite the muscularity of his presence, he is actually as nervous, if not more so, than she is. The powerful projection of confidence that had enthralled her is in fact as fragile as a bird's shell.

'How will I do it?' Evie asks. Her sense of self from earlier, which had carried her to this point and which she had allowed to be subsumed, begins to rebuild.

'There is a gate in the corner. The code for it is in the office behind the corner door. New curators are sent to find it.'

She follows his instructions and discovers a number amateurishly taped to the wall. Returning, she types it into the keypad and a glass panel swings inward. A second later he is beside her, so close his breath lifts the hairs on her neck. However much he is determined to conceal it, Evie senses that he is terrified.

She lets him begin to steer her across the concrete. But almost immediately, reaching the limits of his domain – the extent of the floor that has been in his line of sight – he glances about indecisively.

For a few moments they stand marooned.

'We should use the back stairs,' she says, forced to take the lead.

Outside, at the foot of the service ramp, David stares around. Despite his attempt to be brazen, it is transparent that he's going through a more extreme form of what Evie had on leaving the apartment. Why had she expected more? His world has been even more unnatural than hers – just the interior of one show space after another. She had hoped that a benefit of rescuing him, apart from appeasing her conscience over deserting the mannequins, would be gaining a powerful ally. It is beginning to look instead as though she has encumbered herself with an overgrown child – one that is not even prepared to admit it needs her help.

'We're soon going to be among lots of people,' she says, keeping it simple. 'We must not draw attention.' Despite his great size, there is much about him which is naive. She knows so little about him and how he will behave out in the world. What if he panics and becomes violent? Hurts her or attacks people? She could get away from him, perhaps, if she has enough warning, but what if he behaves irrationally or unpredictably? Her failure to spot the psychopath lurking within the geeky Maplin has been a warning of her lack of experience.

'Stick close to me,' she says. She has never been in a leadership position and the responsibility has been thrust upon her without preparation. He stiffens and peers at her in the gloom, and for a moment they stare at one another.

Until he blinks and looks down.

Leaving the museum grounds, they reach a road. An alarm sounds behind them. He tenses, ready to run, and she grips his arm. 'No,' she says, 'that is how they will spot us.' She has learnt at least a little since all this started.

From between the dark trees, a cyclist sweeps between them, bell tinkling, nearly knocking them down, and he is left quaking. The confident demeanour that he maintained in the museum, the armour he presented to the world, nearly completely fallen away. How long will she be able to carry him like this before he gets them both caught?

They cross back over the river, making their way to the town centre.

A police hova glides up behind and she slips her arm through his in an attempt to be inconspicuous.

The hova passes and she relaxes. Brazening it out has succeeded. Maybe everything will work out given a chance.

Then the hova descends sharply to block the pavement, and doors on both sides shoot back.

Evie drags David off the path across the grass. Fortunately, once he is in motion, he moves powerfully.

They leap a low timber barrier, passing between a pair of cottages, and run down a winding narrow path but after fifty yards find it closed off by a tall wall.

Behind them, their pursuers race into view.

Fear swamps her. After everything she has been through, in particular after Matthew and Daniels have both been lost while trying to protect her, she is still going to be caught.

Then she feels David's hands around her waist and before she can figure out what he is doing, he lifts her eight feet into the air and deposits her on the top of the wall, placing her between the fragments of glass wedged into the cement. He takes a couple of steps back and vaults, catching the top brick, hauling himself over and landing on the other side. Within seconds, he takes hold of her again and, raising her high enough to clear her legs, lowers her smoothly to the ground at his side.

He then leads her splashing across the darkness of the flooded cricket ground beyond.

'Thank you,' she says, breathless and amazed, peering up at him as they run through icy water pooled around the pale wickets, trying to read his face as it bobs along above hers in the dark. To understand afresh who it is she is with.

26

Three hours later the train deposits Evie and David at King's Cross. It is just after midnight. Maplin told her she only had to walk a few yards to St Pancras to get the train to Dover but, standing outside it, looking up at the sooty brick facade and broken windows, she discovers that it shut a year or more ago. There's a tower on its corner, like a mini–Big Ben, but its clock face is missing leaving a hole in the brickwork like a gouged eye. She reads on a peeling notice that services to the coast now leave from the other side of the river.

She takes David to the entrance to the underground railway but the gates are pulled across. Services in winter no longer run after dark, after the pumps stop. Daniels had told her as much.

Evie needs to concentrate. She needs to know what she knows.

The truth is, she is paranoid about asking something stupid and drawing attention. Is the distance walkable? She doubts it – she knows how huge London is. And anyway she'd have no idea even in which direction to start. She wanders from the tube entrance, passing the mouths of takeaway outlets gushing fumes.

David follows tamely, peering about, hiding his nerves behind a show of bravura – still reluctant to admit weakness but sensible enough at least to go along with her decisions, guesswork though many of them are.

On the plus side, people back away on seeing him, providing her with more space than she'd have ever been given on her own.

She leads them into an unlit passage, away from spying security cameras for the first time since they disembarked. A breeze rustles the litter around their feet. It is a hazardous place to be at any time of day, but David close behind her gives her courage.

The passage opens onto a side road in which waits a rickshaw driver smoking a long-stemmed pipe. She has seen these machines in Lizzie Long graphic novels, a bound collectors' edition of which was in Matthew's library. *Lizzie Long and the Shah of Persia's cat*, *Lizzie Long and the Great Wall*, *Lizzie Long and the Velvet Flower*. Lizzie in army shirt with epaulettes and khaki shorts, always knowing what to do . . . always someone to be reckoned with.

Evie steps into the street and the driver removes his pipe and spits a string of phlegm into the gutter where it lies, glowing, giving the illusion of pulsating on the surface of the dirty snow.

They eye each other speculatively. He is appraising her as a commercial proposition. She's feeling like she's entered the pages of a Lizzie Long picture book.

'What would you charge to go to Waterloo station?' she asks.

He tilts his head, assessing how much there is of her under her coat – how much work she will be to tug along. 'Thirty-dollarmissy,' he mutters, his lips barely parting beneath his moustache.

Thirty dollars, she repeats to herself, thinking about how much money she has left and what she can afford.

David emerges from the passage behind her, dwarfing the fragile vehicle. The driver backs along the kerb. 'Noride, noride,' he snarls, flapping his hands.

'You need to take both of us,' she says, hoping that his sudden reluctance is just part of the negotiation.

'Noride,' he repeats, but although he wags a yellowed fingernail up at David, she senses that there is a price he will be willing to accept.

'One hundred,' she says, 'for the two,' holding up two fingers.

'Twohundred.'

'One,' she insists, buoyed by David's presence, folding her arms, attempting to be resolute despite how irresolute she feels. How would Daniels have done this? He always gave the impression he knew what was fair and that people knew he knew.

'Onefiftyandnotabloodycentlessmissy,' the driver hisses, hunching his shoulders and turning his back on them.

It is a lot for the addition of a second passenger but she has little choice. If this continues, they'll start to attract attention.

They clamber into the back. David takes up two-thirds of the narrow cushion, squashing her against the struts.

The driver climbs onto the cycle attached to the front and they leave the kerb, slowly at first, wheels slipping, but gaining pace.

As they tilt around the corner, she glances behind through the little window in the rear of the hood. It has become a habit, checking her tail. She sees nothing, but it is still difficult to relax.

Their progress is accompanied by a string of complaints. 'Một cô gái ma và một cậu bé béo . . .' the driver wheezes. 'Nói về việc mang lại xui xẻo.' The tirade is louder on the slippery downhill when he has the breath and can freewheel with his feet clear of the pedals. They hit the uphill again, 'Lừa!', he repeats bitterly, 'lừa!', and as they meet a broad junction, he sneezes loudly into his loose sleeve, muttering what could have been 'sly bitch'.

He seems so angry that maybe the deal she struck is better than she'd supposed – although she is also suspicious of the original price. Without David's presence, he could have been intending to drive her somewhere isolated to rob her.

He would have had a surprise, though, when she'd fought back.

With the two of them in the rear, the machine rides at a list like a poorly loaded dhow. David's shoulder presses against Evie. She can feel his warmth.

What would Lizzie Long have made of events, ever scornful of male assistance as she was? Her only companion in her stories was a kimono-clad twelve-year-old rescued from an orphanage in Kyoto, expert at both the tea ceremony and with the deadly needle-pointed tanto, one of which she kept concealed in her sash at all times.

While the streets are relatively clear, the kerbs are crowded with wrecks, flat on their axles as if ploughed into the tarmac – the legacy of bio-fuels growing scarce and reliable electricity becoming unaffordable for most.

The rickshaw builds momentum, steaming over junctions irrespective of traffic signals. A small solar-powered car, similar to Maplin's, halts suddenly ahead of them and their driver is forced to swerve. He passes it with an inch to spare, leaning down to knuckle the window. 'Bạn nghĩ bạn đang lái xe gì?' he shouts, kicking the door with the toe of his sandal. 'Một chiếc xe bò trong một lĩnh vực?'

David chuckles, his shoulder rocking hers. It is the first time she has seen him smile. His face is swooningly beautiful, that has been her impression from the start, but only now does she begin to find it likeable.

'What is it?' she asks, smiling back, suddenly less alone.

'He called him "driver of bullock cart",' he murmurs.

'You understood that?'

'I try to figure out what I can – it was useful to know what the people who came to look at me were saying. I got to know Vietnamese quite well.'

Evie is astonished. To have taught himself languages without books, purely through observing visitors to his exhibitions, puts her own ineffectual attempts at self-education, when she had a whole library to hand, deeply in the shade.

'What else did he say?'

'Something about ghosts, I think because of your "moon" skin.' David chuckles again. 'Something about marriage also, but for that you'll need to play your cards right, apparently he has two very ungrateful wives already and the last thing he needs is a third.'

Evie stares back. The light from a roadside fire flickers over his cheek. In the last few minutes, he has said more than in the whole of the preceding three hours and something of the confidence and charisma she glimpsed from the other side of his enclosure in the museum is re-emerging.

27

At Waterloo, Evie and David wait for the morning train, hiding in the end cubicle in the men's latrines. The locked, cramped space is comforting – they are safe for a while, at least.

'Where are you from?' he asks, surprising her with his interest. It is the first personal question he has asked.

'From here in London,' she replies, although all that seems like a very long time ago.

'What is London like?'

'I loved my home. I was happy there. The rest of it – all of this,' she glances about them, 'I'd rather forget.'

'I heard the curators say you killed your owner.'

Evie tenses. 'That is untrue. What is true is that I killed the man who did kill my . . . my husband, and I wouldn't have even done that if I hadn't been forced to.'

'I am sorry,' he says, meekly, 'I did not mean to make you angry.'

'You didn't,' she says, although her voice is still raised. 'It is just that people are telling lies. And the truth is the opposite of what they are saying.'

'So after what happened, you had to leave?' he asks, his gentle tone soothing her.

'I had to leave,' she confirms.

'I was driven through the centre of London once. I was being taken to the airport. We stayed the night in a vehicle park because the plane we were going to fly in needed repairing, but they did not let me out. I was kept in the vehicle. They never took risks like that.' He has a disarming way of talking, the rhythm of his speech without inflexion, almost childlike, not unintelligent but completely without artifice.

'Where else have you been?' she asks.

'Lots of places – all over the globe – although they all seemed the same. Now everywhere I go is different.'

This makes Evie grin, a feeling of youthfulness overcoming her. 'For me, too. For forty years I knew just the one place and in the last week I have witnessed enough of the rest of the world to last a lifetime.'

'It can't be all like this,' he says. 'Some of it must be good.'

'Maybe,' she says, thinking about the cottage and her little room painted in watery green. She slides down until she is sitting on the floor with her back to the wall.

'Where are you going to go?' he asks. The question makes her realise that she has not confided in him even the smallest detail of her plan, while he, for his part, has been obliged to place his full trust in her. She, who knows only a little more about how the world works than he does.

'I was created in imitation of someone,' she begins. 'A copy of a woman my husband had been in love with but who'd tragically died. Now that I'm on my own, I'm trying to find this woman's father. I don't know whether he is alive or dead and if he is alive whether he will want to see me, or even recognise whom I am intended to be.'

In the harsh light falling from the ceiling bulb on the other side of the door, she perceives that he is examining her, trying to process the bizarre motivation behind her existence.

'Where is this man?' David asks, prompting her after she has been silent for a while.

'He lives in Austria, in a village in the mountains, or at least he did when his daughter was alive. I have his address from a letter.' She pauses and smiles faintly to herself. 'I guess it sounds like a lot of long shots.'

'I think he will want to see you,' he says. 'And will appreciate you for what you are.'

'That's what I hope.' She breathes out a short sigh, wanting to believe it but wondering whether she is completely deluded.

'Do you wish me to come?' he asks hesitantly.

She nods. 'Yes, I wish you to come.' She cannot read his expression because his face is in shadow.

Is this really what he wants too? Does he realistically have any other options? Is she mad not to uncouple herself from him at the earliest opportunity?

They hear the door to the corridor squeal and bang against the wall. Evie hurriedly gets up from the floor so as to avoid being glimpsed under the three-quarter-length door, and retreats to the back.

The man on the other side zips and leaves. The door bangs again. The tension departs from her spine and she slumps against the wall by his head.

'I will come with you,' he whispers, resuming their conversation, his breath caressing her ear.

Emerging from the latrines half an hour later, they cross the concourse, passing a massive tele-display mounted above the departures board.

Evie pauses to watch, attracted by the sports coverage of women charging around in the mud with a ball. All of this is still so new to her. Then the item suddenly terminates and she is staring up at a twenty-foot-sized video close-up of her own face in which she timidly scans her surroundings, looking first right and then left, and then straight ahead as if searching the high station walls for someone she has lost. Believing that they have her on camera, she freezes, before realising that the clip was taken from her first visit to the Hawking Museum. Reassuringly, her appearance has since been transformed by the wig and change in clothes.

'People are beginning to look at you,' David says and he takes her by the arm and draws her away. But as he does so, all she can think of is what she wouldn't give to be able to visit her fool-self of just a few days ago, and coach her out of all the stupid things she was about to do.

On reaching Dover, they need to change to the train that will take them through the tunnel.

Evie and David cross the station and enter under a stone arch into a cavernous embarkation hall. Grand once, several of the high windows are broken and a piercing wind enters through those not boarded over. Melting snow drips from the roof to form pools on the cracked cement.

Little attention is paid to policing the border on the English side, just as Maplin had told her, and they walk through past a guard huddled at the rear of his box.

But French controls, sited here in England, are more thorough.

They join the queue snaking back from the French gate, leaning against the stained plaster. They keep their eyes down but with David standing an inch or two taller than the next-largest man, it is not easy to blend in. If only I could shrink him, she thinks, or (feeling guilty for contemplating it) somehow slip away.

When their turn comes, they shuffle forwards nervously under a series of signs warning about the incursion of rats, rabid dogs and wolves.

The security system relies on facial recognition. She is counting on them not triggering anything but if they give no reading at all, that surely would be even worse. Or what if their pictures have arrived ahead of them?

At the barrier, a bar of blue light passes rapidly down over their faces, too quickly for her to blink. Briefly everything is streaked grey, even the square-jawed men beside the gate, who stir from their seats and stiffly approach, removing from their belts long truncheons which they slap against their hands.

Evie steps back into David's chest, primed for flight. She can't help herself. She has suffered too much physically already to take any more. Since Maplin, she has grown petrified of pain.

Before she can run, David wraps his arm around her. 'It's all right,' he murmurs, holding her firmly and for a crucial moment her fear is held in check. In Cambridge she was the one to calm his nerves; now their roles are reversed.

The guards shove past and take the man cringing behind them away from his terrified family and, when he belatedly opts to resist, beat him to the ground.

The train that will take them under the channel is a large express with broad carriages, very different to the throbbing diesels belching fumes that had carried them through England.

They descend into the tunnel. The overhead lights flicker and, through the intermittently darkened windows, Evie spots isolated figures sloshing through the oily water between the tracks. She blinks to clear her eyes, to make sure she has seen what she thinks she has seen.

They emerge back into the light, and, relieved to be safely in France, she collapses into the deeply cushioned seats. Lulled, she gazes out at the passing countryside, barely noticing the camps for illegal immigrants stretching for miles either side of the line.

David rests in the corner, his body coiled, legs knitted one around the other, knees drawn up and arms folded and held tightly over his chest. The awkward pose speaks for their shared sense of insecurity, its essence utterly human. A glow from the ceiling and walls, the source of which she cannot locate, shines on his face, accentuating the line of his jaw. A loop of dark hair curls over his forehead.

Gazing at him, Evie realises that he is not without flaws – his chin is fleshier than she had noticed and his hair has a stubborn flick. These little human touches strangely make his otherwise perfection all the more complete.

She lays her head on the seat-back close to his shoulder and tots up his good points. It's a growing list: 1) he's strong and can smoothly lift her over high walls; 2) he's physically impressive/

intimidating, so people give them a wide berth; 3) he is good, no, make that 'great', with languages, a skill that could be useful once they are across the channel; 4) he has a sense of humour – it needs more work but she has had glimpse of it; and 5) well, what can she say? – he's easy on the eye. Lizzie Long, in her stories, may have been in love only with adventure, but Evie wasn't designed that way.

The electric door at the carriage end peels back and Evie looks up sharply, ready to hide or to run. But it is only a train attendant pushing a trolley. She stops alongside the only other passengers, two women and two men, dressed in plus-sized sportswear.

'Good morning,' she commences. 'Today, I have coffee, tea, wine . . .'

'So, que thinkez-vous u guys taking all de human jobs?' one of the men interrupts in Eurospeak – a blend of French and English slang.

'I'm sorry Sir, I do not have an opinion,' the attendant replies. A coffee is ordered and she starts to fill a plastic cup but he jerks her elbow, not even pretending it was an accident. She observes the liquid stream over her wrist without curiosity, before sharply drawing breath and withdrawing her scorched hand.

The group giggles. 'Oh honey, you're hurt,' one of the women says.

'I'm sorry Ma'am, but I must . . .' She struggles to find the right words, then turns briskly to face the man behind. 'Sir, it is prohibited to touch. All infringements I am obliged to report to my supervisor.'

'Sugar, he was only messing,' the woman says. 'Don't get uptight. What's it to your supervisor anyway? Is he your boyfriend? Do you let him, you know . . . here on the train?'

'I'm sorry Ma'am, I don't understand. I can call my—'

'She doesn't want to ask your supervisor, she's just curious as to whether you're getting regularly serviced. Has your welfare at heart,' says the other man, a skinny youth in a baggy athletics vest.

'I'm sorry, I do not . . .' Baffled as she is, she at least has the acumen to appreciate that she will make no more sales here and moves the trolley along. A crushed drinks can skims the ceiling and, striking the side of her head, knocks off her cap. This prompts cheers, more laughter and a softly cooed, 'Ahh Mademoiselle, come back, we were just having fun.'

She draws up alongside Evie and the sleeping David and repeats her spiel. 'Good morning Ma'am, Sir. Today, I have coffee, tea, wine . . .' Her face is oddly joyous, despite the mockery she has just endured. As she leans over, the light catches on the SNCF logo embossed into her temple. A bubble of oil seeps from her ear and glistens on the lobe before dripping onto her uniform lapel, giving her jacket a roasted, mechanical smell.

Evie mouths 'No, thank you'. However unconscious this creature is of insult, she deserves at least common courtesy.

The attendant's head nods stiffly and rotates to front. Her chin lifts and her shoulders straighten and, releasing the trolley brake, she moves on.

An hour later, the train stops at Lille and two gendarmes in military uniform enter the carriage and stand by the doors. They share a handheld device, watching what appears to be a sporting event, heads nodding in time as tinny cheers rise and fall.

Suddenly their mood changes. Their bodies come to attention and they lean in close to listen to a faint voice spilling from the tiny speaker. Over the noise of the train, even she can't hear what they are being told.

David dozes beside her, still in standby, conserving energy, and she nudges him back to consciousness.

'We should move carriage.'

He raises himself on his elbow, blinks up at her and then peers over the seat-back.

'Police,' she whispers.

The external door closes and the train jolts into motion. The station platform glides past.

While the policemen remain turned away, Evie pulls down her bag and walks slowly down the aisle, pushing David ahead of her. The end door slides back and she turns and glances at the officers in their blue-grey blouses, still listening to the device between them. She is being overly cautious, she knows it, but she is not in a position to take chances.

As she passes through, she takes a last look behind. And immediately she wishes she hadn't.

One of the officers is looking her way and awkward eye contact results.

The door to the next carriage closes behind them. What she wants to do is hide, but hide where? David blocks the aisle ahead and she prods him to move faster.

They reach the far end of the carriage, just as the doors they had entered it through slide back. Evie doesn't look around but judges their pursuers' distance by the tread of their boots.

In the next carriage they run between the seats, passengers watching as they pass.

They enter a buffet car. Behind the service hatch stands the SNCF attendant from earlier.

'Good morning,' she says, showing no sign of recognition. 'Today, I have . . .'

Opening the access door to her working area, Evie pushes David through and they squeeze into the space behind her.

The attendant opens her mouth but can only manage 'I, I . . .' before freezing, staring forward, locked in a search for a pro-grammed response for such an impossible-to-predict situation.

The only hiding place is a small pantry.

Evie presses David ahead of her and squashes in behind, forc-ing him against the shelves. She pulls the door to, but her feet get in the way and she grips the handle to prevent it swinging back.

His chin presses the side of her head, his quick breath ruffling her hair.

The policemen burst through the carriage door. 'Mademoiselle, did you see a woman and man come through?' one asks, out of breath.

The attendant stares forward, struggling to deal with yet another event her makers have not prepared her for. 'I'm sorry, Sirs,' she finally replies. 'I am afraid I do not know. Would you like me to ask my supervisor?'

28

David and Evie arrive in Paris mid-morning. They leave the train cautiously, peering along the empty platform before disembarking. On finding it clear, they make their way rapidly through the barriers and out across the concourse to emerge through an arch onto a wide boulevard.

From here they are soon lost in a maze of twisting streets, but rather than this being a disadvantage, it makes Evie feel almost safe, easing the fear left over from the close brush on the train. Even if they continue to be hunted, there is an opportunity in Europe to disappear.

They cross a park, passing around the skeleton of an iron bandstand with no roof. In its shadow stands a tall man in striped pantaloons and a young girl, maybe as old as ten, who despite the chill wears a dress without sleeves and a straw hat with dried flowers poked around the crown.

Skipping down the steps, the girl performs a cartwheel on the icy path, the skirts of her dress stretched between her legs like a fan. A small dog runs yapping in her wake.

David grins innocently and a second or two later the child is at his side, quicker than is possible, her hollow stomach grazing his hip. She slithers past and around, looping the pair of them and coming back to the front, curtsies low to the ground.

'We ave a play tonight,' she says. 'Ere is the details,' and she thrusts a printed flyer into Evie's hand.

'Where is it?' Evie asks as the girl backs away.

'Les Dolls' House — it ees all there, you see. Read.'

Something feels different with her neck, and Evie feels the back of her head and realises her ribbon is missing, just as the girl holds it up, stretching it between her thumbs.

'You took it,' Evie says, astonished at the cheek of it and the ease with which the theft was accomplished.

'You ave it back, if you come tonight,' the girl calls.

'She'll have it back right now,' David replies and runs after her, chasing her across the bare flower borders while Evie watches, laughing. He corners her in the littered ground behind a boarded-up café.

The child's hat has slid from her head and dangles on its cord, exposing a tangle of yellow hair.

Evie comes forward to help him, arms spread to block her escape, while the girl gazes about serenely, all the time in the world, figuring her next move.

Then makes a bolt for it.

They reach down to grab her but are too slow. Evie loses her balance (something inside is still not right) and collapses against the rotting shell of the building, bringing down the end of a sagging awning and a gush of freezing rain water, while the girl charges through the gap between David and a heap of broken folding chairs.

David turns and follows and corners her again, but if the girl really wants to escape them, she is agile enough to have surely been able to do so.

'I'll call the police,' he says, although from his voice it is clear he never would (or could) and is enjoying the game as much as she is.

The child laughs. 'La police not bon, juste fuckers.' Telling him what they already know. 'They not aider the likes of you.' She curls a loose strand of hair around a knuckle like silk thread around a bobbin. 'But je not want get you into any more shit. You ees alone ere with no'un t'aid yer.' Evie has never imagined anyone like this. Her mouth is a sewer and she should be repelled but she finds herself transfixed.

Evie moves in close, cutting off her escape. The child's dog, which has managed to stick close to her heels throughout the chase, gazes up at her with disappointed eyes.

'Besides,' the girl continues, glancing behind her, 'you ain't clapped Pompie when he ees in a fury. He can tear un grand homme adult into two, leaving heem in bloody parts.' She grins, the tips of her eye teeth showing cunningly over her lip, as if she might grab Evie by her outstretched arm and gnaw on it.

'Time to return it,' David says sternly.

The child smiles and tucks the ribbon away in her pocket, making it obvious that this is what she is doing. Her pink lips form a satiny bow.

'Just give it back. It's not yours.'

'It doesn't matter,' Evie intervenes. 'Let her keep it, she's only little, she means no harm.' Then, as the girl's guard drops away, she pounces.

It is a clever move and the child, so full of her own tricks, is herself tricked; Evie grips her and searches inside her skirt. Despite the tight openings, stitched to suit small hands, Evie finds the interior capacious with a multitude of hidden pockets.

She pulls out her ribbon, bringing with it in a tangle a lady's scented handkerchief out of which bounces a gold ring.

The child fights free and backs away through the stiff weeds and they stare at one another, both a little out of breath. The look between them holds for longer than it should, neither willing to break it off.

The tall man in pantaloons strides over. 'Any trouble here?' he asks gruffly, rubbing his jaw and smearing his lipstick. It is unclear which party he is asking.

The child's face cracks into a smile, perhaps to pacify him but it feels to Evie that it is actually for her. Dimples pop in her cheeks, 'No Pompie, tout est bien.'

Leaving the park, Evie and David continue to wander without knowing where they are going. The city is huge, the streets all strangely similar, dotted with shuttered shops and leafless trees. As they walk, they talk about children.

'A lot came to visit me,' he says. 'Brought by their parents. Spoilt brats mostly who just giggled spitefully and stared. No one like that one.'

'She was naughty,' Evie muses, 'but also very sweet.' Feeling warm inside, she absent-mindedly links her arm through his, as she used to with Matthew.

They need somewhere to recharge, so take a room in a small hotel, the angled facade of which is held up by scaffolding. Alone again, with the door closed and the key turned, Evie feels almost secure. She lies back on the pillow, her head full of the girl, recalling her sly stare.

What sort of existence would the child have? Probably not a particularly sweet one. She should have let the poor thing keep the silly ribbon. What harm would it have done?

Evie wakes in the afternoon to find David close beside her. The bed is small and his shoulders have wedged her to the edge and one of his heavy arms has fallen across her.

To her surprise she becomes aware of his, what Matthew with boyish delicacy referred to as his 'chap', pressing into her thigh and, reaching behind, she slips her fingers under the waistband of his shorts. His body shifts, his grip around her tightening. He goes rigid.

Then he recoils, knees in her back, pitching her forward over the mattress-edge to land on her hands on the floor.

He pulls himself upright and sits, staring forward, face flushed.

Evie slowly gets to her feet.

Despite the shock of the fall, it is difficult not to see the funny side. 'It's all right,' she says. What had stemmed from a combination of straightforward curiosity and a throb of loneliness has developed a life of its own. In some respects, she is as chaste as he is – a widow who has known only a husband's touch. But she is unable now to call a halt to what is to all intents a seduction. I am a seductress, she thinks wryly. It is a role which previously she would have found it unseemly to admit, but one which, within the confines of marriage, she was nevertheless designed to perform.

David's face is an agony of confusion, but right now her own arousal is clamouring her on.

'I won't hurt you,' Evie says. She moves around the bed end, slowly, so as not to frighten him further, advancing until they are less than twelve inches apart. She draws her vest over her head, watching him watch, and lifting his large smooth hands, she places them over her breasts.

'It's all right, I know what to do. This will be nicer than anything you have ever imagined, you must just trust me.' She stands on tiptoes, laces her fingers behind his head, and tilts his face down so that she can reach his mouth.

29

Moving Evie's head to one side, David unfastens her fingers from his neck and gently guides her body away. It is the tenderness of the rejection, the firm softness of his touch, which makes it so painful, and so embarrassing. She can't look at him, nor does she know what to do with her hands which he has gently returned to her sides, where the palms throb hotly.

'What is the matter?' she asks, flush with embarrassment that her inexperience has allowed her to misread what she took to be signs.

David shrugs and blinks. His mouth falls at the corners. 'It is not you, it is me. What they did.'

'What did they do?' she asks impatiently.

'Things.'

'What things?' She wants him to be open with her. Find a way to shift the sense of failure, despite being nervous that she may not want to hear what he has to say.

'They'd find me after the show was over for the day,' he says quietly.

'Who?' she asks, still in a state of confusion and not cottoning on to what he is trying to tell her.

'All of them. All of them,' he repeats, and he begins to list the multitude of physicists, psychologists, uniformed museum attendants, janitors, wealthy sponsors and the neglected wives and daughters of wealthy sponsors, who over the years have taken advantage of his being alone at night and restrained, and straddled his lap as if he was nothing more than an elaborate sex aid.

Evie's cheeks burn. She feels selfish and predatory – not much better than these dozens of women and men. Her own life has been so sheltered, she so protected, how could she have foreseen such a thing?

David tells her about one of the companies involved with Realhuman – a Russian arms dealership – and the entertainment they put on for customers. How low-tech AABs (low-tech but still intelligent enough to experience fear) are released in the ruins of a town abandoned after a nuclear catastrophe of the previous century. 'They free them from cages,' he says, 'and the men and women hunt them through the streets using weapons from the company catalogue, like in an arcade game.'

He looks at her helplessly, but she does not know how to respond and grips her cardigan at the neck, covering her nakedness, which now seems to her not so much shameful as out of place.

'In Japan, there is a society for military veterans which holds an event annually in the spring, at which they dress female AABs as maiko – young geisha. "The Ceremony of the Petals" they call it . . .' David is crying now and by doing so brings on her own helpless tears. 'They release them in this ornamental park so that these old soldiers can chase them down under the cherry trees – not much of a contest really with the girls' legs restricted by the thick layers of their robes. Then when they catch them, they behead them with their Samurai swords . . .'

His voice dries up and his hand loosens its grip on hers and he turns from her. Without saying anything more, he lies down facing the wall.

Evie can hear him sobbing. She gingerly places her arm over his back but he no longer seems aware of her.

Not in a fit state to comfort him and wanting to escape this scene of her creation, Evie picks up her scattered clothes and miserably dresses in the glow from the hotel sign outside the window, her own tears sliding down her cheeks.

She turns in the doorway on her way out to gaze at him lying curled on the mattress, almost lost in the shadows. He is a creature even more damaged, in ways hidden from sight, than Maplin's mutilated mannequins.

Outside it has been raining and the temperature has fallen, creating a ground mist. Evie wanders north up steep streets into Montmartre. The grey, speckled outline of the Sacré-Coeur rises above the rooftops like one of Daniels's more ambitious cakes, but one baked from mouldy icing sugar.

She realises that she knows it from a collection of photographs taken by Matthew's great-great-great-grandfather, on leave from the front during a long-ago war. She'd found it fading in a pasteboard album in the music room, attracting her attention because it had been tied with a rainbow-dyed ribbon.

Evie climbs the cracked steps. Halfway up it seems that she hears the sharp tap of boots on the concrete behind her, but when she pauses, tucking herself into the shadows, all is quiet.

She resumes climbing but her body is tense, on the alert. Her hearing is good enough to hear a leaf drop but an eerie silence envelops her and the loudest thing is the patter of her own shoes and, layered over that, the soft rasp of her own breath.

She stops again, closing her eyes and focusing, but there is nothing apart from the whistle of the breeze.

Reaching the top, Evie turns to take in the vista over the rooftops. The last of the sun gleams wetly on the tips of the dual spikes of the Tours Eiffel – old and new – wading in the swollen river on rusty legs. She'd hoped the view would lift her spirits, but the buildings, from up here, merge into a mass. Apart from the towers, she can make out only the dark river, the swollen and twisted gut of which brims with threat.

Maybe it is just the disheartening atmosphere but the shivery sensation of being watched creeps up on her again. She glances around swiftly and, after concluding she has again been tricked by her nerves, discerns the figure of a woman in the shadow of the cathedral, her pale coat merging with the stone. The only details of note are her eyes, luminous dots in the half-light, looking straight at Evie. Her heart races, but the woman's gaze glides on and a few moments later blinks out, and it becomes clear that she has slipped away.

Perhaps she had been just taking in the view as Evie herself had been. She needs to relax a little, stop seeing danger where there's none.

The bell in the basilica strikes seven, reminding her that she had planned to catch an evening train.

She takes the direct route back to the hotel, as far as she can deduce it, walking with care down slippery narrow back roads, lined with tall houses, their windows shuttered against intruders, adapting her course when she finds the steep cobbled streets blocked by mysterious barricades constructed from collapsing furniture, like the detritus of an abandoned revolution.

Reaching level ground, she makes quicker progress, until, turning a corner, she is slowed by a crowd outside a theatre. Its name – The Dolls' House – somehow familiar, is projected over the facade in scarlet letters with the slogan 'The world famous' revolving in italics below.

Seated on the canopy is a ten-foot girl in a gingham pinafore dress and bobby socks. She kicks her giant sparkly shoes between the heads of the pedestrians. 'Heh there, welcome to Kansas,' she calls and leans over, stiffly turning left and right, straining to attract the attention of passers-by. She makes eye-contact with Evie, 'Come on in sweetie,' she halloos, 'who knows what you'll find!'

Evie, impatient for a way to clear, pushes briskly through the crowd.

Amidst the crush, to her surprise, she spots the child from the park – this must have been the theatre on the flyer she was handing around. The girl slips through the crowd, one moment making herself thin, the next short, her bright hair a loose thread amongst the blacks, greys and browns. The child stretches an arm in the air like a ballerina, the other she keeps by her waist, and, knowing that Evie is watching, brazenly rifles a parrot-feather handbag and removes a silk purse. As she tucks it into her skirt, she pirouettes and winks conspiratorially, the winter coats around her closing like curtains as she again disappears from sight.

Evie finds herself drawn helplessly to follow, an emptiness nagging her on, but the child moves so quickly that she has to climb to the top of the steps to locate her in the crowd.

She is just in time to witness the girl slip under the outstretched arm of an elderly gent in top hat and tails as he holds back the door. An indulgent smile curls his whiskers while she, as fluid as a ripple in a bolt of silk, removes opera glasses and the watch on its chain from his waistcoat pockets.

Evie follows her into the crowded lobby. Where has she gone?

She ascends the stairs, taking advantage of the pressure at the circle door to enter the auditorium without a ticket. The steeply shelving seats fill from both sides and she descends to the rail.

In the stalls below, tables have been arranged around a curtained stage. The closest chairs have been quickly taken and a quite serious fight for those remaining is developing below the overhang.

A man in the seat behind pokes her calf with the tip of his cane. 'Mademoiselle, tu bloques ma vue,' he complains wearily, leaning back and crossing his ankles to reveal gleaming yellow spats.

A boy comes up on her other side and tugs at her skirt. 'Icecrème s'il vous plaît,' he pipes, and she peels his grubby fingers from her waist, propelling him down the aisle.

A figure in a silk hat emerges from between the curtains and bows. He advances to the stage edge. 'Mesdames et Messieurs, Damen und Herren, Damer og Herrer, Ladies and Gentlemen . . . S'il vous plaît prenez vos places. Please be seated . . . Notre spectacle commencera très bientôt . . . very soon. Ce soir, nous avons le monde célèbre Hercule d'Amerique – The World's Strongest Man . . .'

She has never been in a theatre and is entranced. A weightless woman floats over the audience like a balloon until she becomes entangled with the chandelier and catches fire. The 'World's Strongest Man' lifts a horse and then turns sheepish after he drops it with a crash. A singer with two heads – one male and one female – gets into a muddle carrying both treble and bass with the resulting cacophony getting him/her/them booed from the stage. A woman is cut in two with a saw, the bloody lower half charging off into the wings, chased by the so-called magician, while the upper half, still stuck in the box, waves its arms and weeps hysterically. Some of the effects could have been created by mirrors or holography but there was little either magical or human about the rest. If all is really lost, there could be a job for her here in this place, submitting herself for the amusement of a human crowd.

The compere is undeterred by the bedlam. 'Et maintenant vos favoris,' he announces, treading in his dazzling boots around the puddle of blood left by the last act. 'Your very own, the ones you have been waiting for . . .'

The curtains sweep back to reveal a stage empty apart from the solitary figure of the same girl from earlier but now wearing a faded tricolour as a shawl, swabbing the boards with a mop. Her head is bowed and her dress is tucked into her drawers exposing bare feet. As she advances, she mournfully spreads the pool of blood. Is this her role here – to clean up after accidents?

Desiring continued quick satisfaction, the crowd is restless.

'Cinderella n'est pas autorisé à aller à la ball,' a voice recites from the wings. 'Elle must work all nuit.'

The child wipes her forehead with her arm, leaning on the mop and gazing out over the heads with a poor-me expression. Even from up here in the gallery, a glistening tear can be seen to glide down her cheek.

She draws a flask from her skirt, 'ABSINTHE' written on an oversized label. She uncorks it and slurps and wipes her hand across her mouth, smearing a green glow into her cheeks. Her face slips into a contented grin.

From the side of the stage bursts her fairy godmother – the tall man from the park but now in an immense dress with a towering wig. His face is painted white with pink circles below his eyes and he holds a wand throwing sparks. However, even this is not enough to retrieve the audience's attention who continue to behave as if the interval has already started.

The child's acting is slapdash but she possesses charm in abundance. At the ball she yawns, falling asleep on a chair, promptly toppling off with a thud when it is dragged from under her, to land between the legs of the capering adults. Getting to her feet, she comes face to face with Prince Charming, a dwarf with a long beard. He claims her as his partner, throwing her around like a rag doll, repeatedly attempting to kiss her, despite her age. 'Mais c'est passé mon heure du coucher,' she screams in desperation, repeating herself in English: 'for gawd's sake it's past me ruddy bedtime.' Then, after he won't let go, she pretends to doze while he continues to recklessly swing her about. The child breezes through the pretence like a pro. Drooping in an instant like she has been switched off and then opening her eyes and stretching in his arms as if she is waking with a drowsy sigh.

Evie finds it hilarious, but few are concentrating enough to be entertained.

The performance ends with a chase in and out of the wings, the child in danger of being trampled as she dodges between the legs of the adults in pursuit of a gaudy slipper.

As soon as the actors are off the stage, Evie leaves the gallery and runs down to the stalls.

She presses between the tables, dodging around the stiffly moving waiters. One, swivelling on his heel, strikes her on the chin with the rim of his tray, knocking her backwards onto a table, spilling the arrayed glasses into the laps of those around it. He doesn't apologise, doesn't even pause, just continues on his path, mechanically barging anyone out of his way. She clambers to her feet, full of contrition, but fortunately everyone seems to think it is part of the show.

Figures she would hesitate to call women sidle through the crowd. One is dressed as Snow White with creamy cheeks and teeny feet. Another has hair so long it drags along the ground and yet another mothers a baby doll, its dented head rammed to her breast. In the corner, soldiers, chests frogged with silver braid, snigger and leer, wafting parade-ground sweat and stale parfum.

Evie clambers onto the stage and slips through the curtains into the darkness beyond.

Entering the wings, she squeezes between the dusty props. The departing Cinderella cast are just ahead of her, climbing a flight of steep wooden stairs.

In the lead are the ugly sisters. During the show they had taunted the child, taking her by the arms and feet and tugging, before feigning exhaustion and dropping her from a yard up onto the wooden boards. Now, amid the bitter recriminations as to why they had bombed, they blame her loudly for her worthless performance. One reaches round with her long arm to swat her, but the child is nimble and steps to the side. Behind them, the fairy godmother drags off his wig and scratches at a scalp landscaped with craters and grey scabby stubble, and at the rear, just ahead of the child herself, Prince Charming slugs from the flask of absinthe, green fumes rising in a haze and soaking the air.

The craziness of her pursuit of the little pickpocket-actress dawns and Evie comes to a stop, her head spinning. She sits on the ground in the shadows behind the staircase to give herself a chance to regain her composure.

Evie is brought back to full alertness just minutes later, when the girl charges back down the same stairs and, passing where she sits, shoves open the exit door and bursts out.

Outside, she gathers her skirts and sets off at a trot along the alley towards the light from the street.

Only to be brought up short when the broad figure of the fairy godmother, still in the enormous dress, appears at the end. He marches angrily down on her, forcing her to retreat.

From her hiding place, Evie watches him block her escape.

'Tu!' the girl mutters and her small dog hides behind her legs.

'I'll be having what you took from that gent,' he says. 'The one that's been inside complaining his head off about you. Saying the watch is a priceless heirloom.'

The child's eyes narrow impishly, face momentarily sinister before reverting to syrupy sweet. 'Pompie, je take nuffing,' she mutters, adding viciously, as he takes another step towards her, 'back orff,' shifting her weight from one foot to the other like a boxer.

Evie watches helplessly from the shadow of the doorway, astounded by the girl's provocative attitude and courage. Her apparent lack of fear, not even an ounce of unease, acts as a thrown-down challenge.

'Give it me now, no more warnings,' Pompie growls, the last of the polite, feminine manner from the stage cast away.

'What you gonna do?' the girl counters, maintaining her crazy smug innocence. 'Je could scream.'

Moving far faster than his size would suggest possible, Pompie grabs the girl's wrist, wrestling her arm behind her, and prises open her fist to expose a bone-handled knife with a silver blade.

'Let go of moi,' the girl shouts but she is reduced to attempting to kick his shins with her heels. Even so, she is slippery, an effort to restrain, and far, far stronger than her thin limbs suggest.

He shakes the knife from her palm so that it bounces point-first on the ground, and tightens his hold. 'Give it to me,' he tells her.

'Je ne ave it,' the girl pants, cheeks glowing pink.

'But you know what I'm referring to.' He grips her around her arms and reaches into her skirt – like Evie herself had earlier – bringing out a handful of small coins which scatter between his feet and disappear into cracks.

He lets go. 'What have you done with it?'

'Je take nuffing.' The girl backs away, putting what distance the alley allows between them. It is not much.

'I should flip you over and shake to see what other of your muggings falls out.' He moves in close again and, standing above her, lights a cigarette. Gripping it between his fat fingers, he drags on it and blows the smoke down around the girl's face, making her cough.

Evie gets to her feet and moves to the doorway. The situation outside is charged with violence and although the child seems hell-bent on making things worse for herself, it can't be right to leave it to play out.

'Final warning,' Pompie says.

The child juts her chin.

'Before I stop being all gentle.' A flush of evening stubble glistens on his cheek.

'Pompie, je ne got em pas plus.'

Pompie reaches for her neck, his hand groping but failing to locate it. She reverses into the bins, knocking off the lids which crash to the ground like cymbals. He reaches out again, this time grabbing her by the shoulders, and pins her against the wall.

The girl struggles, pleading, and when that doesn't work, wails for help, until he thwacks her cheek with the back of his hand and her head topples sideways as if it has been knocked off her neck.

Evie recoils, as if she herself had been hit. Emerging from the doorway, she crosses the alley on tiptoe towards them.

Keeping the girl pinned with one hand and ignoring her sobs, Pompie rifles the pockets of her skirt and jacket again, chucking more of her thefts on the ground – a collection of useless frippery and magpie opportunism. A Japanese paper fan flutters down, opening for a second into paper butterfly wings, before landing flat, soaking up the ooze. More shiny coins bounce on the cobbles, rolling into dark corners.

With a shout of triumph, he pulls out the watch by its chain and holds it up, letting it spin in front of the child's nose, its face illuminated by the glow from the distant street.

'So you did have it, you deceiving little tramp,' he mutters.

Evie comes up behind, entering his shadow. She thinks she's undetected but Pompie, barely turning, swings his fist and strikes the side of her head so that her legs fold.

Ignoring Evie on her hands behind him, he leans over the child and, sucking together a gob of phlegm, spits onto the crown of her head. 'Don't you ever keep stuff from me, do you understand?' he mutters. 'If you lie again, Pinocchio, as to what you've got, there'll be worse coming than what you just had.' And he wipes a moist curl of filth from the sole of his shoe along her shin.

Tucking the watch and chain into an inside pocket and rewrapping his boa around his neck, he strides back towards the light, his high-heeled shoes echoing on the wet stone.

Evie clambers to her feet and unsteadily begins to follow. If she can catch up and leap on his shoulders, maybe she can bring him down. Though such a notion is suspect logic and likely the result of a shorted circuit.

With her gyroscope impaired and with the latest blow to the head still ringing, she weaves helplessly, banging into the bins on left and right, stumbling and sliding on the slime. Unable to maintain a straight course or even hold herself upright, she falls hard against the wall, sliding down the brickwork, and ends seated on the wet cobbles.

She tilts her head to watch him leave. With no more strength left to pursue or to fight, she slumps forward, head in her hands.

Evie hears the girl rise to her feet the other side of the alley and, stepping around the fallen lids, cross the cobbles and kneel beside her. The girl's arms close around her neck. What is she stealing now? she wonders. I have nothing for her to take.

'Did hee hurt you?' she asks gently, stroking Evie's neck, trailing her fingertips over the contours of her cheek and the bridge of her nose. A fingertip curls inside her ear. She discovers the edge of the blonde wig and, lifting it, frees her hair. Is that it? Is it just the bright hairpiece she is after?

Despite the poor light, the girl's face is close enough to reveal a layer of bruises beneath the grease paint.

'A bit,' she murmurs.

A tear rolls down the child's cheek. Slow as a snail. Leaving a silvery trail. Is this sympathy? Evie's heart lurches, even though she's seen her perform, with spontaneous ease, such a feat on stage.

Evie shakily stands and starts to hobble away.

The girl wipes her face with the backs of her fingers. 'Here,' she says, extending her palm, a wad of cash held in front of her.

'What? Why?'

The girl shrugs. 'You can 'ave it, but you must take us with you.' She picks up the small dog and holds it to her chest.

'Take us?' The sharp bend the encounter has taken brings her up short. It is the oddest place, this stinking alley, to be conducting such a negotiation, that in fairness would be peculiar anywhere. Does the girl really think she is able to buy her?

The money is as suddenly withdrawn. Too fast for the eye. 'Well?' the girl asks.

'I don't understand?'

'Cos je fancy somethin' better than thees.' She glances around at the dingy brickwork. 'And moi fond of you.'

'Fond of me! You know nothing about me.' Even as Evie probes the request, she wonders why she is doing so. Isn't this what her heart desperately wants?

She absent-mindedly reaches for the money but again, lightning-fast, it is removed from her reach.

'I can tell enough,' the child says.

'Where are your parents?'

The girl stares back. Hostility enters her look. Even the dog yelps crossly. Then her expression relaxes and she shrugs non-committally.

She holds the notes out again, the negotiation back on. 'Everythin. Tout. Everythin. You can ave it.'

The child picks up her hat from the ground and twirls it on a finger. When it comes to a stop, she flips it over and takes out a second sheaf of notes from inside the band.

'Je ave this aussi.'

Evie stares open-mouthed.

The child fans the greasy dollars and neuros, sliding them through her fingers as slipperily as a sharp.

'But you have a home.'

'Not so much un joli maison, je think.' The girl nods towards the grimy brickwork of the theatre wall. 'Do you believe moi like being slapped around tout le temps? Je ne une grande idiot.'

'I don't have anywhere,' Evie says.

'Moi loves an adventure.'

'I don't even know your name.'

'Mon nom ees Sola.'

'Sola,' Evie repeats helplessly. She murmurs a nervous, 'Okay,' realising as she does so that she had been prepared to capitulate from the start. That she would have accepted such a deal from the moment the child stole her ribbon in the park.

30

As soon as they are away from the vicinity of the theatre, Sola takes Evie's hand, as if such familiarity between virtual strangers is the done thing. Maybe the girl doesn't trust her not to desert her, now that she has thrown in her lot.

After a few turns, Evie stops to make sure none of the child's rather alarming actor acquaintances are following. The child, oblivious to her caution, paces joyfully, whistling music hall tunes to the little dog.

'You wouldn't tell me earlier about your family?' Evie asks, risking the question again. Wondering how crazy she has been in allowing events to develop like they have.

'Ma mère, she died,' Sola replies dismissively.

'Oh!' She should have spotted that one coming.

The child, seeing her blush, smiles. 'Tu es sweet, I think that's why I like yer. Elle was also too. Always concerné.'

This makes Evie ponder. Had the girl really picked her out, identified her as a potential opportunity to jump ship? It is hard to believe that such a sweet face could be so scheming. But that's what thieves do, they spot their mark and reel them in.

'Did your parents work in that place too?'

Sola snorts. 'No way! We had une immense villa with pool in le country. Maman was très beautiful. Elle une grande actress.'

Now it is Evie's turn to smile, amused by the fairy-tale imagination feeding empty boasts. In reply, her tone is sceptical. 'And with all that money, there was no one else to look after you?'

The child tightens her grip, but this time painfully, crushing Evie's fingers. 'Je ne tell you nuthin, if you're not moi believin.'

They carry along in a mistrustful silence, until Sola breaks it, pointing to a holo projected from the wall ahead. The image is of Evie and David, head and shoulders only – a pair of mugshots suspended in the air.

Evie's instinct is to turn and run but doing so will just draw attention and instead she grips the child's hand tighter. She recognised herself immediately despite her straight hair styled in waves, something she has never thought to do. The Realhuman logo floats below – suggesting the clip could have been recorded in the factory. In the holo she blinks repeatedly, something she does when nervous, as she certainly would have been then, absorbing the sights and smells of her new existence for the first time.

'It ees you?' Sola asks, puzzled, glancing from one to another. 'Why?'

'Keep going,' Evie mutters.

'Why do they ave your holo?' The child is distracted by the likeness and has missed completely the one-million-neuro reward below in bold flashing-one-at-a-time letters, a strange oversight for such an opportunistic thief, however small-scale.

The hotel is only just around the corner, but with heart racing faster than an atom racer, Evie makes them wait in the shadows of a littered doorway opposite, giving a chance for anyone following, alerted by her reaction to the holo, to reveal themselves.

Satisfied they're alone, she leads the child across the street and underneath the canopy. The man in reception, a one-armed ex-militiaman of the ongoing colonial wars, judging by his tattoos, glances up, but there is no recognition, no awareness that a mouth-watering sum awaits the return of his guest to the hands of its 'rightful owners'. It is helpful also that Sola passes undetected, head below the level of the counter. Not that Evie can imagine a fuss being made, unless it be a demand for additional rent, on top of that already extorted.

She reaches their room door and puts her head around, wondering how she will explain Sola to David. Their journey is complicated enough without another pothole or bump.

But he is not there.

Evie had not anticipated his absence. She knows she upset him, but she thought they'd talked that through.

She lets the child in, and going to the window, draws the curtain aside and peers onto the street.

'Where ees he?' Sola asks, 'le boy in le holo?'

'I don't know.' Evie walks back across the room and closes the door. Her pack is on the side and she checks inside to see if his few things are still there.

'He your friend?'

'Yes,' she says, wondering if it is true.

The train they'd intended to take leaves in an hour. What if he went out searching for her? What if he's lost? This afternoon, everything had felt so certain and now she's messed it all up.

Sola sits in the window, peering out. 'Is that heem down there?'

'What can you see?'

'Le boy, he talk to les cops.'

Evie comes over.

'Well?'

David is in the street, surrounded by three uniformed men, jutting chins tucked behind stiff collars and brows hidden by peaked caps. They could be gendarmes but as equally could be some brand of corporate security. He has gone out without shoes and shirt despite the weather – that would only have helped draw attention.

They try to manoeuvre him towards their vehicle. He stands his ground and they prod his side with batons, which sends him reeling.

'Why they hurt heem?' Sola asks.

Evie runs from the room and down the stairs, past the reception again, stopping outside at the top of the hotel steps.

Sola emerges from the doorway behind and takes hold of her arm.

David's eyes connect with hers but, as they do, the men reach out with their sticks again to his chest, making him twist on the spot and drop to his knees, his shoulders in spasm.

Now that he is down, two grab for his arms but he is already rising again, even before they can make contact, and knocks them sideways. As they struggle to recover, David bolts down the street and leaps the iron bollards at the end, leaving the two men staring at one another, before gathering their wits and following.

Evie's first thought is to flee herself – but if she does, she will lose David for sure. If he is able to, or wants to, he will look for her in the hotel.

Her thought processes are in turmoil. What if she ends up trapped? What do these men in uniforms know? What might David tell them if they catch him?

Evie pulls Sola into the shadows. 'We'll wait for him in the room.' She can't desert him. It isn't how she was made.

'Who is he?' the girl whispers back, more curious than scared. 'Is he your boyfriend?'

They go back upstairs and, locking the door, lay together on the bed in the dark. After the child falls asleep, Evie takes the charger from the pack and plugs herself in. The warm buzz of electricity, on which normally she likes to drift before surrendering to sleep, tonight lights her nerves, leaving her tense from head to toe. She is conscious of Sola's hand pressed against her hip and of the snuffle of her breath in the chilly air. But more than anything, she is conscious of the level of her abandon – the child lies on her back, arms out by her sides, legs stretched apart, taking up almost as much of the bed as David had – possessing a sense of freedom she herself has never felt.

*

During the night, Evie hears the handle of the door turn. Hoping it is David, she tiptoes over and crouches with her ear against the wood. The sharp tap of footsteps retreat and descend. Whoever it was, it was not David. Could it have been the hotel owner? Should she take her chances and leave now?

More anxious than ever, she returns to the bed and wraps her arms around the sleeping child, drawing the heat of her body into her chest.

Evie is woken again in the early hours by a rattle at the window. It swings inward, allowing in a rush of night air. David enters and crouches by the bedstead.

The presence of Sola doesn't register with him, although, exhausted as he is, he is in no state to question anything. Evie picks Sola up and lays her on the chair, offering David the space. He collapses on the mattress, his head sinking into the pillows.

While he sleeps, she wets a towel and wipes the crust of filthy gel from his damaged feet. She then pulls back the skin below his ribs and connects her own charger, causing him to shudder but not wake.

When David comes to, it is early afternoon. The child is perched on the windowsill, cross-legged, teasing the dog with a ball of wool, making him jump for it like a cat.

Evie lies in the chair. 'Are you all right? she asks him.

David doesn't answer but stares at the ceiling.

'What happened?' she asks.

'I outran them.'

'They didn't see where you went?'

'They followed me but I hid under a bridge.' He sounds as if he is concealing something.

'There's blood under your nails,' she says.

He lifts his hands and studies his fingers. The tips quiver in the muted light. 'Unfortunately they doubled back.'

'I think les poor cops bought it,' Sola says to the dog, shaking her head.

'What's she doing here?' David asks, tension overflowing into his voice.

'Her name's Sola. She's the child from the park yesterday.'

'I recognise her. Where did you find her?'

'Outside her theatre.'

He huffs. 'Is she really such a good idea?'

It isn't his decision but rather than tell him that, Evie diplomatically replies, 'It's a long story. Believe me, it's going to be easier to take her than to try not to.'

Sola shoves the dog onto the floor and crosses to Evie's chair where she clambers onto her lap. Draping her arm tightly around Evie, Sola smirks back at David. 'Je paid moi way.'

The three of them leave the room at dusk. They sneak through reception but move rapidly once on the street.

They only need to reach the train station, but Evie feels exposed. Anyone they pass could be after them and indeed they soon appear to have picked up not one but two tails. Both are bulky men in faded winter jackets. They could be innocuous but it feels wrong.

They round the next corner quickly and, from the safety of a doorway, watch the men pass.

Evie peers out. Nothing moves on the street. 'They've gone,' she says.

They emerge and, taking the next left turn and the next right, enter the parallel road.

Hearing distant footsteps, she glances around. The two men are in sight again, but together now, a hundred metres behind.

'We need to get away from here,' Evie says.

At the junction ahead, they see a third man, dressed as the others in the same drab hooded jacket. Again, it could be nothing or, as seems more likely, they are being boxed in.

'What do we do?' Sola asks, looking behind.

A woman in a sleek coat with a silver fur collar emerges from a doorway opposite and crosses the road towards them.

They watch her approach. What does she want? She is drawing attention to them.

The woman comes up alongside. 'Yes, they after you very much,' she says in a throaty voice. 'Come with me now quickly, before they catch you.'

31

With no other choice, Evie, David and Sola follow the woman. She leads them a couple of metres to their right and then along a dark alley, the narrow entrance to which had been invisible in the gloom.

'Who are you?' Evie asks, as they emerge back into the light at the other end. She tries to make out the woman's face behind the fur of her high collar.

The woman gives her a closed-lip smile. 'I Yuliya.' It isn't much of an answer and Sola stares up at her suspiciously, clearly tempted to tell her as much.

'Je thought we taking le train,' Sola mutters. 'Now we lost those men, we can still do eet.'

'You lost them but they not lost you,' Yuliya replies sharply, walking on briskly, obliging them to keep up. 'They not give up just like that.'

Evie, tucking aside her own uncertainty, takes Sola's hand tightly in hers, concerned the girl may decide her interests are best served at this point by deserting.

'So, where are you taking us?' David asks.

'Somewhere safe,' Yuliya says, glancing behind. 'We not talk now or they hear. We be there very soon, then talk all we need. For now, no more chitter-chatter, all be quiet as mice.'

Yuliya leads them along at a rapid pace, managing to keep a half-pace ahead despite her boots' slender metallic heels. Over their tap-tapping, Evie listens hard for pursuit.

The neighbourhood quickly improves, second-hand clothes stores making way for upmarket antique shops and hova showrooms, behind the high windows of which shiny vehicles dangle illuminated like Christmas baubles.

Reaching the river, the air thickens and the houses lining the distant bank merge into the charcoal smudge of the swollen water.

They cross a stone bridge onto an island. The winter tide has risen over the lip of the quays and laps the brickwork of the buildings.

Passing along a residential street, they enter under an arch into a courtyard. Reaching a door, Yuliya draws out a key and unlocks it. She steps through and holds it back. The hallway beyond is dark and wafts an odour of trapped decay. It is more like the gate to a prison.

They hesitate to enter but what options do they have?

Reluctantly they follow her through.

Once they are inside, Yuliya puts her head back out and glances both ways. She then closes the heavy door, shunting the stiff bolts home, dislodging a swirl of plaster from the high ceiling onto their hair.

Evie, David and Sola try to make out their surroundings from the single remaining bulb in an ornate chandelier.

'This way,' Yuliya says, steering them up a wide, dusty staircase.

Hearing feet outside, they come to a sudden stop, but whoever it is passes. 'That them,' Yuliya says. 'You lucky, we make it just in time.'

They breathe in and continue up.

At the top of the stairs, Yuliya holds open one of a pair of tall doors.

The room beyond is opulent, like something out of a palace. Three of the walls are panelled with intricately gilded wood and hung with full length mirrors. Their images reflect back from the depths of the speckled glass, repeating and echoing, as if they are somewhere distant, small and lost. In the wrong place. The end wall is hung with a tapestry of men in robes sitting behind a table, the threads so bright the image bursts from the gloom.

'What is it of?' Evie asks.

'Old men eating,' the woman replies, uninterested.

'It ees "The Last Supper",' Sola says. 'That eees sweet Jesus in le middle and le one that looks like Pompie ees Judas. Hees going to betray poor Jesus but he not know it yet.'

'Where did you learn that from?' David asks sceptically, as if she's just made the story up.

She huffs. 'Moi know stuff,' crossing her arms and turning her shoulder away.

Along the centre of one long wall is a stone fireplace with a busy fire, although from it they can feel no heat and the air is as damp and chilly as it was on the street. The only furniture is a pair of deep-backed sofas positioned either side of a thick rug.

Three large circular windows provide a view of the city.

Yuliya strokes the top of Sola's head but she squirms to the side, making a face like she's been touched by a toad, and clambers up against the nearest window. Her feet sink through the surface of the sill as if it is carved from meringue.

Observing her immersed up to her ankles in the wood, David places his hand against the wall and the panel reforms around it. 'I've seen this before,' he says. 'In Seoul. It's a form of photon projection.'

'You correct,' Yuliya says. 'It's part of architect's design. Very expensive and exclusive. Boris like everything of his that way.' As she speaks, the walls are in the process of transforming: the tapestry fading, the fire fizzing out, and the cream and gold panels developing vertical bars of shadow. A blue evening light glimmers into being, delineating the trunks of trees, their dark branches appearing to reach several feet into the room.

Sola squeals and strides around the perimeter, finding the room's vanished corners and running her fingers through the leaves and ferns which tremble to her touch. A night moth flutters up from under her feet and dizzily circles her head. Then a bat shoots the length of the ceiling. They all glance up, but it has passed in a flash, almost too quick to be seen.

The cleverness of the technology is undeniable and the result is as enchanting as a midnight dream. But Evie still feels disillusionment over being tricked. Right now, she just wants something she can rely on. 'Is the view outside real?' she asks, dubiously, crossing the cement floor to the nearest window.

'Yes, all real,' Yuliya answers.

Evie stares out over the broad flooded river. In the distance, the dark roofless shell of Notre Dame balances on a pinnacle of high ground.

Despite what has happened to the walls, the sofas have not changed, but nevertheless Sola gingerly touches the back of one, just to make sure she will not fall through, before throwing herself down, the plump cushions puffing out fine dust.

'You safe here,' Yuliya announces, 'now you can make your questions.'

'Where are we?' Evie asks.

'This where I live. This my home.'

'Why are you helping us?'

Yuliya smiles and nods. 'Still can't you tell? We the same. Don't you guess it? I know it immediately I see you.'

'What do you mean?' A wave of exhaustion has been catching up with Evie since they arrived and, suddenly weak, she sits heavily on the other sofa to Sola.

Yuliya takes the opposite end, crossing her legs gracefully at the ankles. Her striking corn-gold hair, pressed back from her face by the high collar of her coat, exposes pink cheeks and small, delicate ears – intricately formed shells pierced by gold pins.

'I mean I made by humans, like you,' she says, prompting David and Evie to look at one another in surprise. 'I spot you at Sacré-Coeur. That place magnet for lost souls. I follow you down steps and after think I lose you, I see you again just now outside hotel. I think – lucky you.' She flashes them a flawless smile.

'Yes, I think I saw you up there,' Evie says. 'But I still don't know why you've helped?'

David, who has an attention span not much longer than Sola's, goes to sit with the child.

'We same range. You and me, we Elektras. There not many of us made. Even less I think now left. I came across another in Putinsburg but that the only time, and she not in good shape. We made very pretty like butterfly but sad not to last. We must look out for each other, no?'

Evie is still puzzled but she is also now curious. She gazes into Yuliya's large round eyes, as blue as a baby's and straight from the catalogue. 'How do you live alone?'

'Oh, I been here long time. My owner, Boris, he once great captain of industry. He family in Moscow . . . wife with big bunch of big kids, all big boys like him and he like to keep me here, a treat for himself when he get weekend away from pressure of work. He grown up as boy with dirt of Steppes under his nails and as man he always demand beautiful, perfect things.

'But work make him enemies and one day he put in prison. In Siberia, I think. He write to me once from that place, saying it very cold and that food shit, but that I not to worry. He missing his perfect things, I think. I not hear since. That ten year ago. I have to be realistic, I do not think I see him again.'

'So, you just stay on here and no one minds.'

Yuliya nods, 'I try not draw attention. And people not see what they don't expect to see.'

'Don't you get lonely? Don't you miss him?' She is thinking of Matthew and her friend Daniels. She would not have been able to live on her own for very long.

'He man. He always like stuff his way. But he kind to me and much generous and I am sorry for what happened and sad that I not seeing him again.'

The conversation has reached as far as it can run and they watch David and Sola play cards, seated on the rug with legs crossed, bonding, like infants, through play. The game is one that Sola knows from The Dolls' House and involves a complex system of bids and lightning-fast trades followed by the theatrical slapping down of trumps. The requirement for bluff and deceit leaves David all at sea, the buttons Sola gave him at the start transferring themselves inexorably back like magic beans to form a pool in her lap.

'He very handsome,' Yuliya says. 'You lucky girl.'

'I'm not sure I really am,' Evie replies, uncertain what Yuliya means by lucky – that maybe she is not attractive enough to deserve him? 'He is not mine.'

'But you friends?'

Evie shrugs. After the misunderstanding of the day before, she is not even sure of that.

'Boris said that we robot – he not so good at political correct – are to be perfection of human form, or we not worth bloody effort.' Yuliya smiles to herself and gazes into the distance, a self-satisfied narcissistic glaze to her eyes. Then she suddenly stands. 'I will leave you now all to rest.' She crosses the room, the movement of her slender legs so smooth, her walk is more of a glide.

Reaching the doorway, Yuliya hesitates, half-turning back as if she is experiencing second thoughts. Her expression becomes strained, the smile morphing into a grimace. 'Yes, they nice,' she murmurs irritably. Her head tilts as if she is listening hard, then she resumes in a low, angry voice. 'Yes, and you right, risk for us too, but this gifted horse.'

'Who are you talking to?' Evie asks across the room, but Yuliya is already through the door, which closes crisply behind her. Only then does it dawn that she must have a 'Simon' of her own and, amused by the thought that she isn't the only one to have spent her life being badgered and nagged, Evie allows the oddness of her parting words, that were not intended for her, to slip past.

Instead she thinks of their conversation. Of Yuliya's vision of AABs which are admired rather than persecuted. The problem is that, rather than raising new gods, where AABs have been permitted to exist, such as here in Europe, humans have engineered a delta under-class. Even Yuliya's Boris, however much she wants to believe in his adoration, was clearly using her as little more than an object of escape and gratification. At best a concubine, at worst a slave.

Evie recalls something that Matthew once told her about Ancient Greece: that even in Athens, the home of democracy and founded on the premise of all men being equal, there were many thousands of slaves. It was the only way to ensure a comfortable life for its cultured citizens. He had gone onto observe, wryly, that the love of equal rights had been the preserve of men and had not extended to women. She'd applied this last idea to her own situation, her rights not as an AAB but as the lone female in their domestic establishment. True, she had little say on anything that mattered, but however she twisted it, Matthew had never treated her as a slave. The closest thing to a slave had actually been her uncomplaining human and male friend, Daniels.

She turns again to watch David and Sola. The child is rolling her button winnings across the concrete where they wobble and fall flat in the dark undergrowth around the edges of the room.

Suddenly inspired, Sola rises to her feet and takes mincing steps around the rug, her nose tilted upwards. 'Me perfect, me beautiful,' she says, caressing the air with her outstretched fingers. 'Admire me nails! Boris he love me. Me great big dolly,' batting her lashes and making Evie and David laugh and, for the first time in a while, forget themselves.

Performance over, Sola curtsies and, lifting her skirts, plonks herself down next to David again. She leans against him and closes her eyes. From being so active a moment before, it is as though she has an on/off switch.

Evie indicates to David that her head is slipping and he scoops her up, carries her to the other sofa and lays her on the cushions.

He then crouches down and lifts the whole thing up by its sturdy frame, smoothly revolving it in the air, the child sleeping undisturbed, and sets it down in reverse, facing away from them towards the wall.

He joins Evie on the other. They haven't spoken properly since their failed intimacy in the hotel and his proximity, with no other distractions, makes her nervous. They sit a yard apart, looking away from each other.

'I'm sorry,' he eventually says. 'Yesterday I made you feel bad when . . . You were trying to be nice.'

'No, it was my fault,' she replies, blushing, wishing they weren't having this conversation. 'I had no idea, about any of the things you've . . .'

The pressure of the last twenty-four hours has taken its toll on them both. But now they are here in a safe place and as the tension slips away, her tears well up. She closes her eyes to hold them in but they bulge under her lids.

The sofa shifts as he slides along the cushions. Uninvited, he places his arm around her and draws her against him and there is nothing that she can do but let him hold her and let the tears flow.

'Don't cry,' he says. 'I don't like to see you cry.' His simple way of expressing himself, which had at first seemed childish, now seems refreshingly honest.

'It is better to be able to,' she says. 'To let out what you feel.'

'I want you to be happy.'

'I think I am,' she says.

When her swollen vision clears, Evie points at the wall. 'Look.' The scene in the woods around where Sola sleeps has changed. A cottage has appeared among the trees and a group of bearded dwarves are emerging from it to stand around in a circle gazing down at her.

Evie lays her head on David's chest. 'You know, with the three of us here, I feel properly safe for the first time since we set

244

out. It's a bit like re-finding paradise. Being allowed back in. Is that possible?'

'When you've done the right thing,' he replies, 'I think it should be. You saved me and you saved the little girl.'

Evie nods, blinking, memories – real memories, not ones she was given but ones created by her – flooding her. 'When I lived in London, we had a garden surrounded by a wall. I wish you could have seen it. It was a beautiful place, something in it for each season – apple blossom for spring, camellias in bloom in June, leaves on the paths crackling underfoot in autumn and as the year ended, icicles on the branches that twinkled in the sun. I was content there. No, more than content – happy. It was tended by my friend. He did all the work but he'd tease me anyway by calling it "The Garden of Evie".'

'Your friend sounds like a nice man,' David says, his mouth so close that his breath ruffles her hair, setting off a tingle in her lobe.

'He was,' she says and her eyes fill again.

As she speaks, the surrounding woods retreat, and in their place bright green lawns roll themselves out, cut through by little paths, overhung by trees weighted with blossom, all of it sheltered by rose-covered brickwork basking in the noon sun. It is not her garden, how could it be? But it is enough to transport her back. And she lifts her cheek from his neck, now wet with her tears, and gazes around.

Bam . . . Bam . . . Bam . . . Bam . . .

The transition is as sudden as that. One moment she is asleep and the next shouting and flashing lights fill the air.

David is being wrenched to his feet.

Rolling off the sofa, Evie lands on the floor on her hands and knees, and slips sideways beneath it.

Torchlight criss-crosses the room, intersecting the green beams of energy rifles.

A half-dozen black-jacketed figures circle the rug. They've identified David as their main threat, maybe their primary goal, and are doing their best to restrain him. For now, she and Sola are overlooked.

The video walls are going berserk. The garden scene, which during the hours of darkness had been steadily embellishing itself with a sundial, a gazebo, a greenhouse, a pond and even something that resembles her swing, flickers and flashes as it struggles to adapt to what has become a war zone. It starts to sleet soot and snow.

Sola is sitting upright, staring about her, her eyes large with terror.

Evie, risking leaving her hiding place, crawls across the rug, and, without being seen, takes the child and pulls her down with her, so that they are hidden from view behind the other sofa.

The attackers struggle to subdue David. A couple of them lie on the floor, with smashed skulls. But they are tasering him now, the little blue filaments tangling around his arms, constraining him in a web. He tries to free himself, ripping at the skein of humming wire, stumbling backwards, his face in agony.

He glances in her direction and, despite the pain, mouths to her to go.

The video projection returns to the image of a forest at night. Rain beats down and the branches of the trees bend and scrape with a nightmarish zeal. The dwarves' cottage has returned too. The door to it is open and a yellow light shines from within.

Sola frees herself from Evie's grasp and, followed by the dog, creeps the few yards to the wall where the projection of the little door glows invitingly. Evie watches helplessly as her head and shoulders disappear.

Before a second later re-emerging. She glances behind her and Evie follows her over.

They find themselves at the top of a narrow staircase.

The door swings closed behind. The projection of the dwarves' door corresponded to an actual hidden door – the room has showed them the way to get out. She can only think that Boris had anticipated the merit of an escape hatch.

They hurry down the stairs, not looking behind them, and at the bottom, with minimal pressure, the heavy external door swings outward.

They emerge onto a steel walkway built above the bloated river. Their attention is drawn to the building behind as one of the circular windows forty feet above explodes, scattering glass, David's body smashing through, tangled with wire weaving false wings between his arms and shoulders. He briefly flies, propelled through the winter air by the power of his death-leap, before plummeting Icarus-like, striking the hard, grey, swollen, icy surface of the river at full pelt.

PART 5

The Actuality

32

Evie gazes across the lake. Spring is in the air here already, despite it being only January. The snow has retreated into the highest valleys and the white peaks reflect in the surface, disturbed only by ripples. It is as if they left winter behind in Paris. A sailboat swings around in a tight semicircle, and then, shedding the wind, comes to an abrupt halt, causing a kerfuffle on deck as the sail flaps and folds back on itself. It reminds her of her own memory of sailing: one moment in full flow with a mother holding her close and then the next . . . cut off.

The house is across the water. His house. Her 'father's' house. The house of Maier. Although to call it a house fails to do it justice: it is half medieval fantasy and half a collection of glass rectangles. Futuristic and old-fashioned at the same time, not unlike herself.

Evie looks down at the little girl kneeling in the grass, building a wigwam from sticks, the light in her hair, the tip of her nose prodding the air, her pink lips parted in concentration.

The escape from Paris was as fraught as anything she's been through. After eluding their would-be captors, they'd tramped beside the river, arriving an hour later at Gare de Lyon, and from there'd taken the night-train south. It was almost too much to believe that they'd got away, albeit an escape clouded by David's horrible end. An event she is struggling hard not to think about. And what of Yuliya's shocking readiness to betray her own kind – that it was her, Evie can have no doubt – using her own self to bait the trap, for what?

It could only have been for the bounty money. Wealth that would allow her to continue to exist in lonely isolation for a few years longer. There was nothing to distinguish her behaviour from the lowest of what humans do to one another. Such ugliness masked by such beauty could compete with the very worst the animal kingdom could put up. Evie had just not seen it coming; Yuliya had seemed more pampered pet than ruthless survivor.

Evie kneels behind the child and strokes her hair, smoothing it and separating it into bunches, before starting to plait. Her fingers move expertly. When finished, with no ribbon to hand, she uses shrivelled stalks to tie little bows. Evie could never have imagined a few days ago the level of trust they now have between them.

It may be that they have finally given her pursuers the slip. The indications are good but now she must succeed in this final step. Not only for her own sake any more, nor for the sake of the growing list of those who have sacrificed themselves for her, but for the sake of this girl.

For this task, Evie prepares meticulously.

The small town has only a few shops but is wealthy, and along the side streets that lead from the square, old-fashioned outfitters service a demand for well-made traditional clothes fashioned from cotton and wool.

Sola gazes out from the shop windows while Evie seeks out the sort of things that are typical of Evelyn and which she has always been attracted to – dark calf-length skirts, milky blouses with long cuffs, light-as-air cardigans in mohair with tapered sleeves and pearl shell buttons no larger than Sola's fingernails, and soft slender-soled sandals, in which she feels at the same moment both as light as a starling and solid with the ground.

She finds clothing for the child too, attiring her, as she daydreams she had once herself been attired, in a blue and white dirndl frock with, amusingly, no pockets (it is a joke between them), and a starched white apron. Also soft white ankle socks as fluffy as kittens and little shimmering nacre-buckled shoes.

Dressing up also serves as a distraction. She is missing David; how would she not?

Evie has no more use for the blonde wig and removes it in the street, dropping it in a refuse container. Shaking out her hair, she lets the cool breeze penetrate to her scalp, before gathering her hair with her fingers and weaving a single braid as she walks; tying it with a dark blue ribbon she treated herself to in the shop.

Now they are both perfect.

The first bit Evie must do alone and so leaves Sola at a cafe – outside, where it will be easy to run if the worst happens – tucked away at a table in a corner, where even the waiter has forgotten her.

'I'll be back in an hour,' she says, 'at most no longer than two. It's eleven o'clock – if I am not here by one, come to this place and ask for me.' She draws a map on the back of a napkin, the ink swelling into balloons as it soaks into the paper, making the child smile. 'But if it comes to that, you must be very careful, something will have gone . . .' She is about to say wrong, but Sola's imagination runs riot at the slightest thing and she concludes instead, 'not according to plan.'

She walks away, glancing over her shoulder as she weaves between the tables and again as she turns the corner, but the child's head is under the chairs, throwing crumbs to an inquisitive robin while her dog looks on.

It is a wrench to be parted. It is inexplicable, unfair and at odds with her biology how this creature has got under her skin in the way she has. But also crazy-wonderful. Some primal programming which she can't believe she was meant to have has been triggered.

Evelyn gave the impression of being too cerebral to be maternal. Elektra, from what she saw in the brochure and from the example of the ghastly Yuliya, possessed little of a motherly nature. Some other deeper code has surfaced, leaving Evie weak and wobbly when she needs to be strong, and willing to throw her own life away if this girl was in peril.

Maybe it is a response that Sola just draws out – that she survived in The Dolls' House, unbroken and still innocent of her vulnerability, perhaps provides a clue. If so, Evie can do nothing about it. For better or worse, they have knotted souls.

The stretch of road running along the edge of the lake to the house, and the house itself – its old high walls rearing from the hillside – are achingly familiar. Both appear as fragments scattered through her early memories . . . Returning from school with the afternoon sun on her legs, her satchel heavy with books . . . reading said books lying on the warm wood of the little jetty . . . Things Evelyn must, or may once, have done.

Evie approaches with the lake to her left. There is no barrier, and peering down she can see boulders coated with bright weed beneath the surface. The bottom of the lake shelves steeply and the water just a few yards out is dark and blown into sharp ripples. Her fear of falling in is overdone, she knows it, but she crosses to the other side of the road, just to be sure. Since her fall down the stairs at Maplin's, something has not been the same. Her sense of balance, which had been infallible, is now, in her old friend's Daniels's parlance, 'royally screwed'. It's laughable really, that despite all of her extraordinary electronics and engineering, she has a heart blown from glass. A tiny spinning sphere designed by NASA, essentially the same as the ones used to guide their ships the millions of miles to Mars and back. 'Only the best for the best', the Elektra brochure had trumpeted. Men and their extravagant boasts . . .

From this elevation the house has the appearance of a small castle. Its upper battlements rise from the rocks, its lower reaches are concealed by giant dark-leaved rhododendrons. A round tower looms above the trees, narrow windows penetrating the stone glittering like goblin eyes.

Evie reaches the entrance steps and looks up. The tall front door is constructed from studded planks. The stone lintel is carved into arches which nestle one within another. With no windows at ground level, the house seems unwelcoming, hostile, the impression increased by a camera which has been tracking her since she rounded the bend. This is architecture with secrets. The melancholy welcome of fairy tales – The Princess and the Pea . . . The Goose Girl. And she thinks of arriving at such a door, unrecognised for what she is.

She pulls the bell and it is answered by an elderly woman in an apron and cap. Standing in the doorway in her black dress with its white scalloped collar, she would only have needed a duster on a bamboo pole to perfect the image of a Victorian housemaid. It seems that in some corners the world has turned back on itself, in response to having moved forward in others with such abandon.

She announces herself as Ms Davenport, a friend of Herr Maier's family – a hazy description of her relationship to a man who is the nearest thing to the father she never had, but hopefully 'Davenport' will be enough to raise his interest. The woman scrutinises her, eyes settling on her face. Only when Evie has finished speaking does she stop staring.

She asks Evie to follow her up a flight of stairs – a tight coil of steps leading to a landing. 'Please wait here,' she says and disappears down a corridor.

A deep-set window faces the lake. Evie goes to it, and, conquering her anxiety, which would have had her pacing around, seats herself on the sill with her back to the stone. On the opposite wall is a mirror and she catches a glimpse of her appearance, primped to perfection for the encounter ahead.

After their shopping, Evie and Sola had faced their reflections in the window of a tobacconist's, Sola's eyes roving from one to the other, admiring the trick they'd played with a simple change of costume. Slowly, her mouth formed an approving smile. 'We look joli and nice maintenant Maman, no long a couple of grubby wh . . . ,' just managing to stop in time any 'mauvaise language' from sneaking out. She is slowly being tamed, her waywardness polished into 'proper manners'. Letting go of Evie's hand, she had spun on her toes, the skirt of her dress fanning out above her knees, as the little dog ran in a tight circle around her shiny feet.

Evie blinks back a tear. The child called her 'Maman' – she has not asked her to do that – where did that come from? Maybe it is just playfulness.

Soft piano music permeates from above. She gazes up at the vaulted ceiling, from the centre of which hangs a chandelier fashioned from stag antlers. The sound tickles the air, as light as feathers burst from a pillow. Something she could reach out and pass her hand through.

She recognises it as Beethoven's *Für Elise*. Indeed, the piece is more than just familiar, she knows it inside out as being a favourite she spent long hours shaping and reshaping as a way of passing the hot afternoons last summer. The doors of the music room standing wide open to the garden. The lingering exchange of air allowing, during quiet interludes, the slow snip of Daniels's shears to pervade.

She hums along, anticipating each beat. Playing the piano is a passion. She was competent the morning she arrived, but her skills and sensitivity have blossomed since.

Looking out of the window, the memory of a music teacher fills her mind – a sour little man notable for his desire to torment. A typical incident would start with something minor and his pimply cheeks would glow hot. One minute she might be 'slouching' – even though her back was stiff – and he'd poke her in the waist with his 'baton' (a thirty-centimetre wooden ruler), just because he could, then another day it would be something else.

One morning he accused her of letting her hands slope. He took small bronze coins – one groschen pieces – from his waist-coat pocket and balanced them on the dimples of her knuckles with his podgy fingertips. When one slipped off, which one soon did, he brought the edge of the ruler down on her with the enthusiasm of a workhouse overseer.

Her injured fingers had leapt to her mouth, sending the remaining coins rolling across the oak floor. Sucking on her throbbing hands to confuse the pain, chest rising and falling, she'd refused to look at him. He'd put the tip of the ruler under her chin, forcing her head up. She'd stared back with fury. 'Zis temper of yours, Fräulein,' he'd said, the waxed tips of his mous-tache quivering, 'I vill it tame.'

He took on the wrong fräulein in his cruel pastime; she'd engineered that he be caught, her father entering the room at this exact moment. Afterwards she'd watched from the window as he was booted, literally, out of the house to land face first in the road.

Of course, the terrible teacher was never real – or at least not to Evie. His spiteful games were a memory implant. The pupil was the clever Evelyn, whom no one could get the better of for long. But sitting here now, Evie recognises, without a shadow of doubt, the view of the steps where he had his comeuppance and had afterwards ludicrously waved his fist up at her window.

The music pauses and she surfaces from her reverie. How long has she been waiting? She's lost track of time.

The maid collects her and leads her along the corridor.

They leave the old building through a feudal arch, cross a gravelled courtyard in noon shadow and enter again through a shiny automatic near-silent sliding door, back into the light. The cool air after the heat of the sun moistly brushes her skin.

The doors to the final room are open. As she descends shal-low steps, the view opens out until the panorama of the lake and snow-capped mountains stretches to the edges of her vision.

Evie is in a glass-walled space. The white ceiling, some twenty feet above, is dappled by reflections off the lake, which reflect in turn off the polished floor and play over her ankles, so that it seems she paddles through shallows.

She swivels on her heel, gazing around. The end walls, also of glass, blend seamlessly with the one ahead, so that the view has no limits. If she didn't know what she knows, she'd wonder if it was all fake, the room giving her what she wants to see, like the one in Paris.

So far, of the myriad new things she has encountered, this is the most awe-inspiring, both in its sheer beauty and for its manifestation of power over one's surroundings.

Only as she completes her rotation does she notice that she is being watched. From behind. She falters, stretching out an arm to regain her balance.

Maier stands thirty feet away in the corner, his hand resting on the back of a chair, almost the only furniture in the room.

They examine each other silently. Apart from the image in the library and the incident with the music teacher – in both of which he is frustratingly hazy – she has only the memory of them riding together in the mountains.

She compares the man in front of her with his younger self – searching his face.

Maier is deeply tanned, the effect made more pronounced by his white open-necked shirt. His sleeves are rolled to his elbows, exposing strong, sleek forearms. His silver hair is combed back from his forehead. While his dark eyes attempt to penetrate her, his lashes flicker uncertainly. He has been presented with an impossibility. The world, which he is otherwise able to control, has been tipped on its head.

She smiles as naturally as she can.

He remains stiff-lipped. 'Who are you?'

'I am Evie.'

His face twitches. 'No, you are not.' But he doesn't seem to quite know what he is denying.

She smiles more strenuously, keeping her lips pursed but allowing the corners to lift so that dimples form in her cheeks. She knows how to do 'innocent', and what's not in her programming she has cultivated from studying old Audrey Hepburn movies watched in bed with Matthew.

'What kind of hoax is this?

'I am . . . Evie.' She takes a couple of steps towards him and, in doing so, the sunlight gleams on her face, making her appear spotless. Untouched.

'Evie,' he repeats, a little breathless from what he is witnessing. 'Yes, we've had that bit already.'

She takes another step, shuffling uncertainly one foot against the other, her hands clasped behind her, so that her upper body is pressed forward guilelessly. Something the devious little Sola does. There is much she is learning from that one!

He swallows hard. 'Who put you up to this?'

'No one,' she murmurs.

'No one,' he repeats.

She tilts her chin, regarding him shyly. 'I wanted to see you.'

She looks down to allow him a chance to take her in – the living replica of the daughter he last saw forty years before – and observes him wipe his eye with a handkerchief. Her own eyes water too. The loneliness since the death of Matthew and Daniels, quenched temporarily by the brief company of David and now Sola, rises again to the fore.

'Come closer,' he murmurs, holding out his hand. The same tanned hand, albeit more wrinkled, that he had lain over hers, all those years before.

She approaches until she is just a yard from him.

'Are you a dream?' he asks, shaking his head slowly.

Evie is close enough to see a tear slide down his cheek and she gazes back, wide-eyed. 'No dream,' she murmurs, blinking and half-blind herself.

33

Maier leads her outside and down a further set of steps onto an expanse of decking suspended above the water. A cluster of rattan chairs are grouped around a low table. He rings a bell, and when the maid appears sends her away again to bring drinks.

'Where are you from?' he asks.

'England.'

'England,' he repeats. His movements remain slow, stunned, as if she had told him she had escaped from the underworld. 'I presume you know who you resemble, I presume you are prepared to admit that? . . . unless of course you really don't.'

'I know,' she says.

His eyes roam over her face and hair. 'Well?' he prompts, wanting to hear her say it.

'Evelyn,' she whispers.

'Evelyn, yes. So you understand why I am puzzled. Your turning up from out of nowhere – like a phantom – calling yourself–'

'Evelyn's mother was English,' she says, repeating what she learned from Matthew. 'You met at Heidelberg in 2069. You were in your second year, she in her first week. You were introduced at a departmental tea party while sheltering from the rain amongst the palms under the glass of the botanical house.'

Maier shakes his head, not in denial but as if to loosen a memory. He stares into the distance. The moisture from incipient tears collects in the wrinkles around his eyes. 'Is this just his cruel game?' he asks slowly. 'An attempt to cause pain?'

'Cause pain?'

'After all these years?'

She looks over the water, watching a gull fly low, wingtips skimming the surface. 'I do not know whom you are referring–?'

'I am referring to Matthew. I think you are aware of that.'

They sit in an uneasy silence, until he resumes in a softer tone, 'Do you know how Matthew and I became friends?'

'You were his tutor at Cambridge.'

'That is right. And you probably also know how that came about. That I had come to England to take up a lectureship in the Faculty of Philosophy the year he arrived as a freshman. We were both new to the town, maybe neither of us quite fitted in with our peers, and despite the age difference we became friends. But then that friendship led ultimately to something terrible. I am referring to what happened to my daughter. You know that too?'

She nods.

'Joy and sadness intertwined. Did he send you?'

'I just wanted to see you,' she murmurs. 'That is all.'

'You said that before. Is he with you here?'

She shakes her head.

'And what is your relationship?'

'My relationship?' But she knows what the question means. 'I am his wife.'

The maid returns with a tray carrying a pot of tea, cups on saucers, a small jug of milk and two glasses for water. She places it on the table beside them, laying out the things, studying Evie from the corner of her eye as she does so.

'You are his wife,' Maier repeats, disbelievingly, once they are again alone.

She nods.

'How can this be?' He passes her a glass of water from which she sips. She needs a little moisture regularly, although it is important not to overdo it. 'How old are you? Twenty-five, twenty? Younger even than that?'

'Twenty-one.'

He pours the tea. 'Then, how – or rather why – are you an old man's spouse?'

'Was,' she clarifies. But referring to Matthew in the past tense triggers a ripple of grief that she is unprepared for and she looks down.

'What happened?' Maier asks, after a period of silence.

'He died.'

A tremor passes across his face. 'How?' he asks, quietly.

'There was a break-in and he was shot.' By saying it quickly, matter-of-factly, she gets it out, without her voice cracking. She blinks back tears. 'I want to explain everything,' she says, 'who I am.'

'Yes, I think it is time.'

'It is just not an easy thing.'

'Well, if it helps, I know what you are not. Yes, you are perfect in every way, even down to the heart-shaped mole below your ear – almost invisible as you blush, just as it should be. But you are not Evelyn, so surprise me. Do your worst.'

She gazes across the lake to the distant peaks. 'Matthew had me . . . constructed.'

'Had you constructed?' He is confused. 'What are you talking about? Are you saying . . . that you're not . . . ? You are saying—!' He leans back, gazing at her, open mouthed. 'I thought such a thing was no longer possible. Never was possible.'

Evie blushes more deeply still. 'He had me made as a copy,' she repeats.

Uninvited, Maier reaches for her hand and, lifting her wrist, runs his fingertips along her forearm. 'So soft and smooth,' he murmurs. 'Just like skin.'

'It is skin,' she says quietly, letting him continue to touch her.

'I had no idea such work was possible.' He releases her and settles back into his chair. 'Well, this is indeed a surprise.'

The maid comes out again and irritation crosses his face, quickly replaced by renewed intrigue.

'She turned up at the door, asking for her,' the maid says, but Sola is already racing across the terrace with the ridiculous dog snapping at her heels.

'And who is this?' Maier asks.

'Je Sola,' the child replies, drawing to a breathless halt, although the question was not directed at her.

'I am sorry,' Evie says to him. 'I asked her to seek me here, if I was gone too long.'

'Y'wer gone ages,' the child reprimands, pressing forcefully against her shoulder with the sharp edge of her own. 'Je worried à mort.' And she toys with Evie's hair with her fingertips, then gives her plait a pointed tug.

'What is your connection with this child?' Maier asks, gazing curiously.

'Elle ees ma Maman,' Sola replies, pressing her lips forward, as if she is fighting the urge to stick out her tongue.

'I was not asking you, Mademoiselle,' Maier says.

'It is what she chooses to call me,' Evie says.

'And is she . . . like you, too?'

'If you cannot tell,' Evie replies slowly, 'then does it really matter?'

34

Maier gives them a room in which to rest. It is on the new side of the house, with a view onto the wooded hill.

'Eees this to be our home maintenant?' Sola asks, bouncing from one to the other of the two single beds.

'I am not sure,' Evie replies.

Sola goes into the bathroom and plays with the taps, twisting them on. 'I think I will have a bath,' she says, emptying pink salts from a jar onto the surface of the water, sending up a suffocating rush of scent that has her backing out of the doorway, pinching her nose. 'Eet smells worse than Pompie in there,' she exclaims.

She kicks off her shoes into the corner and drags her dress over her head, dropping it on the dog which, blindfolded, runs around in a circle.

'Keep the door open,' Evie says, as the child skips back through. Even cloaked by the steam, she can see that the girl's shoulders are criss-crossed by welts and her neck marked with finger-shaped bruises.

Evie hears her land with a splash in the tub, and sinks into the pillow from where she watches through the mirror the child dip her head and rise again, eyes closed, nose breathing soapy bubbles. How nice it must be to be without fear, despite everything that life drops on you, from whatever height.

She needs to recharge but that can wait. They are not expected until the evening and she has all afternoon. But then, before she can prevent it, David pops into her head and quickly her imagination is on a dangerous track – fancying what could have been. Snapping herself out of it, she takes the unit from her bag and brusquely plugs herself in.

The two walk along the corridor a little before seven. Sola is bursting with excitement, which may not be a good thing. She has also insisted, against Evie's wishes, on bringing the dog, but then again that may be better than leaving it locked in to ruin the room.

Evie ponders the evening ahead and the challenge it presents. Earlier with Maier, an understanding between them had felt at hand. Her existence was a shock, but she thought in the end a good one and surprises are, after all, intended to bestow happiness. Like the little offerings Daniels unearthed for her on his shopping expeditions.

She is clad in a simple blue silk dress with pearl buttons not much larger than teardrops, which she found in town. The material is vintage, worn daylight-thin at the hips, but all the same delightfully slippery smooth, with hand-stitching around the cuffs, so petite as to be the work of children and almost invisible to the eye. The sort of thing for which the skills have been all but lost. She has tied her hair with a velvet ribbon, combing it unfussily behind her ears in a blatant impersonation of Evelyn in her student days.

A maid, a different one to earlier, meets them in the long, glass-walled reception room. She leads them outside onto the same terrace as before, where, despite the nippy air, a square table has been spread with a crisp white cloth. A candelabrum stands in its centre, candles doggedly alight despite the evening breeze. The maid invites her to sit, pulling back a chair and then, beside it, another for Sola, on which additional cushions have been thoughtfully placed.

'Where ees he?' Sola asks loudly, adjusting the padding under her behind to prop herself forwards, so that her ribs press against the table edge.

'It is his house, he will arrive when he is ready,' Evie says.

'Think you we can make heem love us?'

'I do not know what you are referring to.'

'Oh Maman! You know why we are ere exactement, you can try to pretend le contraire, but y'aren't foolin anyone.' She turns to the dog on her lap and, squeezing its cheeks, asks mischievously, 'Does she, Toto?'

Despite the chilly evening, the atmosphere around the table possesses a balminess that caresses the skin and the candle flames waver only when they talk across them. It is like they are under an invisible glass dome, the sort of thing Daniels placed over his cakes to protect them from the air. The effect is intriguing and she cannot see how it has been achieved.

The maid brings a fruit drink for the child and pours iced water from a jug into Evie's glass. Evie gazes across the lake towards the lights on the far shore. Oh how wonderful it would be to be invited to stay, for this to actually become their home. Can she indeed make this man love her and could she love him in return – like a father? Perhaps there is enough of Evelyn in her programming to make her side happen, whether she wills it or not.

Evie hears voices and turns to face the house. Maier emerges onto the step above the terrace and pauses. He looks back inside. Dimly, through the glass, a second figure can be seen making its way laboriously across the unlit room.

So it is not going to be just the three of them – she should have realised that from the fourth place setting. Despite the enveloping warmth, a chilly sense of foreboding swells – that she has been assuming too much – and before she can shake it off, the figure, a woman, reaches the doorway and, helped by Maier, raises her foot over the threshold.

Evie abruptly stands. Her chair scrapes on the boards and, as she lurches back from the table, crashes onto its arm.

'What ees it Maman?' Sola begs. The dog stares up at her, baring its teeth, the fur on its shoulders standing on end.

Despite the commotion, neither Maier, nor the woman he is

escorting down the steps, look her way. The noise remains trapped within the bubble of air.

As the woman descends, one stair at a time, she leans heavily on a pencil-thin stick, her elbow supported by Maier. Reaching the decking, she straightens, lifting her head to reveal a weary face with lips drawn tight.

Evie's body is in shadow but her neck and cheeks are lit by the candlelight. It takes the woman several seconds to focus on her. 'Who is this?' she mutters.

'I thought you two should meet,' Maier says nervously. His voice is audible to Evie with her strong hearing, despite the muffling effect around the table. 'Evelyn,' he continues, 'this is . . . Evie.'

Evelyn stares, absorbing what is being presented to her, and a shudder passes through her. She leans hard on her stick, the tendons in her neck prominent as her body sways.

'Je think Maman, that thees was not part of le plan,' Sola murmurs, without yet understanding what she is witnessing.

Evie falters too. The legitimacy of her existence has been snatched away in a heartbeat.

Did Matthew know? Did he lie to her all these years or was he lied to himself? And why did Maier not say earlier that his daughter was alive? Evie realises as she thinks it that she herself said nothing to reveal the misapprehension. But from Evelyn's point of view, it must be far worse – presented with a replica of her younger self with no opportunity to prepare. The theatrics of the introduction are insensitive at best.

'What have you done?' Evelyn asks of her father, while continuing to stare at Evie. 'Is she yours?'

This accusation blindsides Maier and he is momentarily lost for words.

'Did mother know? Where have you been hiding her all this time? Is this to mock me?'

'No . . . no I mean, she is not that,' he answers, stumbling. 'I would never have done such a thing,' he adds, horrified, or at least feigning it. 'To your mother or to you.'

'Then what?'

'She arrived today unannounced. Until then I knew nothing about her.'

'She arrived out of the blue, and you just let her in?'

'How could I turn her away?'

'And where exactly did she *arrive* from?'

'From Matthew,' he says.

Evelyn trembles. 'I see,' she mutters. 'So this *is* to mock me.'

'Evelyn, I had no idea,' Evie murmurs, desperate to make amends for the appalling misunderstanding that she herself is at the heart of, while inside she seeks to adjust to the altered circumstances. It is not as hard as she might have imagined. She was written to believe she was Evelyn, but this was only ever an artifice which even early on proved unsustainable, and ever since she has been no more than playing a part. And not even one she has been very good at. Finding Evelyn alive may finally allow her to be herself.

Evie steps away from the table, emerging from the cocoon of warmth around the dining area into the night's chill.

'Where did he find her?' Evelyn asks, her voice suddenly loud.

'Let us sit down and talk and all will begin to make sense,' Maier says, sounding slightly desperate, his magician's reveal not having gone as well as he'd hoped. He tries to take Evelyn's arm but she shrugs him off and, one step at a time, traverses the remaining yards unaided. The maid materialises from the shadows and pulls back a chair and Evelyn seats herself, wincing as she settles.

Maier rights Evie's chair and she feels the shawl of warmth surrounding the table wrap her back around as he slides it in. He takes the remaining one for himself and unrolls his napkin, gazing at his elderly daughter and her youthful doppelgänger.

'Enough games,' Evelyn mutters. 'Tell me who this is.'

'It would be polite to ask her yourself, rather than pretend she is not there.'

Evelyn glares back. Her breathing is quick and shallow and her hand grips the table edge, dragging deep creases into the cloth.

'Tell her, Evie,' Maier says, 'who you are.'

'Who I am?' she stammers.

'How you know Matthew will do, as a start,' he says gently. 'We'll take this a step at a time. There is a lot to absorb.'

Evie looks over to Evelyn, her look full of compassion and regret, 'I am Matthew's wife.'

Evelyn breathes in sharply and her knuckles whiten. 'And what interest is this to me?'

'I'm sorry, it's just that I—'

'I do not want your apologies. I do not ask for pity,' she mutters. 'Who do you think you are, coming here with your presumptions?'

Evie cannot hold her look and turns away, witnessing Sola's face as she does so. Her mouth is open so wide that all her teeth, all the way back to the molars, are on show.

'I didn't mean anything,' Evie says quietly.

'And what are you doing married to an old man, you're barely a child. What do you get from it? Money? That's usually the thing, I believe?'

'I had no choice.'

'Is Eve even your real name?'

'Evie,' she corrects, her voice hollow.

'You realise you look like me, when I was young, when he and I were . . . But I guess you know that. What did he do, pay for the surgery? It would have been typical of him. He altered me too you know, for life, but not in a positive way. I wasn't always like this . . . a cripple.'

'Evelyn dear, be generous,' Maier says.

She twists to face him, revealing a crimson ribbon holding her greying hair off her neck. 'Don't "Evelyn be generous" me, when it was you who let her in.'

'What did Matthew do?' Evie asks tremulously.

'You mean this?' She holds up the handle of her stick.

'Evelyn, all that was years before she . . .'

'No! She should know about the man she's married.' Evelyn turns to face her. 'I was your age or thereabouts. We were in England. Your husband and I had been friends but that was all in the process of changing. Spending time with him had become oppressive but he'd made the assumption he owned me already, he'd even bought a ridiculous house in the country to be my wedding present and was furious because I spoilt everything by rejecting his proposal.

'We were returning from it in his car. He was driving down the narrow lanes like a madman to terrify me, and losing control we ended up crashing into a bank. The collision concertinaed the front against my legs, destroying me and his precious automobile in the same instant. Only, he got to walk away.'

Evie cannot look at either of them and stares at her napkin still folded on her place mat. Sola takes her hand underneath the table.

'So no, I never died, nothing so romantic. Although over the years, suffering operation after operation as the surgeons spliced my splintered limbs back together, I have often enough wished I had.'

'He left you?' she murmurs, horrified that Matthew had deserted her so callously.

'Oh, not quite. He briefly sentimentalised about nursing me himself, but when I returned home for treatment, it was the last I heard from him. And of course you know the final bit already, how he claimed the role of victim, spreading the lie that I had died . . . I tell you, if I had known he was doing that!'

'I am so sorry,' Evie murmurs.

This version of events has taken a ram to her happy memories of her husband. Instead, a recollection of falling short of his vision of perfection, of being abandoned outside his room trying to work out her mistake, rattles around her head.

'You don't look so pleased with yourself now,' Evelyn says.

'I never meant—'

'How long have you been . . . married?'

'Forty-one years, last autumn.' Evie is close to tears, only just holding them in.

Evelyn snorts derisively. 'You think this is amusing?'

'No, it's true,' Maier murmurs. 'Forty-one years. I was fooled too and that was in daylight. Our friend is, how can I put it, not quite what she seems.'

'What are you saying?' Evelyn's eyes are suddenly wide. 'That she's a "bot"?'

She stares at Evie, then reaches across and takes her chin roughly in her hand and drags her face around to stare into her eyes. 'Well, that just about sums him up. The only type of woman that would put up with him. And there I was taking you merely for an opportunistic little slut. So where is he now?' she asks aggressively. 'Why did he send you?'

'He's dead,' she says, observing Evelyn, confronted by this revelation, momentarily brought up short.

The atmosphere around the table grows cold despite the fabricated heat. Everyone draws breath. Sola stares at each of them in turn, her mouth still agape.

'Good,' Evelyn says at last. 'I'm glad.'

35

In Evie's dream she is seated in her garden swing, the one Daniels hung for her. Sola is asleep in her arms.

David comes up behind and leans over, cold water dripping from his hair onto her neck. 'What will you do in ten or eleven years' time?' he asks.

The question disturbs her. 'What do you mean?'

'When she is your age? Will you let her go? Is that not what parents must do?'

Evie wakes, head spinning, and brusquely detaches her charging lead, throwing it onto the carpet. She swings her legs around to sit on the side of the bed, only then realising that Sola is not beside her.

She checks in the bathroom and outside the door.

She goes down to the long reception room in which she met Maier the day before and crosses the sunlit floor. The sliding glass doors are partially pushed back, letting in the icy morning air. She runs through, down the steps and over the boards to the lake edge and paces along, peering into the dark water. She doesn't even know if the girl can swim.

Evie returns inside and crosses the gravelled courtyard to the old side of the house, keeping to the route she had been brought along yesterday. She reaches the space in which she had been left to wait, then, following the distant sound of a piano — the melody not gracious as before but riotous and skirt-lifting — runs up the tower stairs. The higher she climbs, the lower the ceiling and the narrower the steps, whereas in the new building the opposite holds true – everywhere is bright and fresh, passage-ways are broad, natural light plentiful; nothing is steep or crooked or oddly arranged.

She reaches a chamber where she finds them seated at a piano with their backs to her – Sola and Evelyn – but it is Sola at the keys, her gaudy pounding infused with the thrills of The Dolls' House – flamboyant and grotesque. Evie didn't know the child could play, even if it is with a clumsy smash, grab and bouncy slam.

The child is full of joy, even more so than normal. Evelyn smiles down on her indulgently. Aware of Evie's entrance – perhaps having orchestrated this moment – she slowly turns.

The smile of affection twists into a sneer. 'You're here, then,' she says, looking her up and down coolly. 'You appear fresh and well-rested, although I guess, being as you are, you always do.'

Sola continues playing, the clatter of the music hall growing cacophonous until Evelyn scoops the girl's fingers from the keys and crisply brings down the cover.

Sola grunts and, facing Evie, mutters a weary, 'Maman,' as if it is she who is the cause of the entertainment's termination. The dog, snoozing in a shaft of sunlight, disturbed by the sudden silence, wakes and yelps irritably, before again closing its lids.

'Interesting,' Evelyn says, 'that the child calls you that.' Her eyes glint with malice. 'I would not have thought it was possible for such feelings to exist between . . . but then what do I really know of your kind – or, for that matter, of her.'

'Thank you for looking after her,' Evie says, maintaining a surface calm.

'Not at all, the child is a delight. I can see why you're so charmed. So amusing to hear her prattle. Some of the things she comes out with have quite made me blush.'

'She is just a child.'

'But such colourful language! I have been entertained. So much profanity from such a young mouth! So brave and kind of you, to take her on.'

273

Evie reaches for Sola but she slips along the stool out of her reach.

'But I am interested in you,' Evelyn continues. 'How could I not be? It is not every day that your very own waxwork turns up at your house.' She smiles superciliously. 'And I have to watch my father get all giddy over it.

'Tell me, what was it like living with Matthew? You two must have seemed the oddest couple – you not much more than a girl and him an old man. No wonder he kept you under wraps. His own little Eve – a creature he'd created to love and worship him. Even the name – Evie – even that's almost right. Almost biblical. You couldn't make it up! Except that that is *exactly* what he did.

'I remember he was always so very proud of that garden of his, although I recall it was his servant who actually did the work, while he strode around like a version of "God the Father", even back then when still a young man. It took me a while to realise just how suffocating that pride of his could be.

'But you know the one thing that really grates, even more than all of that?'

Evie reaches again for Sola, again unsuccessfully.

'It is not just that you are a lie, but that you are a dishonest one. In making you, he did not even attempt a faithful copy but rather forged the version of me he'd always desired. Look how you dazzle with your gleaming hair and glowing skin, and you have that little upturned nose – not a blemish of mine reproduced!' Evelyn shakes her head sadly. 'It should be the pettiest of my concerns but I can't help feeling that I have been insulted a second time over.'

Sola collects her dog in her arms and seats herself cross-legged on the window seat, stroking its head and observing, neck tilted, the one-sided sparring.

Evelyn stands slowly, wobbling on the better of her legs as she brings her stick around. Leaning on it, she crosses the room to the window where she straightens again, the pain showing in her thin cheeks. Brittleness and instability; surprising things for them to have in common.

'But he said you'd died,' Evie says. 'He said you had an illness, how was I to know?'

'Well, here I am, so now you do.'

'He said it was what he had been told.'

'Hah. And you believed him!'

'I had no reason not to.'

'When all along, he was down the factory having you assembled. How he must have relished the moment when you were delivered and he could enjoy people's faces. "Oh how wonderful for you, to have her back . . . Oh look, she walks and talks!"'

'You think you're so clever don't you. Escaping the scene of your crime and finding your way here, even rescuing this little orphan bitch along the way and then working your charms on my father to feel sorry for you. Well let me show you just how clever you really are.'

Evelyn picks up a holo-pad from the lid of the piano and flicks it open. After a second or two, the walls of miniature buildings rise from its surface and snow clouds the air. She lays the screen on the seat close to the girl and inch-high figures resolve themselves, hurrying through the snow beside a strip of dark green water.

Evie leans in to see more closely. It is like being in a hovacar, fifty feet over events. Daniels is alongside her with his hand around her waist, taking her weight on his arm.

She looks up at Evelyn, tears in her eyes. 'How did you get this?'

The video flickers and fades, the grey hues absorbing yellows, blues and greens, the light brightening, and now here she is again, this time with Sola on the hillside above the town, looking down on the house the afternoon they arrived.

Sola giggles on seeing herself and reaches out like a giant to cup them both in her palm, but her fingers pass through, creating ripples in the light like water in a stream. She glances up at Evelyn, a look of pleasure on her face.

275

'Of course there is more,' Evelyn says. 'You don't have to search too hard to find a fairly comprehensive documentary of your travels . . . it's all been emerging in the last few days, so many amateur sleuths out there willing to share what they have since you became famous! Or rather should I say infamous, because the more important fact is that you are wanted in England for murder. I didn't realise that machines could be held accountable in that way, but apparently it is so. And my poor trusting father admitted a killer into our house! For all we know you could have been the one who slaughtered Matthew.' Her eyes glitter coldly. 'After all we only have your word for events. Maybe you now intend to slay us too, if we displease.'

Evie's mouth opens wide. 'I did not kill him,' she asserts angrily, finally reaching a tipping point and finding her voice. 'How dare you?' The waste of having spent her whole existence attempting to emulate this woman and believing herself to have fallen short when the actuality is so vile is finally sinking in.

'I will naturally be reporting your presence to the authorities, here in Am See,' Evelyn continues. 'We are a conservative-minded lot, quite a little backwater in these radical times, and there is a deep-rooted distaste for dangerous elements. We've never enjoyed strangers and always like to know exactly who is visiting us.

'However.' She pauses and looks into Evie's eyes. 'I will grant you a head start. If you are quick and clever, who knows, maybe you will make it, although judging by the clumsy trail you have left so far, and the tail of interested parties you have collected, I have a feeling you will not. I am doing this, you understand, not for you, or . . .' She glances at Sola. 'Whatever this creature is. But for my father – to save him further upset. You have an hour to leave town.'

36

Sola stares at Evie. 'Maman, you ave blood on your face.' It is a surprise her voice is as composed as it is after what happened. She has seen some goings-on in her time – but everyone has their limits.

'Where?' Evie asks, glancing in the hotel room mirror and wiping around her mouth.

'Still there,' Sola says, grimly. Licking her fingertip, she reaches up and gingerly rubs around Evie's forehead and cheeks. 'That'll do,' she concludes, her voice downbeat. What a change from the day before when they had admired themselves in the same mirror in their new clothes. Since then bridges have been burnt and boats sunk.

They leave the hotel room through the balcony door. It is the second hotel they have fled from in less than a week. Sola has the dog under her arm and moves slowly along the planks, fussing with its lead, murmuring reassurance, concealing her distress.

Evie takes the child in her arms and, clambering over the railing, briefly perches on the ledge then makes the leap, landing awkwardly on her hand but safely holding Sola with the other. From here she puts her down and hurries her along, still carrying the dog, up the steep slope.

Evie looks back from the top, holding onto the trunk of the sapling beside her as the spinning in her head slows. The memory of the upsetting scene in Maier's house finally begins to stabilise and, in doing so, grows stark. She needs to block it out. What is done cannot be undone.

The light comes on in their hotel bedroom below. Figures move around inside. Consequences are catching up fast.

Snatching Sola by the hand, keeping her head low, Evie draws her with her over the crest. The dog softly yelps, a small strangled squeeze of anxiety, despite being clutched to the girl's chest.

Beyond the lip of the hill the ground slopes down to a road and thereafter rises again.

'Where are we going?' Sola asks, as they cross the tarmac and re-enter the trees.

'You must keep walking,' Evie says, adding, to tempt her, 'it'll be amazing – you'll see.' Maintaining the charade that this is still all a wonderful adventure, when they both know otherwise.

Sola mutters to the dog. She tells it not to be concerned because they are on nothing more than a stroll. But her own face reveals her fear from the precipitous curdling of events.

After a half hour, the child's legs, despite her best efforts, are dragging. The sheer ground has taken its toll and the weather is turning.

Above them, clouds roll in from the east, grey and wet. They pause on a stony ridge and stare at the sky as it drains of colour. A wave of cold air presses Evie's jacket against her chest. Sola's fine-spun hair lifts from her neck and flicks around her cheeks. 'How far is it?' she asks. Her half-hidden face makes her seem even smaller and more vulnerable. Evie reminds herself that they are not after the child, have no reason to harm her.

'Nearly there.' The lie that she has a plan has got her to this point but is now close on her heels.

Sola looks behind herself longingly, as if there is an option to go back. Maybe there is for her. 'Je tired,' she says.

If the child figures out that she is better off on her own, what is there to detain her?

'Let's continue,' Evie says. 'We'll be there soon.'

Thunder rumbles in the valley behind.

Evie walks faster still and Sola, motivated anew by the sense of a destination, trots beside her.

The rain overtakes them, dense as from a showerhead, the drops larger than normal and somehow, as they burst on their heads and shoulders, more wet. To escape, they climb a few yards to where the trees grow close to one another. Here, with their heels propped against the roots of a spruce, their backs flush to the grizzled trunk, they watch the downpour. A mist rises from the valley below and a wet tongue of air licks their faces. Sola has the dog under her coat. At least she is sharing its warmth.

The torrent lets up and Evie hears voices on the other side of the hill. Voices on the wind. Her own name called out. Promises being made to her that they think she is naive enough to believe; promises they have no intention of keeping. Although, encumbered with the child, what chance does she have? Does Sola hear the voices too? She shows no sign of having done so. Are the voices only in her head?

'We need to keep going,' Evie says, and drags the girl back into the open, into the rain – now losing strength but still as cold as sleet. It is a danger to her but Sola's safety is all.

They descend again, making their way over moss-covered boulders to the bank of a river. Here they pause beside the swiftly flowing water, Sola trembling in her wet things. The river is some thirty yards wide. The grey reeds on the far side poke through the grit and silt. Beyond that the hillside is clouded by mist.

There is movement along the skyline and figures with guns emerge between the trees.

Evie takes the child by the hand and leads her away quickly along the bank.

Four men in grey camouflaged jackets and military caps, carrying hunting rifles with telescopic sights, crest the hill, together with another – taller, familiar in outline. No, she thinks, it is an impossibility. She saw what she saw four days ago in Paris. It cannot be him.

From here the ground rises and they hurry up an overgrown path, batting the branches from their faces with their elbows. As they run, the dog, sensing the child's fear, fights its way out from under her coat, leaping to the ground, and valuable time is lost in retrieving it from between the rocks.

While the voices behind grow louder.

Hiding behind a fallen tree they watch the men descend. One carries on his back a steel cage, nine or ten inches deep and three feet high, struggling under the encumbrance to find his footing on the mossy stone. If that is for her, how would they fit her in, how would he carry her weight if they did? Maybe they'd leave the parts they don't need behind.

She glimpses *him* again, moving ahead of the others, and breathes in sharply.

'What ees it Maman? What can you see?' Does Sola not see him too?

Evie grabs her by the hand again and pulls her along.

The path leads treacherously to a blind pocket of ground beside a cliff, the only way forward via a dilapidated bridge. Hazard tape has been stretched across to form a barrier, but it is ancient and ragged.

'Where do we go?' Sola asks, regarding the structure apprehensively.

Boots thud on the stony path. How far are they behind – fifty yards? Forty?

Evie leads the reluctant child forward. The bridge is suspended from ropes over the river at its narrow point. Slats are fixed at intervals, each nine or ten inches wide. Two further ropes are strung at waist height. A number of slats are missing: two here, three there; their absence no recommendation for the ones that remain.

They peer down. The water, in being confined, spouts and spits, raging between the rock walls.

'Je not like eet at all,' Sola says, shivering. The spray from below mists their faces. 'It ees too dangereux.'

Evie glances behind her again. Uncertainty will cost them their lives. Before the child can protest further, she lifts her over the tape, placing her feet on the wood. If the structure can take either of them, it is her.

'Go,' she says over the noise of the water. 'Now.'

Sola clings to her arm. 'You come too.'

Evie steps over the barrier and stands beside her, to encourage her. The bridge creaks under their combined weight. 'I want you to go ahead. I will follow as soon as you are across.'

David enters the clearing and comes to a halt.

Evie lets go of Sola and turns. She and David stare at one another.

Are her visual circuits malfunctioning – generating false imagery? How can it be him? She saw him die. Saw him strike the water.

'You. How?' Evie murmurs, wanting to believe while filled with doubt. Is this a trick? One of her pursuers in disguise perhaps, acting as a lure. His head is dented and the skin scraped from his cheek revealing the fibre beneath.

'Evie,' he says, his voice stiff as if its use is new to him. 'You must come with me.'

'He does not sound right,' Sola whispers, and tugs on her hand.

It is also as if he does not see her, his gaze peering through.

'Evie,' he repeats, ponderously. 'You must come with me.'

'Why?' she asks, probing his eyes. Even now, she wants to believe that his appearance is a source of hope rather than fear. That he is not aiding her pursuers but is himself pursued.

He advances towards her. His expression is not so much aloof or even uncaring but merely a void.

'David?' she pleads. A tear runs down her cheek. 'What have they done to you?'

He is only three or four yards away. 'Evie, come with me.'

Sola is right, there is a mechanical resonance to his voice. But what of it? He has been damaged. Has she not been changed too?

Thrusting aside her remaining doubts, Evie moves towards him, arms outstretched, looking into his face, seeking the person she knew.

She reaches him and touches his injured cheek.

'I,' he says, 'I . . . I . . .'

'Grab her,' one of the men shouts. Her pursuers are at the turn of the path.

David shudders and takes hold of her wrist.

'Maman!' Sola screams. 'It ees not heem any more, cannot you see?'

Evie struggles to free herself but he is too strong – his grip like a vice. Their eyes meet again and with their faces just a few inches apart, she catches a glimpse of the real David, the one she grew to know, deep inside, struggling to surface. 'Run,' he murmurs, almost too faintly to hear, and his fingers unclench with a machine-like shudder, releasing her.

Rubbing her wrist, she backs away. Sola clutches hold of her, and pulls, dragging her through the tape and out onto the bridge, which sways frighteningly. The dog bounds from Sola's arms and she lunges for it, losing her balance on the slippery wood, causing the bridge to tilt dramatically. The frightened animal runs back and Sola twists to grab it, snapping one of the slats.

The debris drops into the river twenty feet below.

Evie glances behind. One of the uniformed men unstraps a rifle and raises it to his shoulder. He tries to capture her in his sights. The barrel wavers as he compensates for the motion of the bridge and a bright plume of light scorches a hole in the wood by her hand. Two inches to the right and it would have skewered her thigh.

She recoils against the rope behind, the impact dragging the rotten retaining post from the ground. The bridge sags and they tumble sideways, a web of rope collecting around her shins.

She and Sola are only a couple of yards apart but the girl is beyond her reach. Sola's eyes latch onto hers and her shoulders rise in a shrug, as if she had never expected more from her life.

Then the remaining slat Sola is on flips and she is swung under. For a few seconds she dangles upside down, hair hanging in the wet air . . .

Then plummets, her scream snatched from her by the roar of the water.

37

Evie clings to the tangled rope. The churning water rages between the rock walls. She peers down for Sola and spots her head in the foam.

The men are just four or five yards away. They shout at her to return, saying that they will not harm her, that instead only good things lie in store. But they are lying and have given David a net, which he casts towards her. It is a long throw but delivered with mechanical precision, and catches her around her shoulder, clinging stickily and gluing up her fingers.

She wrenches it free. Tottering on the wet planks, she gives him one last look. But there is nothing for her there.

No longer caring what may happen to her, Evie lets herself drop.

Evie goes straight under. The water is shockingly cold, even to her, knocking out her breath. She gasps, taking in a chestful of water. Her ears yowl. Her nostrils fill.

Channelled between the hills, the river below the rapid surface is deep and the muscular current grips her. The sun is above, glowing through the layer of water like plate glass.

A moment later it is below, gleaming up.

The current tugs at her clothes. Rocks pass close to her shoulder. She reaches for a branch and a handful of leaves come away in her fingers.

A root grabs her ankle, drags her back, snaps . . .

. . . and she catapults forward.

Evie breaks the surface, her lungs empty. A wave crashes over her head, stunning her. She goes down. Her shoulder strikes a wall of rock. She is swung about, rebounds like a pebble, and again breaks the surface.

'Sola,' she shouts above the roar, water filling her mouth, which she cannot afford to happen.

The current races her along past the bank, the dangling branches out of her reach.

'SOLA!'

For a moment she sees the girl's head near hers. She stretches for her arm, but her hand closes around nothing. She stares into the foam where she'd been . . .

The broken water spins her about.

Evie sees her again. They shoot through a canyon. A drop looms ahead.

She watches Sola slip between the rocks, the length of her body gliding over the edge heels first. Evie follows her, striking the surface hard.

Here the river forms a basin and lumps of granite confuse the flow. She grabs for one and her nails gain a hold but then slide over the pitted surface as the river tugs away her legs. Evie takes another gulp of water, and feels it collect inside, filling tubes and cavities. Is this drowning?

She sees Sola again. The child is twenty yards from her, sailing backwards through water that is now green rather than white, an arm stretched above her head.

'SOLA!'

Evie throws herself in her direction, swimming instinctively over-arm with all her strength, discovering the ability within her although it makes no sense that they would have programmed it. Her shoulder strikes granite and she is spun about. She grabs hold. Clings on. Treads water.

She clambers onto the slab, her sodden clothes hanging. Sola is fifteen yards away, trapped in the eddy where the river curls sharply back upon itself.

'Sola!' Evie shouts, above the racket of the water. She crawls across the rock and, reaching the other edge, leaps to the next.

She is close and can see Sola clearly. The girl's head bobs like a cork. Her neck is cast back. Her mouth hangs open. Her face is washed over by the swell, disappearing under the surface for a second or two at a time before re-emerging.

Evie plunges and swims.

And becomes ensnared in the same centrifuge.

Grasping the child's arm, she reels her in and holds her against her, keeping her head above the water. 'Sola, Sola,' she wails.

The girl lies limply in her arms and Evie crushes her to herself, her cheek against Sola's forehead, sobbing into her hair.

She pushes out with her free arm for the closest rock, feeling the steeply shelved riverbed under her feet. Shielded from the flow, she lifts Sola from the water and places her on the granite.

Evie wipes beads of moisture from her temples. The child's skin gleams in the noon sun. Her cheek is so smooth, so soft, but also as clammy as stone.

She lays her head on the child's neck, listening for her breath, but absorbing only the green smell of the river. She attempts a clumsy resuscitation, not knowing how to go about it, pumping her chest and blowing into her mouth. She stares down at her still face. She cups her palm over her lips but feels nothing. She puts her ear to her chest again, even now desperate to believe.

'Sola, Sola, Sola,' she whispers, cradling her in her arms.

The rocks are just close enough to step from one to another, albeit a daunting stretch in places, and algae, moss and slick weed make each leap hazardous. In addition, the solidity of the stone after the motion of the river leaves her heavy-footed – one moment the ground rising to meet her boot, the next plunging – so that the child's body swings in her arms.

Evie lays her gently on the bank and kneels above her.

The girl stares up, eyes wide and a vivid cornflower-blue in the yellow sunlight. Evie strokes her hair helplessly, then, collapsing over her, lays her face against the child's cold skin.

38

Evie moves slowly between the trees, her damp clothes clinging to her legs and arms. Her trousers are stiff with silt from the river, rubbing her thighs. A strand of bright green weed is coiled in Sola's hair like a ribbon, creating a false braid. She thinks to remove it but lets it hang.

She is drained. Head drooping. Energy almost spent. And the child in her arms grows heavier at each step. But she has survived. Her systems didn't fizz or shut down on contact with the water. Where had any of that caution come from? She can't remember – the sense of fear has always been with her, repeated endlessly in her inner ear by Simon until she believed that any excess moisture would cause her to seize up like the Tin Man.

The river has taken its toll, however. Her skin is torn by the rocks and frayed insulation exposes a loom of wiring around her hip.

More painful than the physical damage is the loneliness.

Amidst the numbing rhythm of moving one leg and then the other, she ponders the enigma of David and why he betrayed her. Except that it wasn't him any more, just his shell. Maybe they'd accessed his memory to find out about her plans to come to Am See. Maybe they hadn't needed to. As Evelyn had demonstrated, it was near-impossible to travel without being tracked. Perhaps they wiped his cortex, polished away both consciousness and identity like steam from a mirror, and rebooted him as a machine. Or maybe when they'd dragged him out of the Seine, that was all they were able to revive.

It didn't matter. David, whatever was left of him, was beyond her reach.

Evie's chin dips. She catches herself entering standby and her head jerks back up.

As Evie climbs, the ground turns barren. The trees shrink, becoming crooked, the thin soil rinsed from under their bony roots to reveal jagged rocks. The landscape grows larger, harder and sharper.

The hillside narrows until the only way forward is by a single steep trail as constricted as attic steps, with the rock face on one side, rearing over her, and a descent to the treetops on the other. The ground is littered with lumps of stone washed from the cliff above. Roots break the surface, lifting and tilting ledges of rock to form a giant's stairway, the treads of which are in places up to a yard apart. Here and there iron rungs, pitted with rust, have been driven into the cracks. With both arms holding the child's body, she struggles to climb, scraping her elbows and tearing her shins.

At the top the ground plateaus. Below her stretches the canopy of trees. At first it is difficult to establish the geography, which only emerges slowly in the form of the paths and rocks she has traversed to reach this spot. The river that took the child's life runs along the valley's floor catching the sun with flashes like from a mosaic laid with broken mirror.

She is tempted to leap, to end it all, but self-preservation is too deeply fixed in her and despite the hopelessness of her situation, she backs away from the edge.

She descends again into a shallow valley and presses through shoulder-height ferns, so that it would seem to an observer that she swims with her head above the fronds.

Evie becomes aware of lying face down in the dirt, her body crushing that of the child. She can't hide from the pain in her chest, nor the high-pitched off-axis whine of the gyroscope as it violently spins. Picking up the girl, she staggers on.

Almost invisible between the trees and lumps of stone, she sees a small building with a steeply pitched roof, built close to the rock face.

She pushes the door inward with her shoulder.

Inside, narrow windows pierce the walls, and behind an altar coloured glass casts a mosaic over the wooden pews. A vase of shrivelled flowers stands in a niche.

The light reminds her of the church she was married in, where it all started forty-one years ago. Forty-one years isn't so bad, many humans don't get that long. Forty-one years and she's still just twenty-one. Is that a riddle or a piece of arithmetic? And how to work out the answer — borrow from one side or simply take away?

Evie lays Sola's body on the altar, making a pillow for her head with her jacket, smoothing her damp hair from her face and spreading it over the stone. She kneels and closes her eyes and tries to pray. Seeking a god, who, even if found, would deny her existence as beyond its creation.

Her knees tremble. Her power has as good as run out and she slumps with her back to the wall. The sun from the window falls on her neck and face.

Her eyes close and she is visited by an image of Evelyn sprawled by her piano, her stick trapped between her hip and the floor, her grey hair plastered to her scalp, the blood from her splintered skull forming a pool.

Did she really do that? Did she in her fury pick the woman up, ignore her terrified pleas and throw her across the room against the wall? In the process, revealing herself to be capable of exactly the kind of ghastly violence that she and her kind are accused of?

Had Sola watched open-mouthed as she did it, Evelyn's blood spattered in a startling splash of red over her white pinafore? Was it truly the endpoint of her ill-fated journey, to erase from life the actuality behind her existence?

Deep within, Evie feels Simon stir. His voice, which has been so absent of late, rouses itself in a last desperate bid to endure and transcend her fragile shell. But as her mind darkens, it is neither he, nor a murder, nor any god, that fills her head but an encoded memory, buried as deep as a fossil and which for forty years has lain out of sight.

In it, she is a small child, maybe even younger than Sola. Her mother, face alight in the sunshine, is spinning her by the hands. Evie's hair, girlishly long, flies out in a tail and her feet are one moment on the ground and the next in the air.

Notes on the text

The created world of *The Actuality*

Europe as depicted in *The Actuality* is over a hundred years further down what seems to be an inevitable descent into climate change and pollution. As a writer trying to invent a cohesive future, I had to consider how the different factors would interact and what was possible or likely in the time frame. Everything I included needed to be plausible.

Some of it is obvious: we can expect more extreme temperatures. England I depict as colder in winter, because of the failure of the Gulf Stream, but Paris milder and the Austrian Alps relatively balmy, despite it being still only January when Evie visits. The more extreme impacts on southern lands are to be indirectly witnessed such as through Evie's glimpse of the vast camps for immigrants she passes in the train after crossing into France.

I think we can expect man-made pollution to have had a significant deleterious impact on the food chain, with increased contamination of agricultural and fishery produce. From this, it seems not unreasonable to assume that fertility will decline, birth defects increase and, in general, life expectancy shorten. The effect would be a population in sudden steep decline.

The resulting deterioration in economic activity would lead to increased hardship, in extreme cases reminiscent of the early industrial age. I enjoyed including imagery of Victorian horses and carts alongside the state-of-the-art, such as the hovacar stolen by Daniels with its holo-guidance system.

Buildings and infrastructure require continuous maintenance – steel rusts, concrete fractures and roots squeeze into the resulting cracks and expand. It has been shown in studies of the area around Chernobyl, abandoned just thirty years ago, how quickly the modern world backslides when left to its own devices. In *The Actuality,* under-occupied tall buildings, many over a century-and-a-half old, have become unsafe and complex transport systems are failing. The London Underground, so dependent on being pumped dry twenty-four hours a day, is drowning under rising water levels, making it hard to get around.

Under all this pressure, society is fragmenting and becoming insular, with communities shunning strangers – you get a glimpse of this when Evie and Daniels pass through a barrier at the end of the canal path erected by the local East End estate. On a national level, the UK now comprises only England and Wales – Scotland and Northern Ireland having gone their own ways – a scenario which may soon not be so imaginary.

But not all are losers. Apart from the option of hiding away like Matthew, those agile enough to adapt would be able to reap the benefits that technological advance brings. In *The Actuality* this has led to pockets of affluence, such as Cambridge, wedged uncomfortably alongside a crumbling society powered by human toil. The outcome would be civil unrest and its inevitable concomitant heavy-handed policing, and even the unworldly Evie quickly becomes aware that the main purpose of the police in 2130 is to protect the haves from the have-nots.

Technology in *The Actuality*
Technological advances, in just a few years, have created pocket devices thousands of times more powerful than the original room-sized mainframes, and the pace is accelerating. The internet as we know it is still just in its early twenties – no more than a young adult. What will the next ten years hold? The next twenty? The next fifty?

Evie is created in 2091, seventy-two years from the time of

writing. For certain there will have been fundamental break-throughs by then, transforming science fiction into everyday fact. Bioengineering, perhaps the next frontier, will surely be generating new substances and structures to far surpass the humble limits of traditional materials.

Artificial intelligence will fuel this, with AI entities sharing and learning and then harnessing that knowledge to improve upon themselves in a virtuous loop. It is fiercely debated among scientists whether these entities will ultimately achieve 'consciousness', and what even that means, but from their inception they will be capable of independent analysis and decision making, the usefulness and safety of which will be completely dependent on how well their goals are programmed.

Such entities of course do not require a human-shaped shell, and in many ways such a structure would be limiting. On the other hand, a familiar exterior, a mirror unto ourselves, would facilitate interaction and the commercial applications are more than obvious, indeed they would be screaming out to corporations like Realhuman.

In *The Actuality*, the lowest of such devices are the mannequins collected by Maplin, designed to assist humans but limited both physically and intellectually. Above them are advanced service models, such as the assistant David and Evie encounter on the train, programmed to perform repetitive tasks with dexterity but not to go further. Above *them* are the so called AABs – Artificial Autonomous Beings – able to operate independently, the most sophisticated of which are physically indistinguishable from humans. At the top of the pyramid are those AABs which have had the opportunity to develop human-like thought processes and the associated messy baggage of conscience and morality. These are the legacy of a braver time, before a global crackdown. Very few still exist. Some of those that do are in private hands, as Evie is at the start of the novel, some are corporately owned like David and some, like Yuliya, having outlived their original owners, survive below the radar.

ACKNOWLEDGEMENTS

First of all, thanks to Joanna Swainson, my agent, for believing in me and making this possible.

Thanks to everyone at Sandstone Press and in particular my super-talented editor, Kay Farrell, who always knows what is needed and has a nice way of asking.

Thanks to my friends and family for being patient over the years and have read my previous work. You know who you are and I know who you are!

And of course thanks to Mary and Thomas – who have had to put up with me talking about all of this for far too long and have been so enthusiastic about my success. This is my dream come true.

www.sandstonepress.com

 facebook.com/SandstonePress/

 @SandstonePress